SLIPPERS ON A FIRST DATE

JOANNA WARRINGTON

Disclaimer and Background to the story

As I write this, we are emerging from a pandemic. Billions across the world were in varying degrees of lockdown. Somehow life still carried on. Despite the challenges and obstacles, us singles continued to date. Some couples had dates over Zoom, but others met in parks or went for walks. *Slippers On A First Date* is inspired by my own experiences and those of my friends of dating through the lockdowns of 2020 to 2021.

This book highlights the challenges of finding love in the later years and the utter futility of it all!

The characters in this story are fictitious. Any resemblance to actual persons, living or dead, is coincidental. All the places mentioned in the book though are real. The opinions of the places are the opinions of the characters and not necessarily the opinions of the author.

CHAPTER 1 - THE CUTTING REMARK

 onna

'NO OFFENCE, Mother, but you literally are a loser.'

It's late one Saturday evening, and we're discussing my chequered relationship history.

It stuns me how easily the cutting words slip from my daughter's mouth. Laced with mischief and designed to hurt. You'd think by her age, having just turned twenty-one and studying psychology at Leicester University, she'd be more subtle, consider other people's feelings and be sure to engage brain before putting mouth in gear. Her career goal is to become a psychotherapist. Heaven help those poor souls in need of her reassurance and support.

Shocked, I feel her words numb me to silence. I think of making a joke, reminding her that variety is the spice of life and all that jazz.

Kids are so rude these days. You hear a lot about parental verbal abuse, but what about the other way around? Parents aren't allowed to be upset; we must take it on the chin, get over it, they don't really mean it. I wouldn't have dreamt of calling my mother a loser back in the day.

When I text back telling her she's being nasty, she doesn't retract her words or apologise. Instead, she accuses me of being oversensitive. 'But Mother, you are a loser,' adding a row of laughing emojis.

It's not too late. I will find Mr Right, Mr Normal, to stop these snide remarks. Even if it means signing back into a dating site. I hate being the object of ridicule in this family, the butt of jokes. Not my fault that I have a list of failed relationships longer than a shopping bill. She should be understanding of my situation and proud of everything I've achieved.

She doesn't know what it's like to be me--useless in love. There's still time for her to screw up. Twenty-one years old-- she's barely out of nappies.

I almost miss the brat years. Those years when Olivia was obnoxious and had full-blown meltdowns in Asda. They were a picnic compared to now. When she was little and didn't get her own way, she called me a poo-poo. Now, her language cuts to the core. So much of my identity as a human being seems bound up in what she thinks of me. Her assessment of me weighs more than almost anyone else's. And let's face it, adults are crueller than kids. If any other adult called me a loser, I'd cancel the relationship for good. But she's my daughter, and quitting isn't an option. I don't want to lose her; she's all I've got.

For your information, in case you are wondering, I, Donna Ratcliffe, am most definitely not a loser, although I'm sure you'll make up your own mind. Things haven't worked out for me. I've been unlucky in love. There's a big difference. We can't all be lucky. Olivia needs to filter her thoughts. I have no control over the hand I've been dealt. She makes it sounds as if I deliberately make bad choices when it comes to men. That I'm somehow too emotionally unintelligent to make wise decisions, or too weak to resist unwanted advances. Or maybe she thinks that when I do meet someone nice, I get bored easily. That I'm programmed to fail through some inbuilt mechanism inside my brain.

Despite my operating an Australian-style points system over the years, I admit, there were occasions when I abandoned my list of *musts* when a guy was keen on me. I thought that with time I'd fancy him and come to overlook all that I didn't like. Of course, that never happened. I just loathed them even more. Everyone knows you can't force a square peg into a round hole, but I was too daft to see that. It's not an age thing, something we do when we're young, less experienced, and less confident. I make the same relationship mistakes now that I made back in my twenties. It's shocking really. You'd think by now, at the grand age of fifty-six, I'd be more mature. That's why I gave up on dating and convinced myself that I was happy being single. Except that I'm not. There's a niggling sadness inside me that never goes away. It's more acute when I drift up and down the aisles in Sainsburys watching couples. Anyone who tries to tell you they're happy single, is lying. For most of us singletons, it's just Plan B.

I tried online dating a few years back and look where that got me. Since then, I've tried many lines: like the washing line trick–– pegging my smalls out when I spot Barry, the hunky single dad next door. And line dancing. Never again. I hated the Cupid Shuffle and the Birdie Song and all those turns and kicks. I thought it would be a blast, a chance to connect in a fun setting because sometimes only the dialogue of dance makes sense between a man and a woman. But maybe it's time to give internet dating another whirl. God, listen to me. I make it sound like a coconut shy. Well, the more balls I throw, the better the chances of knocking one off.

Being called a loser is a turning point in my existence. My

rock-bottom moment. I'll show her that I can meet someone half-decent. I can do it. I will do it.

It would be nice to be back in a relationship and after all, there's so much I miss about being with someone. Like sitting in a coffee shop reading the Sunday papers together, an autumn walk through woods, kissing while watching a sunset, throwing my legs over someone's lap while watching Netflix. The good things in life don't always come organically and so I must go out and find them. In my world, the only men I meet are old. Very old in fact. That's because I work as a carer and most of my clients are men. Rickety, frail men who move like badly oiled robots, sprout wild nasal hair, and tell me how much they love me and want to marry me. In a former life they were company directors, lived in big, detached houses. Instead of carrying the keys to a flash car, these days they carry a catheter bag.

There's one problem about dating right now.

Lockdown.

It's the spring of 2020 and mixing with other households is banned unless you live alone or fit the limited support bubble criteria–– which I don't because my house is filled with a jelly-bean assortment of lodgers. A student doctor working on the frontline in our busy A&E, in contact with Covid patients daily. A Glaswegian electrician. And a woman and her eleven-year-old daughter from Hong Kong are in my loft conversion, doing Zoom lessons in the middle of the night. It's a crazy motley household, but the lodgers help pay the bills. Whoever I meet online is going to have to accept that they can't come in my house, not even wearing a mask and visor. As it is, I've a nosey neighbour who stands at his lounge window all day watching who is going in and out of people's houses. My house must be a source of great entertainment and reason for him to snitch on me. It's like having the Stasi as neighbours. One evening my doctor lodger caught him snapping photos so he waved his stethoscope at him and gave him the finger.

Lockdown's not the only problem. I'm over the hill and carrying extra pounds. My boobs droop and despite lathering my neck with Aveeno twice a day to tighten it, I look as if I should be in a poultry farm. Guys are hardly going to say, hi, Donna, wow what an attractive neck. I live in hope though that there might be a man out there who appreciates the beauty of silver hair on a woman and doesn't automatically think of Zimmer frames, knitting needles and incontinence pads. I think my hairstyle is chic, avant-garde. God knows, I spend enough money on it.

~

IT'S EARLY on Monday morning and I head to my first client of the week. I'm still reeling from Olivia's hurtful remark. Couldn't sleep. Once upon a time I had school friends who knocked my confidence, now I have a daughter to do that.

Normally I enter George's bungalow through the front entrance, but because the door is close to his bedroom he'll hear me, wake, and start calling out. 'Donna, my pillow's hurting my back,' or 'Donna, what's the weather like?' or 'Open the curtains.' There's never a quiet moment, he's a demanding chap. So instead, I go round the back, past his greenhouse where he's growing tomatoes and peppers and up the patio steps where I punch in a code to enter the lounge. The bungalow is silent. Good, he's still asleep. When he wakes, I'll pretend I called his name and tried to rouse him. I read the diary the night carer has written, before heading into the kitchen to make coffee. Slumping onto the sofa, I glance at the mantel clock. It's only going to take ten minutes to upload my photo onto the dating site and write a short resume. In the middle of the night, I did a quick search of dating sites. There was a new one I've not seen before, and it popped up in my search. I'm won over by the name, *Lucky in Love*. There's a joining fee and a small monthly fee but that's okay. Paid dating sites are probably better than free ones because they're bound to attract more quality matches. It's the difference between shopping at Waitrose and shopping at Poundland.

I tiptoe into the hall; no peep from George yet, so I return to the settee where I upload a photo of myself--the best one I can find of a recent day out to Bognor Regis. I'm wearing a bright red sundress, low-cut, showing just enough cleavage. I hope they aren't put off by my height; I'm only five foot three and my greatest liability is my legs. They aren't shapely and are covered in purple thread veins and I have a complex about my baggy knees. One ex said I had legs like a pit pony. My best asset is my eyelashes, which are especially noticeable when I wear mascara, yet nobody sees them because I wear glasses.

When it comes to writing the resume, I'm flummoxed. I'd ask a friend for their sage advice, but I don't want my friends to know that I'm dipping my toe in the murky waters again, only to be the laughingstock when it all goes tits up. I don't want to teach these blokes a bunch of facts about myself, I just want to give them a flavour of who I am, so I settle for words like bubbly, chatty, personable. I avoid well-worn cliches like, 'I'm back on here after a long break.' I start with a few basic Google searches to walk me through exactly how to write the perfect profile and before long I realise it's 9.20. I should go and wake George. His catheter bag will be brimming.

As I pull the curtains back, he wakes with a jolt, the sunlight streaming in and dragging him from sleep.

'Morning George.'

He half opens his eyes and mumbles, 'That you, Donna? What's the time?'

'Nearly half nine.'

'You're late,' he snaps. 'You need to make the time up and write it on the timesheet.'

'I was on time, but you were sparko.'

'Was I?'

After washing my hands in the bathroom and putting on plastic gloves and a facemask, I try not to breathe in the odour lingering in the air as I bend beside his bed to release his catheter bag from its straps and point the drainage tube into a waiting bucket.

'You're hurting me,' he yells. 'Jeepers.'

I'm being careful like I always am, but sometimes he winces. What it must be like for him, God only knows. Straightening myself, I glance at his shrivelled willy with the tube running into it and I feel sick. Poor man. Years of toil are baked into him, and this is what it's come to, how it ends for lots of men. Once an instrument of pleasure, his penis is now a source of pain, an appendage to his body he'd probably rather not have.

His skin is bleached of colour, hollowed out cheeks sink into his face like the craters of volcanoes. 'Ready for breakfast?' I ask all cheery.

Decades ago, George would have smelt of London, fumes, trains, and black coffee, but now he whiffs of pee and milky tea. And this makes me think. My partners have always been older than me because this was and still is the societal norm and from an evolutionary perspective, I guess it makes sense. But now, at my age I'm not sure it does. I'm fit and healthy, I'd rather be with someone my own age, or maybe younger. That way our bodies can decay together.

As I stir oats into milk in George's tiny kitchen, more doubts kick in. Carrying the bowl to the microwave, I stop in my tracks, aware of a subtle negativity spreading through my veins. I've always believed that one day the right man would come into my life and stay, and I know that I'd be happier sharing my life. But I want to prove something to myself and to Olivia. I know it's absurd. I shouldn't have to prove anything to her. She should be proud of her mother--the struggles I've faced, the challenges I've overcome--but no, she thinks I'm a loser.

CHAPTER 2 - LIPS

*D*onna
There aren't many rules of dating. The most important ones surround the issue of personal safety. Over the years I made a few of my own rules, one of which was to ignore that old cliché of letting the man make the first move. Unless I begin chatting, they don't bother. And as for suggesting we meet, that doesn't happen unless I ask them out. I'm sure some of these men think the dating site is a point-scoring game to see how many women fancy them, a great way to massage their egos.

It doesn't take long to start connecting with men on *Lucky In Love*, but the messages that fly back and forth aren't inspiring and are just plain dull. They follow a daily pattern of 'Morning, how are you, what you up to today?' And 'Evening, did you have a nice day?' After a few days of this routine, there are no plans to meet and the communication fizzles out. How can you tell if there's a spark between two people without meeting in person? It's just word tennis. They aren't real people until they are standing in front of you.

There are some bizarre profile pictures as I get into practice swiping my screen. Why would men pay good money to be on a dating site only to upload a picture of a random body part like a hairy ear, a foot or a nipple, the corner of a car's interior, or a robot? Who are they trying to attract? There are even pictures of famous people like Grant Mitchell from East-Enders and Boris Johnson among the many tattooed oinks, the grisly-bearded and general assortment of weirdos. One man was even wearing a lampshade on his head with dangly sunflowers.

I don't like it when some men call me darling. It feels fake and I guess they are scammers. James from Brighton calls me darling and sweetheart and sends me pictures of his kitchen and bedroom. One evening he sent me a picture of himself in his library. I zoomed right in to see the ancient volumes crowding on the shelves behind him, then googled the titles but they weren't real books.

Ammar from West London looks hopeful. He's wearing a suit and holding a huge bouquet of roses in his profile picture. He calls me without arranging to and during the chat asks, 'What are your energy levels like?'

'I swim and I walk.'

'I wasn't talking about that kind of energy. You get what I'm driving at?'

'You'll have to explain.' I've already guessed. Why are some men one-track minded?

'Unless you've got energy in the bedroom, it just won't work. We may as well clear that up now before we meet.'

Pete from Pulborough is a definite weirdo. I fire off a friendly message and he replies, 'did you read my profile?'

Shit, what have I missed? Something important. I'm so scatty. 'Have I missed something?'

'You're comfortable wearing black stilettos and a short skirt?'

'And have you seen my age? It's been many years since I

wore stilettos, that's if I ever did. Are you honestly expecting me to go on a lockdown walk wearing high heels?'

JUST WHEN I'M starting to believe that maybe I am a loser, because the quest to find love comes with too much rejection, a bruised heart and knocked confidence, along comes Russell. While he certainly makes a strong impression on me, I wouldn't say that his messages leave me drenched in a golden glow. After all they're just words on a screen, we've not met––yet.

When I find out that Russell works at a golf club as well as being a keen golfer, I send him a stock image cartoon via WhatsApp of a golfer wearing Rupert-Bear trousers, holding a glass of martini and ask, 'Is this you?'

'I like the glass,' he replies.

'And the olive floating in the glass?'

'I don't think my taste is sophisticated enough for olives. I'm a simple guy.'

'Canapes aren't your thing?'

'Could I have chips with a pint instead?'

'Fat greasy ones, or thin, skinny ones?'

'That depends on the location. If it's The Grand Hotel in Brighton, I'd want to be continental and go skinny. What about you?'

'If it's The Grand, just a few skinnies in one of those tiny metal buckets beside a club sandwich, but if we're on the beach then fat greasy ones drenched in vinegar and wrapped in a sheet of newspaper wins the day.'

'Marry me.'

I send him ten laughing emojis. 'Years ago, my friend and I were walking round Superdrug eating chips in cones and I looked behind me to see a trail of vinegar weaving round the aisle.'

'I hope you left, casually pretending you didn't realise.'

'So many funny stories to tell you.'

'I love the fact that you can laugh at yourself. It's a very attractive quality.'

And in the following days the messages continue, but with no date yet arranged. At some point these messages are bound to fizzle out.

'Hey you xxx,' he messages one evening. 'How was your day? And what are you doing?'

'I had a twelve-hour shift today with my old boy, George. Tiring.'

'I'm so impressed by your job. I couldn't do it.'

'One day someone will have to wipe your arse.'

'Charming. Well it shows how amazing you are. You're clearly a wonderful person.'

'Someone has to do it!'

'Much as I'd like to keep you talking, you need your rest. I'm here if you want me. Speak whenever you wish.'

'It's okay, I'm just going to see what's on Netflix. I'll probably watch *Jack Whitehall: Travels with My Father*. So funny.'

'I like that too.'

'You can try everything once, apart from incest and Morris dancing.'

'I think you'll find that quote was from either Oscar Wilde or Winston Churchill.'

'Okay, smarty pants!' He's getting cocky.

'I'm not clever. I wanted to go to uni, but didn't get the grades.'

'You've done well enough.'

'By the way, I like watching Morris dancers,' he texts, followed by laughing emojis. 'They remind me that I'm not the saddest human being on the planet.'

After two weeks of this, I'm bored. It's not leading anywhere. Just as I'm thinking it's time to move on, Russell texts one evening, 'I hope you're having a relaxing evening.'

I need to know where I stand. If he's wasting my time, he's stopping me meeting, 'the one.' At fifty-six time is running out.

'About to wash my hair. It's thick and wild and takes all evening to dry and style.' Washing my hair is about as tedious as waiting for him to ask me out.

'Lol. You're just showing off to a balding man that you have hair.'

Go on, I egg myself on, just ask. 'What about meeting up at the weekend?' I want to add, we've been texting long enough.

'I can't really commit to weekends. I'm playing two rounds on both days so don't know what time I'll finish. I'd love to say yes but if I can't make the agreed time, I'd feel awful.'

'No problem,' I reply, 'I'm sure we'll sort something.'

And then it dawns on me. All the golf courses are closed because we're in lockdown. He's a cheater.

'I thought all the golf courses were closed. And you're on furlough, right?'

'Sorry, should have explained, we play simulated rounds. I can meet on Monday.'

I want to tell him that it's a weird day for a date, but instead I agree to meet on Monday. I can't write him off, not until we've met. I've invested a lot of time in him, texting back and forth. If I delete him now, it will all have been in vain.

'Whilst I'm not confident that you will find me to be what you're looking for, I have to say that there is nothing about you that could put me off. I find everything about you attractive.'

'I'm very flattered but you are underestimating yourself. A lot of men are arrogant and full of themselves. That's not you. You come across as caring and interesting.'

'I'm certainly interested but that's down to you for being so interesting.'

'I guess it's all down to that elusive thing called chemistry, and until two people meet you can't tell.'

'I'm a firm believer that a stranger is a friend we haven't yet met. And so, with that in mind, please know that regardless of how you feel our meeting goes, I will always be here if ever you need something in the future.'

His kind, reassuring message warms me. I put the golf to the back of my mind as we make plans to meet by the kiosk in Victoria Park.

It's a warm summer day and the early morning mist has cleared bringing the world into focus and a deep cornflower blue sky. Entering the park, I weave my way up the path past a thicket of silver birches and an empty tennis court and when the kiosk comes into view at the top of the hill, I recognise him immediately even though he's standing with his back to me. He's a large man, heavily set like Father Christmas. I stop to pause by the beacon to observe him. He's ordering a coffee for himself and taking it to the ledge to add milk. There's a long queue which I will now have to join and by the time I get served, he will have finished his. He could have waited for me. I decide that he must be mean, wants me to buy my own, and selfish too, thinking of himself. I continue walking, my eyes on him, noticing the thickness of his neck, his broad upper body which is not in proportion to his legs. And his baggy, loose fitting trousers.

As I make my way up the steps and onto the veranda, he turns, but doesn't see me because he's concentrating on making sure his drink doesn't spill.

'Russell?'

He looks up and there's a sheepish look on his face. He knows he should have waited for me before ordering. 'Shall we go somewhere else?' he asks glancing at the long queue snaking round to the back of the kiosk.

'Nowhere else is open.' How could he forget lockdown?

'Let me get you something?' Droplets of sweat are breaking out on his forehead, and he looks flustered. Coffee slops from the sides of the paper cup as I watch him decide how to rectify his blunder.

I glance at the queue then to the ladies serving behind the counter. Gill, who I know well from having worked together in a care home years ago catches my eye, sussing out the predicament I'm in and mouths across, 'tea?' pointing to the large paper cup on display at the window. Russell turns to join the queue, but my cup of tea has already appeared at the counter, and I head over to pick it up. 'Pay later, Donna,' Gill says passing me my cup.

He looks mortified. 'How did that happen? I didn't mind waiting in the queue.'

'It's okay, I'm a regular here.'

'So, I see.' He smiles and I notice his piercing blue eyes––by far his best feature. He turns, squinting against the sun to look for somewhere to sit. 'Over here.' We head to the bench next to the beacon with views over the football pitch and a row of three-storey apartments on the fringes of the park.

He takes a sip of coffee and without commenting on the view or the glorious weather, launches into a speech that feels rehearsed. 'I'm under no illusions. You're clearly a wonderful person and everything I see,' he says, appraising me with sadness and love in his eyes, 'confirms you're just lovely. But I'm not holding out my hopes. I don't expect you'll want to see me again.'

Jeez, he looks like he's about to cry. What's brought this on? Such a bizarre thing to say and at the start of the date. We've barely spoken.

'Hey, I remember your profile. Under those standard questions when it asked what you always carry with you, your answer was lack of confidence. You shouldn't tell women that.' I'm not going to pry about his lack of confidence. It's too early for that. I wonder though, is his confidence really that low, or is it a front to make him look vulnerable when really there are other women he's chatting to? Maybe he doesn't want to raise my hopes because he has other dates lined up. God I'm cynical.

He won't let this drop. 'I knew I'd like you, but I think you could do much better than me. I don't hold out hope of this becoming permanent.'

Increasingly irritated, I want to get up and walk away, bringing an end to this date. But I don't. Instead, I change the subject. 'How long have you worked at the golf club?' I notice a glint of red in his thinning ash-coloured hair and ginger hairs on his freckled arms.

'Years now. I was a police officer in Brighton, but it wasn't the job for me. I wasn't tough enough.' He goes on to tell me the story of how he met his ex-wife. 'It was on Bonfire Night, and I had to rescue someone who'd fallen into the river. I was waiting beside the ambulance for the crew to open the doors and when they opened them, the paramedic on board glared at me with a look on her face as if I was dirt on the bottom of her shoe. Weeks later I met her, and we got chatting but over the years together, I never forgot the way she'd looked at me that first time.'

We chat for a while about work and the conversation flows well. Why does he think we won't meet again? He seems to have that fixed in his head.

'It's beautiful down there.' I point to the tall pines in the distance. 'Fancy a walk through the woods? There's a bench by a pond.'

'Get our daily exercise. Boris will be pleased.' He laughs. The government keep encouraging us all to exercise daily during lockdown. Boris, the Prime Minister, is constantly emphasising the importance of daily exercise, described as one journey outside for up to an hour.

'It's like living in North Korea, isn't it?' I get up.

'You could say.'

As we stroll, I glance at his shoes––black and frumpy. It's as if they can't make up their mind what they are. Hybrids. They are neither trainers nor shoes. Brick-like in size and shape, they remind me of those big early portable phones only the rich carried around. I've always thought a person's true personality can be determined by their shoes. His shoes tell me he is not cool, but should he be in his fifties?

We walk past the children's play park. The gate is padlocked. There are notices pinned to the railings saying not to use the equipment. Everything taped to prevent its use. 'Horrible to see it empty,' I comment. 'Especially when the weather's so beautiful.'

'I'm glad my kids are grown up,' he says. 'Don't know how parents are coping. Must be hard.'

This leads us to talking about our children and soon we are entering the woods. He takes my hand. This doesn't feel right. It's too soon, too intimate and he hasn't asked if it's okay. We're barely an hour into the date. And then, without warning he pulls me into an embrace and plants slobbery kisses on my lips. It's not at all romantic and when he pulls away, I wipe my mouth with the back of my hand and stare up at his thick rubbery lips that I've not noticed until now. We continue walking but there's an awkward atmosphere that's descended as we reach the bench and sit.

'Do you like living in Portslade?' I ask, opening a fresh topic of conversation.

'It's great being by the sea. I live with another guy. He's a bit of a rough diamond but it's company.' I want to ask whose house it is, Rough Diamond's or his but don't. If Russell is the lodger, I'm wondering what happened. Did he lose his house when he divorced, or does he have debts and why did he really leave the police force? But I realise I'm overanalysing. Do I like him? That's the only question I need to ask myself.

He puts his arm around me and pulls me in for another kiss. I quickly pull away before our lips have barely touched.

'I'm sorry, this doesn't feel right on a first date.' I feel zero desire, that's the truth. We don't feel aligned, there's no kiss-me vibe. A first kiss should come later, something to look forward to. Something to savour. It should be special. Playful, tender, warm and exciting but it's none of these things. It's clumsy, forced. Like eating dessert before the main, he's robbed me of the build-up. Is he testing the waters, does he only want one thing because if I go along with this, where will it lead?

'Of course, sorry.' He gets up and walks away. Even though I'm annoyed, I join him, and we stroll around the pond. I can't win. If I'd responded to his kisses, what message would it give? That I'm easy and the next stage would be to go to bed together, then he'd discard me like a used tissue.

'I'd like to see you again,' I tell him when we've completed our circuit of the wood, arriving back in the park. I'm not sure I do, but I'll keep my options open. If he's keen, then he won't let the kiss put him off.

Several hours later, after our date, despite a text telling him I enjoyed the afternoon, there's no reply and the following morning he blocks me on WhatsApp. I guess this is the modern world, but I find it despicable. Why can't people be honest? He clearly finds it easier to ghost than have the discomfort of telling me that he's not into me. Despite my better judgment, I'm itching to tell Olivia, just to see what she thinks, even though this is the last thing I should do. It will give her carte blanche to deliver one of her cutting remarks. And I'll only have myself to blame.

Olivia doesn't need to know about my personal life, but despite being a 150 miles away, she has a knack of finding out what's going on. It's as if she has a spy on every street corner. The matriarch, that's what I call her. She has all the tools at her disposal. It doesn't surprise me when she rings to announce in her mocking tone, 'Ha ha, Mother dearest, you were spotted in the park with some weirdo.'

I shouldn't let her get to me, but it's hard not to. 'He's not a weirdo.'

'You admit, you *were* on a date?' She breaks out into laughter which lasts for ages and feels like a deliberate ploy so I can't defend myself.

'He's just a friend.' I sound feeble.

'Holding hands? Yeah right.'

I don't remember seeing one of her friends in the park. But some snitch has spotted me and reported back to the Matriarch.

'How are you?'

'Don't change the subject, Mother. It's not safe to hold a stranger's hand.'

'Holding hands, shaking hands, it's the oldest custom around.'

'I don't want you catching Covid and dying. I worry about you.' Her voice is whiney. 'You shouldn't be mixing with people outside your household.' How high and mighty of her. Little madam. At her age rules are to be broken.

'The rules are less strict down here.' Not sure why I say this. The rules are the same everywhere unless you are in Scotland or Wales.

'I'm pretty sure they aren't. Anyway, how did the date go?'

'Not great. He tried to kiss me. Twice.'

More laughter. 'You're a right doner kebab. You've probably got Covid now.' There's an enormous tut.

'Don't call me that.'

'Because they called you that at school.'

She knows it, but still calls me that.

'Lucky it was only a kiss.' There's relief in her sigh. 'He'd think you were a right slapper otherwise. But anyway Mother, he took you into a wood and tried to kiss you. It's a red flag. But ignore it at your peril, you always do.'

Red is the colour of blood and cherries and stop signs. Hard to shut your eyes and pretend it's not there. It still exists behind closed eyes. I've seen more red flags than the Kremlin. I ignore them, then suffer the heartache—like I did with her father.

'Bet you don't accuse your father of being a loser.' There's a pause while she considers her answer. 'His life is normal compared to your chaotic existence, Mother. He's not dated a load of strange women like you have men.'

It's not fair, I did nothing to ruin our marriage, but Nick was lucky enough to meet someone to settle down with. Soon after we divorced, he met someone online and they married within a year. God knows how she puts up with him. Must be just a fluke that it's worked out for them. But if the statistics on second marriages are anything to go by, they should be divorced by now.

CHAPTER 3 - HYPNOTISED

onna

I MET NICK, Olivia's father the evening I was hypnotised, twenty-six years ago. We were at a Young Farmer's meeting in a village hall. Those who'd been gathering the year's crop on their combines brought with them the smell of ripe earth, soil on their boots and grain dust on their clothes which made my chest rattle, my breathing ragged and my eyes puffy. The woman standing at the front of the hall giving a talk on hypnosis saw me struggling for breath and called me to the stage.

I drifted into a pleasant sleep under her magic and moments later when she snapped her fingers, I woke calmer and more relaxed. The room was silent, everybody waiting with bated breath to find out if the therapy had worked. And it had. My asthma was gone.

As I peered out at the audience, someone caught my eye. A newbie? Dressed in a smart black shirt, dark drainpipe jeans and polished tan brogues, he didn't look as if he was connected to the farming world. Was he there purely for the social side, the parties and pub crawls and maybe to find love? Or had he heard the motto that the Young Farmers were 'not just for those who wear wellies.'

Afterwards, we all wandered over to the Crown and Anchor. At the bar I turned to find a table, nearly bumping into the stranger, and narrowly avoided spilling my red wine down his ironed shirt.

'Whoa,' he said, stepping back to stop my glass from slapping his chest.

Tony stood close by. He was the manager of a local abattoir and a regular at the club. He introduced me to the stranger. 'Donna, meet Nick, our newest member. He joined while you were gallivanting around the world.'

Hardly gallivanting. I'd only been to Tenerife. I swigged my cordial. 'Nice to meet you, Nick. Any connection to farming, or here for the social side?' I kept my tone cheerful, didn't want to come across as interrogatory.

'Hey, Miss Cynical,' Tony said. 'Nick's my accountant. He's got his nose to the grindstone. Knows all about the financial side of running farms.' Turning to Nick, Tony introduced my friend who was standing next to me. 'And this is Fiona, Donna's friend.'

'I bet that's a high-stakes role, doing the accounts for an abattoir,' I quipped.

'Ha ha, very funny,' Nick said, laughing. Now it was his turn to tease me. 'Most people sing or dance, or perform on stage, but you fell asleep.'

'It was so embarrassing, a weird experience. I felt exposed, slumped in a chair, everyone staring.'

'Yeah,' Nick said frowning and scratching his head. 'And come to think of it, you were dribbling.'

'Stop.' I laughed and smiled at him, warming to his humour.

'Yep, you were.' He beamed at me. His eyes, intense and blue were sparkling and under his gaze I felt my cheeks blush.

I retaliated with a wave of my hand. 'Get away with you.'

'You make a great guinea pig.' He made an impression of the small creature by wrinkling his nose. 'And were you aware that your mouth was wide open? Your fillings were glittering under the spotlights.'

I pursed my lips and breathed through my nose. Surely, he wasn't being serious. He had to be teasing. Or was he flirting with me?

For the next twenty minutes the four of us talked about hypnosis, sharing stories about it curing phobias. Nick said he was trying to quit smoking. 'Try acupuncture,' I suggested.

'Eek, I hate needles.'

'How do you cope going to the dentist?'

'I don't. Not been in years. My dentist was a butcher. He enjoyed pulling teeth for the fun of it even though they weren't rotten.'

'Maybe he had a special deal with the tooth fairy.'

Fiona, who'd been standing next to me all this time, picked up her bag and gave me an apologetic look. 'Sorry Donna,' she said, glancing at her watch, 'I know you're enjoying yourself, but it's getting late.'

'Fiona's got an early shift in the morning. She's a nurse.'

'*You* don't have to go,' Nick looked at me. He appeared to have shrunk, as if some of the stuffing had been knocked out of him, and it was then that I realised he liked me, and it was only a matter of time before he would ask me out. 'We can give Donna a lift, can't we, Tony?' he suggested eagerly.

After Fiona left, Nick suggested another pub and we piled into Tony's car and headed along the high street and out to a nearby village. I was in the back of the car and every time I spoke, Nick chuckled and reached out to squeeze my shoulder.

As we entered the Spread Eagle, a cheer went up, with raised glasses. It was like a heroes' welcome and all for Nick.

'Welcome to Nick's local,' Tony said. 'He's part of the furniture in here. It's his second home.'

I glanced around the pub. The lighting was gloomy, but it was warm and cosy with its low beams, treacly paintwork, and brass knick-knacks. In August the fireplace was dusty and neglected and the only concession to summer was a peace lily in a pot perched awkwardly on the bar.

Everyone seemed to know each other. The place was filled with all manner of people: burly men, wizened ladies with freshly sculptured curls, a cluster of spindly young guys by a juke box and a few others playing pool. It felt as if they'd still be here even if they were down to their last pound and pint because it was where they wanted to be. There was something about the place that made me feel at home.

'Yeah, they miss me when I'm not here. Nobody to entertain them.' Giving the barman a high five, Nick laughed and ordered his beer. 'And I know *you've* missed me,' he said to the buxom bar lady, giving her a peck on the cheek. 'You watch the door all evening for my grand entrance. Can't live without me.'

I watched Nick weave his way around the pub, bantering with the regulars and listening to tales before he joined Tony and me at our wobbly table. There was something magnetic about him, something deeply appealing, and part of that appeal was bound up in his life here, in the pub. He was sociable. He had friends. Was charming to everybody. A complete contrast to the boring fart I'd just dumped. It was hard to believe that I'd wasted three of my best years on a pretty boy with long eyelashes and soft dimply skin, whose idea of fun on a Saturday night was sitting in with Mummy to watch *Noel's House Party* with a mug of what he called his warm-milky-milk. Never stepping inside pubs, always declining party invitations, John led a sad existence. Half a sherry with his nan was his only vice.

Nick cradled his pint of Strongbow cider, and when we spoke, he had a flirty look in his eye.

'What's your number?' he asked opening the door for me when chucking out time came, and everybody left. I could smell his fruity breath. 'We can let you know if there are any good events coming up, can't we Tony?'

He gave Tony a nudge. Slow on the uptake, Tony simply shrugged. 'She doesn't need us to ring. She can look at the programme, can't you Donna?'

'I'll jot my number down anyway.' This was embarrassing. Tony was making it difficult.

AFTER WAITING a week for Nick to call, finally he did.

'Fancy coming to the cinema?'

'Sounds good. What's on?'

I waited for his blokey suggestions. A horror, or something violent. Or much worse, James Bond.

'*Beauty and The Beast.*'

I was too shocked to speak.

'You still there?' he asked.

'But that's a kids' film.'

'You don't stop being a kid with one big pop of a balloon. Bet there's a big kid in you deep down. I'll pick you up at seven, Saturday?'

He just assumed I was free. And then the line went dead, but I didn't mind, I liked him, and I'd have seen any film with him if it had meant sitting in the back row of a dark cinema, the pair of us chomping on popcorn.

AFTER THE FILM we stopped at the Spread Eagle for what Nick called, 'a swift half,' a phrase I often heard over the next ten years. That first time of hearing it, it made me smile, but I didn't see the red flag. My heart was open, but my eyes were closed to the drinking problem that would, in time, become worse.

CHAPTER 4 - SLIPPER MAN

 onna

'I HOPE you haven't arranged any more dates, Mother.' The animosity in Olivia's voice makes me flinch. It's posed more as a question than a statement, I pause, about the time it takes to lift an axe into the air and wait for her to slice my head off. 'I knew it. I will literally be so angry if you end up with another loser.'

Even though I'm reeling and can taste a million angry words on my tongue, I don't come back with a retort. She's my daughter and I love her, so I try to dismiss her scorn. 'I miss you, darling. I don't know when this lockdown is going to end so that I can come up and see you.' Face-to-face is the only meaningful way to hold a conversation.

She softens. 'I miss you too.' My heart lurches. 'Don't know how you find the time to go on dating apps. Must be soulless, messaging back and forth. I don't like to see you lonely, Mother, but honestly––just wait till lockdown's over. It won't go on forever.'

After exiting Zoom, I ignore her advice and return to my phone to resume texting the latest, Ivan. I think I've already nudged him into the friend zone without even meeting him, purely because he's got two cats. I have nothing against cat owners, but a man with a cat seems a bit wimpish. How easy it is to be judgemental, but I find it hard not to be.

I can't decide if Ivan is dour and frumpy or interesting and brainy. His job, working for the Home Office, suggests intelligent. It's probably all form-filling and paper-pushing, targets and deadlines. Typical boring civil servant. I doubt he's witnessed a migrant boat arrive in treacherous conditions on our shores or heard a family's tragic tale, but there's a chance he'll have a few entertaining stories. I may as well arrange a lockdown walk. Not much else to do on my day off.

Studying his pictures on his profile, I can see that his clothes are old man and I'm not sure about his hair. It's swept to one side like a freshly groomed pony. Given that he's sixty-two, it's remarkable that it hasn't gone grey. It's the colour of ginger biscuits with fiery undertones, the exact colour mine was when I was home-dyeing.

I'm sure there's a nice person beneath the man boobs straining under his tight shirt and a brain beneath what could well be a wig. Keeping an open mind is all I can do. But pray for good weather. Don't want his hairpiece lifting in the wind.

What am I doing? I'm repeating old habits, arranging to meet up with men I'm not attracted to. It's crazy. Not even I understand why I do it. I've done it so many times and need to break this pattern.

'Fancy meeting on Sunday?' I suggest by text, almost to get the ordeal over with. 'Godstone? It's halfway. Pretty walks around a pond and lakes. Could take our flasks.'

What about toilets? A country wee could be embarrassing. It's bad enough that we have a chronic lack of public toilet provision across the country, but we're in lockdown and pubs and cafes are closed. Hell fire, I can't squat behind a bush on a first date. I could wear an adult nappy. *Donna, stop. This is ridiculous. It's simple, I just won't drink.*

'I've not been out for a week, apart from to the corner shop and a stroll in the park. It will be good to get out.'

'Bring your wellies or walking boots. Anyway, how are you by the way?'

'I'm still plodding along working from home. My two cats keep me company. How's work?'

'I'm sick of wearing a mask and a visor. It felt like I was trapped in a sauna yesterday.'

'Poor you. Can't be for much longer though. I did a makeshift hair cut yesterday. Not easy with only a mirror to guide me, and a pair of glasses that won't stay on my nose.'

'Specsavers is open.'

'Not sure I want to risk going in there.' Scared weasel. Covid isn't the plague.

'How long are you working from home for?'

'Could be for another couple of months. Difficult to maintain social distancing in the office. They can only allow two people in the lifts at any one time and there are 800 in the building. Using the stairs is an option but I'm on the eighteenth floor so I'm not going to attempt that. Can't wait till cafes open.'

'4th of July for them. Takeaway cups are not the same.'

'Yes, I think that's when the barbers open. I've had a couple of takeaway meals, but it's not the same.'

THE DAY of our date dawns and thankfully it's warm and sunny, otherwise we'd be forced to cancel. I stand in front of the full-length mirror in my newest t-shirt--soft and silky with criss-crossed straps across the chest. It's simple and classy and skims my breasts. We're only going on a lockdown walk, but I'm determined to make an effort-- with my top half at least. Jeans and walking boots are a given for the bottom half. I straighten my hair, applying make-up, with pink lipstick. I almost look glamorous. Peering closer to the mirror, I study my reflection. Tiny lines fan out from the corners of my lips and eyes. There's a soft sagging in my cheeks.

It's a beautiful drive to Godstone, the lanes are quiet, and the verges are bursting with cowslip and daisies. Cash-strapped before the pandemic and now with workers on furlough, councils have stopped cutting the verges. It'll be a good year for wildflowers and wildlife.

This is the furthest I've been since the start of lockdown and with every mile clocked, I'm further into forbidden territory, like an escapee tunnelling under the Wall from East to West Berlin. Not sure I should be venturing this far. Godstone must be twenty miles away, at least. Before all this, I'd have thought nothing of driving there. Why didn't I think to check the rules in my haste to arrange this date? I have no idea what the *stay local* rule means in practice. Maybe there's a radius in terms of mileage.

I'm sure the police have better things to do with their time, like catching real criminals. As if they'd stop and fine a middle-aged woman for going on a date. I curse myself for being sucked into the vortex of media fear whipped up daily. Just because two women were fined for drinking coffee on a remote hill somewhere, their faces splashed across every paper, doesn't mean the police budget can stretch to fining every June, Ruth and Sally.

As I round a bend, the sun is blinding. I pull the visor down and as I squint into the midday light; I almost crash into a stationary car and brake hard, swearing. There's a long line of traffic ahead and I crane my neck to see what is happening. I don't remember passing any cars the entire journey, and now there are at least fifteen ahead of me. The car in front turns his engine off. What idiot has caused this snarl-up? Why are there no cars coming the other way?

And then I see blue and yellow Battenberg paintwork gleaming in the sunlight: three police cars parked haphazardly across the road, blue lights flashing. Something's happened, maybe a collision. I hope nobody's died. This is going to take a while and if I sit here waiting for them to unblock the road, I'll be late. I'm not sitting here any longer.

Bugger. My satnav is at home updating and I'm hopeless at using my phone to navigate. Which road do I turn down? My mind freezes. Where exactly am I? I'll have to pull over, message Ivan to let him know. I hate queues. I have no patience. Five minutes pass. I yank the steering wheel, lurching the car round in a screeching two-point turn. I'm in the middle of the road, about to ram the gear stick into reverse, when I see a police officer hurrying towards me, bulked out by his stab vest and batteries of kit. He's at my window, motioning me to wind it down. Damn him, I've got nothing to hide, I've done nothing wrong.

'Madam, you're going to have to wait in line now that you're here.'

'Why?' This is mental. I want to go the other way; I should be able to.

'Where have you come from today?' What's the relevance of his question? What I need is an alternative route. He's a policeman, he'll know.

'I'm trying to get to Godstone, which road should I take?'

He eyes me with disdain and asks again, 'Where have you come from?'

It takes a few seconds for the cogs in my mind to realise what's really going on.

There hasn't been an accident at all. They are stopping all the motorists, and this is about lockdown rules.

'Haywards Heath.'

'And you're heading for Godstone? You're a long way from home. What's the purpose of your journey?' It's not far. Not as if

I'm journeying north, like one MP did, or some other back-of-beyond place.

I could tell him I'm working or collecting medicine but that would be a lie. I'm sure he'll just smile and wave me on my way.

'I'm meeting someone for a lockdown date. A walk round a park, that's all. Good for our daily exercise.'

'And you consider that to be an essential journey?' He's leaning into my window. He's not wearing a mask and I can almost feel his breath on me. We're in the middle of a pandemic and he's a bloody policeman. He of all people should know better. I'm not standing for this. My hackles go up. The hypocrisy.

'Yes, I do,' I say, a bit too forcefully, as adrenaline surges through my body. 'I live alone, I'm not getting any younger, this could go on for weeks and you're denying me love.'

'You just need to maintain social distancing. Stay safe.'

I don't believe I'm hearing this. He's telling me how to behave. 'I do know there's a virus going round.'

'Exercise like a walk in a park needs to be taken locally.'

'But this is halfway for both of us.'

'You're breaching Covid rules, and I need to issue you with a Fixed Penalty Notice. Do you not watch the news, do you think you're impervious?

'How dare you.' I start to shake and am aware of my eyes twitching. 'I work for the NHS,' I lie. I retrieved my lodger's NHS lanyard from the footwell this morning after she dropped it yesterday when we went to the supermarket together. 'It's people like me holding this country together, while you're standing here booking innocent people. I'm underpaid, over-worked and on my knees. You have no idea how hard some people are working. I've been doing twelve-hour days, and this is the first day off I've had in a fortnight.' My voice goes wobbly, my hands are shaking as they grip the steering wheel, sobs racking my body. *Steady on Donna. Don't go overboard.*

He's going to issue a fine. I can't afford to pay it.

Furious, I yank open the glove compartment and pull out the lanyard. 'Happy now?'

He steps away from the car. Those bold blue letters, NHS are my saviour. My golden ticket. 'I'm sorry, madam, I think a mistake has been made. I'll let you go on your way.' He glances down the road and waves me through the waiting motorists.

I pull out onto the opposite side of the road and drive slowly past all the marooned cars. It feels arrogant, I am cheating. All the occupants turn and stare at me. Some appear to be angry that I've been allowed to jump the queue.

One man raises his fist at me and in despair I grab the lanyard, flick down the window and wave it at him. 'Stick that in your pipe and smoke it.'

Jeez, that was a close call. I take a deep breath, the roadblock behind me, the lane empty. I can't believe I just did that. Pretending to be someone else. Giving the police such cheek. I could have been arrested. I'm *Toad of Toad Hall*.

Running late, I increase my speed, and soon I've entered Godstone. There's a pub on my right and a duck pond and car park opposite. Gliding into a space, I glance around me. Such a beautiful day, such a pretty village. Perfect for a walk. A mix of beamed cottages and large detached houses with perfectly manicured front gardens ribbon the village green where cricket won't be played this summer. Through the leaves of a bulging weeping willow, I spy him, Ivan, sitting on a bench, his back to me and the pond, his head, a ginger blob, tilting towards the warmth of the sun. I pull on my walking boots and tie the laces. I'm going to enjoy today and make the most of these snatched few hours of freedom from the confines of my house. I head towards him, planning in my mind the route we'll take--along the pathway by the green which leads to a looped trail past three ponds and a church. My phone is tucked into my pocket; there are bound to be good photos along the way.

He glances up at me as I approach. Doesn't smile, doesn't stand. He's locked in the same position on the bench, too comfortable to move. This simple act tells me he's lazy, both in mind and in body. If there's no effort to get up, what effort will he put into a relationship? As I sit, he smiles up at me and we say hi.

He's much worse than I'd imagined.

A complete frump. A date with my grandad. He has as much sex appeal as a crushed beetle. He's wearing an unflattering pair of grey office trousers made of some nasty manmade fibre, the type of trousers my grandad wore in the 1970s, and I think they're stretchy. And much worse––an old navy cardigan with pockets.

I apologise for being late and while I'm telling him about my altercation with the police, creating a dramatic story to entertain and break the ice, I notice the bulge of a tissue stuffed up his sleeve and a packet of Werther's Original poking out of his cardigan pocket. How am I to get out of this one? He might be the nicest guy on the planet, but this is dire.

He doesn't comment when I finish my tale, but instead stares at the ground. Surely, he has something to say. Afterall, being stopped by the police for breaching lockdown is quite amusing, although a tad scary.

'I know you suggested going for a walk, but…' he says.

'What's wrong?'

There's a grave look on his face. 'I'm ever so sorry, but I forgot to take my slippers off before leaving home.'

My mouth falls open and I stare at his feet. He's wearing a battered pair of old tartan slippers.

A little voice tells me to run for the hills. You learn a lot about a man by what he's got on his feet. Shoes are important. Probably the most important item of clothing. I don't have a Geiger counter for slippers. Slippers are a definite no-no, because let's face it, men just do not look good in slippers. Of any variety. Especially outside. I don't care if they're Birkenstock or suede moccasins or made of silk. No matter who the man is or how much he earns, they are still naff.

'I'm glad you find it funny.' He gives a half laugh but looks well and truly mortified.

'Are you Scottish by any chance?'

'Why? Do only Scottish men forget to take their slippers off?'

'No, I just wondered if that was your plaid? Blue, white and blue.' I'm laughing again.

'How did that happen?'

His slippers are his second skin. I'm glad this is happening to him, not me. I'm always nipping out to the bin in my slippers or to empty compost at the bottom of my garden. They're so comfy and with rubber soles, they could easily pass as shoes, although I don't think I've ever forgotten to take them off before going out. If that ever happens, I'd question my sanity. Olivia certainly would. Maybe Ivan's losing the plot. Lockdown cabin fever. Too many hours spent indoors. He should go for a run round the block. Looks like he needs to.

'This is the first time I've been out in days. I forgot I was wearing them.' He glances up. 'I'll be okay on the pavement.'

'Come on then,' I say. This guy has zero energy. Maybe wearing slippers was a deliberate plan, to avoid a walk. 'We could take a stroll round the housing estate.'

'That sounds nice.' He doesn't clock my sarcasm. We'll be missing out on spectacular views across farmland, lambs running in the grass, an old mill, a Norman church, three ponds. Instead, we are traipsing round a council estate. Sounds as if he didn't bother to Google the village to see what's here.

'I still can't believe you wore your slippers on a date.'

'It's like a Cinderella story gone wrong.'

I laugh mischievously, enjoying the slipper charade. 'I can't see many takers lining up to try them on.'

Glancing at him, he looks as if he's holding himself together with considerable effort. 'You won't forget me in a hurry.'

I could laugh about this all day, but I think he'd welcome a change of conversation.

'So how are you finding lockdown?' I keep my tone cheery.

'Other than forgetting to put your shoes on.'

'I blame bats for causing so much global carnage. If it wasn't for bats, I'd be standing here in shoes.'

'Hey, don't blame an innocent creature for your forgetfulness. Do your cats get blamed for your mistakes?'

'My cats are perfect. They share my bed, my dining table, and every other stick of furniture. They spread love and calmness, never viruses.'

'What do you mean, they share your dining table?'

'Exactly that.'

'They sit on the table and eat with you?' Surely, he realises that cats have roundworm, toxoplasmosis and a million other pathogens.

Alarm bells are ringing loud and clear. This is one red flag I won't ignore.

'Some people would be disgusted, but I know where my cats have been, and I hate eating alone.'

The garden, that's where they've been. To kill birds and mice.

He's glancing towards the road; the beamed pub. 'Wow, it's open.'

People are drinking outside at wooden benches. I'd like to end this date right now, make my excuses, and head home, but it would be rude to rush off so soon. The lure of a pub proves too much, and I can see the look of longing in Ivan's eyes. He's a few feet ahead, making a dash for it, with or without me.

There's a sign at the back door asking customers not to go inside and to wait to be served. A man in a white apron smoking a fag by the bins sees us and stubs out his butt, grinding it under his foot.

'Can we order drinks?'

The man looks shifty. 'I'll grab some menus.'

'We don't want to eat,' Ivan quickly says. I'm disappointed. I'd like a bowl of cheesy chips.

'I know you don't, but we go through the ritual. I give you the menus, you pretend you're eating, I bring you drinks. That's how it works.'

'Must be to get around lockdown rules,' I say after the man disappears inside.

Ivan digs into his trouser pockets. 'I don't believe it. I've forgotten my wallet.'

Now that does not surprise me. He's totally clueless. 'It's okay, I've got money. I think you left your brain behind this morning.' I laugh, but inside I'm squirming. I've been told that I'm a tolerant, accepting person but that isn't a good thing. It means I hang in there when I need to walk away. I can't embrace his flaws, nothing about him leaves me excited and there is no future.

So why am I still here?

Simple--I'm too polite. I have no backbone. I sit it out. If he is keen to meet again, we'll arrange a second date, because it's easier to do that than tell someone they are not for me. It's what I do.

Olivia is right. I am a loser.

Lucky for me, Slipper Man doesn't message the following day. Either too embarrassed, turning up in a pair of crusty tartan slippers, or he can't trust himself to cock up another date, which suits me fine.

CHAPTER 5 - MOTHER'S HAREM

*D*onna
       I took a sneaky pic of Slipper Man's feet--as you do. My mobile was on silent, so he didn't notice. Not sure how he'd react though if he knew that I'm about to post his tartan-clad feet on Facebook. Would he be cross or find it amusing to read the comments?

I'm at work and supporting an overweight disabled lady called Trisha. While she's having her nebuliser, I stand behind her so she can't see what I'm up to. Quick as a flash I post the picture of the slippers on Facebook with a caption, 'Went on a date. He wore his slippers.'

By the time it's lunchtime, there are fifty-eight comments. As I stir soup for Trisha and spread butter on a roll, I scroll the thread.

My cousin is the first to comment followed by numerous friends. 'Slippers creep me out. They remind me of a.) Perverts. b) Serial killers c) Weirdos. Get rid, Cuz.'

'If he can laugh at himself, he gets the thumbs up from me. I hope you kept two metres apart.'

'I hope his mum sent him out with a clean pair of pants.'

'And those kecks. Is he eighty?'

'This is why I don't do internet dating.'

'Dare I ask, will you be seeing him again? If so, ask him to rock the sandals and sock look. He could even throw a hanky on his head.'

'Those trousers. Flanelette?'

'Synthetic.'

'Like Teflon?'

'I work in a charity shop. We sell a lot of those trousers. Got to be over eighty to wear them.'

'I'd deffo notice if I'd walked out the house in slippers.'

'Maybe you could wear your slippers next time, too.'

'Where do you meet these oddballs? He's clearly a dimwit. Was he smoking a pipe and wearing a cardigan?'

'At least you wouldn't lose him in an airport. Message over the tannoy, *anyone seen a man in slippers,* would soon find him.'

'Surely, he'd have felt the difference driving?'

'I wear slippers when driving. More comfortable than shoes.'

I'm wetting myself with laughter reading all these comments, until the next appears.

From my daughter.

'You do pick 'em, Mother.'

My heart jolts. I forgot to block Olivia from the Facebook post. I'm in trouble. The only time she calls me Mother is when she's unhappy with me.

'What, cockroaches?' My sister replies.

Olivia calls on Messenger. I can't ignore her, but I know I'll be reprimanded. My nerves jangle as I brace myself. 'What the actual heck, Mother. You went out with a guy in slippers? And now you've embarrassed yourself by posting it all over Facebook.'

All over Facebook. I only have one hundred friends and it's not a public post.

This is precisely why I'm better off keeping my dating life

private, but on this occasion, I wanted to tell all. Lockdown is making everyone so depressed, I thought I'd raise a few smiles. Should have realised I'd get a snide comment from somebody. Had to be Olivia.

'It was too funny a story not to share.' Surely Olivia can see that. Where's her sense of humour gone?

'Not for me it isn't. I wish you'd stayed with Father.'

I'm shocked by her words which are laced with sadness. Olivia was just four when Nick and I broke up and in all that time she's seemed so accepting of the situation. Why say that? She adapted well, didn't miss him and was happy to spend alternate weekends with her dad, and Pamela, his second wife has never been a problem for her.

'Life would be easier. And you wouldn't be dating creepy men.'

'Easier?'

'I've got to visit you in Sussex, then drive to London to see him.'

'We're in lockdown, so technically you can't see either of us.'

'That's not the point.' She sighs. 'It's hard work having divorced parents. You don't realise.' She blames me. As if I wanted divorce. I just wanted Nick to change.

'I'm sorry.' I don't know what to say; I wasn't prepared for this. The long arms of guilt circle and squeeze me making it hard to breathe. I dearly wish things had worked out, but how could I live with Nick, with the way he was? Olivia was too young to know what I went through. I have never told her, and I never will. Because it's a mother's duty to protect her child from the truth, at whatever cost to herself.

'I don't like this whole broken family thing.'

'There's no such thing as a broken family. Family is family. The problem is physical distance but thank heaven for Zoom.'

'But *you're* broken, Mum, otherwise you wouldn't be going

online. You're not happy. You could have been happy with Dad, but you threw it all away.'

'I threw it away?' I'm astounded. What's Nick been saying to her? Spinning a web of lies, giving her his biased account, blaming me for the marriage downfall and taking zero responsibility. Bastard. This is so unfair, when I've tried hard all these years to be respectful, neutral, saying only positive, kind things about him, and never criticising. If only she knew the bloody truth, she'd think again.

'I don't know,' she concedes. 'You're probably both to blame.'

I'm silent, I'm not giving her ammunition to go back to Nick with.

'I hate coming home to your harem of men.'

'What?'

'There's always a new boyfriend, every time I come back.'

'That's not true at all.' Harem. The word stabs like a knife. Only she could say something so cruel.

'It feels like it.'

I either put an end to this dating madness, or I carry on and find the man who will stay in my life forever.

There are no prizes for guessing what I'll do. I'll carry on. Because the thought of being on my own till the end of time is too sad and painful to contemplate.

OVER THE NEXT FEW WEEKS, I can't seem to get anywhere. Most of my matches don't contact me, only responding when I contact them, or they unmatch me. Some are keen and then fall off the radar. Sometimes I get the feeling they're passing me up for a better option, like in an overinflated housing market when a buyer gazumps. Or they only consider me good enough for casual sex. I don't know what I'm doing wrong but this is my rock-bottom moment. A nagging voice in my head tells me this is not all about me. These fickle idiots don't know me beyond a few exchanges. They can't be basing their decisions on anything beyond superficial impressions.

Take Dave for example. I had high hopes for him. He works for a Dutch bank and lives in Surrey. According to *The Surrey Comet*, Surrey has been crowned as the poshest county in the country with a score of ten out of ten. I assumed anyone who came from Surrey would be sauve and sophisticated and this fella certainly looks debonair. I think I might have ruined my chances though by mentioning my athlete's foot. After a few introductory texts, this is how the conversation goes:

'Hi Donna, how are you this evening?'

'I'm fine, thank you. Shattered after work and a fifty-minute swim.'

'I'm chilling on the sofa.'

'I won't tell you what I'm doing right at this very moment. Might put you off.'

'Try me.'

I hope to elicit a laugh. He may as well know the quirky me. 'Well, I'm sitting here on the edge of my bed with my feet soaking in a bowl of warm water and TCP. I've got painful athlete's foot. They're itchy, burning, angry and inflamed.'

'I don't know what to say to that.'

Sorry you're suffering, would be nice. 'Don't worry, you're not likely to see my feet, just yet.'

'But I'd like to meet *you.*'

'That would be good.' Progress. I feel a rush of excitement because it feels as if we're about to arrange a date.

Then he asks, 'Do you like kissing?' And my heart sinks. What the hell. Only interested in one thing.

At least I only wasted two days of my life texting this loser. I'll block him, after I've teased him. 'Never kissed anyone in my life.'

'Funny girl.'

'It's obvious you only want sex. Goodbye.'

Idiot. Before he has the chance to reply I block him. Shame, I'd felt hopeful about him.

I need to develop plated body armour like a pangolin to survive the knocks and bumps of internet dating. My skin is currently thin like an extra sensitive, feather-light condom. I should toughen my emotional epidermis and stop listening to my inner voice telling me I'll never meet a decent guy, because I swear I will. I've made it my mission. I want to prove to myself and to everybody else that I am not a loser.

CHAPTER 6 - THE SWINGING CROSS

*D*onna

  I start chatting with the next lonely heart and a date is arranged with a fella called Mike. As I'm on the train heading into Brighton to meet him, that perpetual question comes knocking. What on earth am I doing? This isn't pleasurable. These dates with random strangers plucked from the ether feel more like an assignment but without the commission.

There's a cold wind rattling around the station concourse, and it's started to rain. I've no idea what we are going to do. Cafes are open for takeaway drinks, but everything else is shut up. I guess we could take a stroll along the seafront if the rain doesn't turn heavy.

Mike texts. He's driving down the hill and will be here in two minutes. Says he's in a silver Honda Jazz with a dent in the side and a missing wing mirror. Hardly a chick magnet, but at fifty-six, do I need my fancies tickling with a sexy car? If he had a sports car he would be spoken for. End of. A small car suggests he is a saver not a spender, a practical, reliable, and solid sort of guy. Someone who is most definitely not a poser. Maybe the type for me.

With no sense of adventure.

Boring, staid, miserly.

Stop it, Donna. You judge too readily.

When his car pulls up and he stretches over to open the door for me, it doesn't matter what he's driving. All I see are his missing teeth and a metal cross hanging from the rear-view mirror. I don't want to get in, but I can't turn and go, it would be rude and that's something I'm not.

'Hi, how are you?' I say breezily. I'll be cheerful, chatty and hope the time passes quickly.

'Let me just manoeuvre the car away from all the traffic and then we can chat. I can't concentrate on two things at once.' He drums the steering wheel with the heel of his hand, and I can sense anxiety grinding away at him as we weave through busy traffic and negotiate traffic lights. Is this my cue to shut up while he's driving? 'There's a Greek deli in Seven Dials, we can grab coffee and cake there. You'll love it. Delicious pastries.'

I can't get over how thin he is. Painfully so. He looks ill, stick-like and has a very long neck and enormous Adam's apple. What would it be like to hug him?

The rain is heavy, pounding down on the car roof like marbles pinging on metal and the wipers are barely able to carve away the rain sluicing down. As we round bends, the cross sways like a branch in the wind and a book flies from the dash-board. Retrieving it from between my feet, I read the cover. '*365 Pocket Prayers, Guidance and Wisdom for Each New Day.*'

'I brought that so that we can pray together.' Shit? I should have just stayed in bed today.

'Lovely.' I wish he was hot in the conventional sense but the only heat radiating from him is the Holy Spirit.

He glances at me. 'Would you like to pray with me? I'm willing to put my hands on you.'

'Maybe.' Hell, what am I supposed to say?

He glides into a space and after switching the engine off

reaches into the back swinging something long and metal over my head. For one awful moment I think I'm going to be attacked with an axe but realise it's a crook-lock for the steering wheel. To stop someone breaking in to steal his prayer book? After applying the lock, he reaches into the glove compartment and takes out a disabled parking permit. 'I've got a disability,' he says, slapping the blue badge on the dashboard next to the book of prayers.

I don't know if I should ask him about his disability. It seems rude and intrusive.

'Sorry I was late,' he says.

'You weren't late.'

'I was on a Zoom meeting with my therapist.'

Therapy. I don't want a needy man. Am I supposed to ask him what he's having therapy for? Probably best not to, so instead, I say, 'Zoom's great, isn't it?'

'Not for counselling it isn't.'

'Oh, I'm sorry you're having counselling.' I'm curious.

'I've got a hoarding disorder. My flat is overrun with clutter, and I can't seem to be able to get rid of it.'

I wonder why he's a collector of things. Maybe it's his way of keeping hold of memories, each object a prompt, a gentle nudge to his past. I'm not a hoarder but I do find it difficult to get rid of clothes. When I open my wardrobe, everything hanging there, from coats to dresses are my dearest faithful friends. I like to know I can revisit my special moments, bathe in the precious times we spent together. Photographs are important but they aren't the same. I want to touch the fabric, smell the garment, the merest hint of scent lingering, recapture the time I wore my little black dress or my big fur coat.

'That must be hard but it's good you're having counselling and want to change. Sounds like you're doing the right thing.' I visualise his mountain of crap. I don't need a man with issues, but I'm happy to listen to him if he wants to talk about it, so taking a chance, I probe. 'Sometimes problems are linked to childhood trauma or loss.'

He opens the car door in an abrupt manner. I've struck a chord. 'Come on, let's grab a coffee. Rain's stopped.'

Out on the pavement, he pulls a silver walking stick from behind his seat and a rucksack which he adjusts on his back before we head across the road to the deli. At the shop door, he shrugs his rucksack from his back and delving inside it, takes out an enormous Tupperware box, big enough to hold a family picnic. Must be his alternative to bringing a bag. He cares about the planet. Can't be a bad thing. I'm all for recycling and saving on waste. Looks as if he's planning to buy lots of cakes though. That's a tick in his favour. My mouth is watering in anticipation of all these goodies we're going to feast on and the smell emanating from the deli is delicious––sweet with a hint of honey and syrup. But when he opens the box, I'm horrified to see a facemask inside. What the hell am I doing here with this complete weirdo?

'I'm like a kid in a candy store in this place,' he says as we order two takeaway coffees and several baklavas.

'I love Greece,' I tell him. 'To eat figs off the tree in the early morning, my favourite fruit.'

Back in the car, we rest our plastic cups on the dashboard and eat the delicious baklava. He polishes off his last one in a shower of pastry flakes, wiping his face and hands with a napkin, while I nibble mine, savouring every bite, enjoying the syrup and chewy almond.

'Have you always lived in Brighton?' I flick the pastry shards from my lap and bite into my last baklava. It's sticky, nutty and yummy.

'I didn't really live anywhere growing up. I was home-taught and then my parents took me round the world in a sailing boat and I never met people my own age. We were always at sea.'

'Sounds lonely, but exciting at the same time.'

He shrugs. It's not the response I was expecting. I study his face and wait for him to offer me a glimpse of his childhood and regale me with tales of life on the high seas.

'Are your parents still alive?'

'Mum is, she lives in a plastic pod.'

'A plastic pod?'

He looks at me as if I'm stupid, as if this is not unusual, as if all parents eventually retire to a plastic pod. 'It's a sort of ball-shaped cabin. She lives off-grid.'

'Interesting,' is all I manage, even though I want to ask more questions. 'It's probably the way to go, with climate change.'

'You're my first date,' he says shifting in his seat. I catch a whiff of his fusty-smelling clothes.

'On this app?'

'No, ever.'

'Ever?'

'I've never been out with anyone, never had a relationship. I decided it was time. So, thank you. For being my first.'

'That's okay. Pleasure.' No dates, ever? Not a single relationship? How could anyone go through life having never experienced love or sex? This is bizarre and I'm so shocked I don't know what to say. 'But you have friends?'

'One or two. I have God. God is all I need.'

'Right.' I turn my head away from him and glance out the window, silently cursing myself for being here with this strange man. What will Olivia say to this one? I won't tell her. Can't face her laughter and ridicule.

'Shall we pray, for us?'

It's my turn to shrug. 'If you like. I'm not into praying though, it's not something I do these days. Not since I was at primary school.'

'That's okay.' He takes my hands in his and prays for about five minutes with his eyes shut, while I stare out of the window

46

and watch a Labrador cock its leg against a lamppost and do a very long wee.

The praying seems to tire him out because afterwards he says he can't stay out very long because of his condition, whatever his condition is. I still haven't asked. 'I need a lot of rest,' he explains.

At the station when he drops me off, I tell him what he'll want to hear, that I've had a lovely time. It's the kind thing to do.

On the train I send him a text. I've got to treat him with care because if he genuinely is inexperienced, I might hurt him. 'Hi Mike, it was a pleasure to meet you. There were lots of positives and I think you are an interesting guy but unfortunately not for me. You need someone who follows the path of Jesus. My path is to Bluewater shopping centre. I wish you well and you have every reason to be confident but be wary too as the dating world can be a cruel one.'

When I finish my text, I feel sad and concerned for him and the need to protect him in some way. I hope he doesn't fall prey to scammers and lying cheats and that he doesn't have to go through some nasty experiences to find the right one. It would be good to hear from him at some point in the future and to know that he'd found love.

He replies a short while later. 'Thank you, Donna. You have a lot of positives too, you are pretty, you have lovely hair and a great figure. You come across as interesting and intelligent. I enjoyed talking to you very much. I appreciate your comment about being wary. Meeting you has been a meaningful experience.'

Reading such a kind and considerate reply, I almost change my mind and arrange to see him again, then remember my mission--to find the right one, not any old one. No point in dating somebody I don't fancy or have nothing in common with.

CHAPTER 7 - PAPERCLIP MAN

onna

THE TEDIUM of swiping back and forth resumes at the crack of dawn the following morning before I slide out of bed for work. The dating app has become a chore, an activity I don't enjoy. I'd rank it in the top fifty most boring things in life, along with being stuck in traffic, queuing in Primark, and watching BBC Parliament. But it's a means to an end and one I hope not to do for much longer.

So much for the saying, the early bird catches the worm. I'm not having much luck, but it's only six and most people are still asleep. The only ones online are the jokers, fakes and scammers. A man with red and yellow hair wearing a Carlsberg band on his head and bright green glasses. A whole bunch of miseries who can't even smile for the camera. And lots with wild beards today. Is it National Beard Day?

The scammers are easy to spot. They are too perfect, too good to be true and pose on yachts or in front of mansions or sports cars. Their photos often look like stock images yanked from the internet. Conversations are robotic and disjointed or too flowery, like this one:

'You are beautiful lady, my darling.'

'Thank you for the compliment.'

'Please send more pictures to my email address.'

'Can I have another picture of you?'

'I will be offline for a few days on business. I will be in touch soon my darling.'

I PULL onto Mrs Garton's driveway shortly before eight. She's my first client of the day and I'm here to make her breakfast, bath her and get her ready for the day. As I head round the side of the house, the back door flies open, and I'm confronted by the most obnoxious man ever to walk the earth—her son, Richard.

'Oh, it's you,' he says, carrying a bag of rubbish to the bin. 'Last carer didn't bother to empty the rubbish.' He puffs dramatically as he slings the bag into the bin making it look as if the bag is too heavy to carry.

'You're late,' he says wiping his hands and huffing. He has a ghastly Home Counties public school accent and an intimidating air about him. He's a short man, a complete shrimp, and tries to compensate for his height with an overinflated ego.

I bristle. This job was supposed to give me freedom and independence but today it's as if he's my new boss breathing down my neck. 'I'm on time. In fact, I'm five minutes early.' This is a great start to the day—not. Bit odd that he's here at this time of the day. He shouldn't really be here at all. He should be protecting his mother by staying away. Or at the very least, he should wear a mask in the house and keep his distance.

It's as if he's read the question in my head. 'I've come over to order her some paperclips.'

'Does she need paperclips then?'

'I've seen a special offer.'

He eyes me suspiciously as we go inside and follows me into the kitchen where I read the notes and wash my hands, before putting an apron and plastic gloves on.

'Nobody bothers to trim Mother's nasal hair. It will be down to her feet soon.'

I stifle a snigger. 'I'll have a look later.'

'See that you do.'

He's hovering by the door watching me. I wish he would go away and get on with what he came here to do.

'I've seen you on a dating app.'

I wheel round, heart hammering in my chest, face burning. It's impossible to keep my work and private life separate. 'But you're married.'

'We don't get on.'

'You looked happy enough when I saw you together, few weeks ago.' This is none of my business. I don't want to know about his private life or discuss his married life. 'I best get on.' My voice is curt, and I wait for him to step aside to let me go upstairs.

'Sexy top you were wearing in your profile picture.'

I just want him to go. He's invading my space, making me feel uncomfortable. Doesn't seem to understand the concept of social distancing. 'I've got to get on.'

He stares at me through cold eyes making me flush, and for one awful moment I think he's going to stop me leaving the room. His face relaxes and he lets me pass.

Upstairs in Mr Garton's bedroom, I sweep her curtains to the sides, welcoming the grey morning light flooding into the room. 'Richard's here.'

'What's he doing here? He shouldn't come inside the house. I don't want to catch Covid.' I take her eye mask off. She likes to sleep in complete darkness.

'Said he's ordering you some paperclips.'

'Whatever for?'

Richard appears in the doorway, whooping and ecstatic. 'Guess what, Mum? I've got five pounds off your order.'

She cranes her neck to look at him. 'What order?' Her skin is leathery and tough like an alligator's. She glares at him savagely, her frown lines, deep farm tracks.

'Paperclips.'

'I don't need paperclips.'

'You will do, you're running out. I bought a 1,000. You'll be well-stocked up.'

I leave them to argue about her stationery requirements while I go down to make breakfast. I can't help myself, as I wait for the kettle to boil, I check my phone. Shit, there's a message on the dating app from Richard. 'Donna, I've always fancied you. I'm looking for a bit on the side. You're nice and local. Interested? As long as we're discreet.'

I swipe to block him. Filthy beggar. As if I'd fancy him. He's married for goodness' sake. Slimeball. I pity his poor wife.

His footsteps are on the stairs. I wish he'd go, leave me to get on with my job. His rapid steps are in the hall, getting close. The door creaks open behind me as I pour milk into Janet's tea.

'You got my message,' he says bluntly, leaning against the counter opposite me.

'I'm not interested.' I turn away from him, keeping myself busy so that I don't have to look at him.

'Think about it. We're both lonely.'

'Speak for yourself.'

'You wouldn't be on a dating app if you weren't lonely.'

'I'm looking for a proper relationship, with a single man.'

'If you change your mind, let me know. We could have a lot of fun together, you and I, while you wait for your Mr Right.'

'No thanks.' I leave the kitchen swiftly, carrying a tray of tea and cornflakes and hurry upstairs.

. . .

LATER, back at home and sprawled in front of the TV, I'm somewhere in that hazy place between asleep and awake, dreaming and as dreams go, this is the worst ever. There's a foggy image of me and Richard humping away, but thank God, my phone ringing on the cushion beside me comes to the rescue and snaps me awake.

I see that it's Olivia. I hate talking when I'm tired so I'm tempted to ignore it, but I don't ever do that because you never know when it might be your last chance to speak to someone. This is unusual for Olivia to ring without prior warning.

'Liv, you okay?' My head is foggy. I've drained a couple of honey Jack Daniels, medicinal tonic after a long day on my feet.

'Just wondered how you are, Mum?' I'm suspicious. She can't be ringing just to see how I am. Children don't do that. Imagine if I dared to call her unexpectedly. I'm a troublesome boil if I disturb her doing something important like making a TikTok video or applying a beauty mask.

'I'm fine, long day at work.'

'Any more dates?' She wants something, I can sense it in the frilly edge to her voice.

I tell her the full story of how Richard nearly pounced on me in Janet's kitchen, and she responds with a gunshot of expletives.

'You've got to report him.'

'Why? I don't want to rock the boat; I like going to Janet's.'

'Mother,' she says in a stern voice. I'm about to get a lecture. 'You have to report it. Have you never heard of the MeToo movement?'

I make a hissing noise through my teeth. 'Back in my day we just got on with things.'

'And look where it's got you. About time you stood up for yourself. But you're going to let him get away with it.'

'Best to ignore blokes like that. They're just full of testosterone.'

'Mother, I'm worried about you. How do you know he's not a psycho?'

'He's Janet's son. I've known him for years.'

'So that makes it all right?'

Why does speaking to my daughter always lead to a banging headache? 'Did you ring about anything in particular, darling?'

'You never listen to me. I worry about you.' There's a sigh of despair followed by an awkward silence before she announces, 'I'm thinking of buying a puppy.'

'What on earth for? How much?'

'I'm lonely up here in lockdown. I needed the company.' Her voice is whiny. 'He's so cute, Mum, you'll love him. He's a bichon. He was only £1,000. It's not much.'

Not much? I'm stunned into silence. She's living on student loans and is always complaining that she's skint. She's mad.

Hang on. What happened to that money I gave her to fix her wisdom teeth?

'The money I gave you, it was for your teeth.'

'The dentist won't see me. Not till lockdown's over.'

'But the money was for your teeth, not to waste on a bloody dog.' I'm angry now. She knows I don't earn much. It was a lot to hand over, but I wanted to help her. Didn't want to see her suffer, but now she's about to blown it all on a mutt that she won't have time to look after.

'Honestly, Mum, he's so cute, you'll love him. He cuddles up to me and looks adoringly into my eyes.'

'For God sake, Olivia, you cannot get a dog. I won't be able to give you any more money, you know that?' My disappointment in her stabs me hard in the chest. She's really let me down this time.

'I know and I'm sorry.' The remorse in her voice makes me feel slightly better.

'Why can't you just get a boyfriend like any normal person of your age?'

'I'm too busy, Mum.'

'Where are you going to find the time to look after a dog then?'

She laughs, as if I've said something stupid. 'Dogs are easy, boyfriends are hard work. I only have to look at your life, Mum, to see that.'

She's riling me up again, I can't stay on the phone a minute longer, so I end the call. Good luck to her. She'll soon find out just how time-consuming puppies are.

Into the silence of the room, my thoughts come thick and fast. It's not really about the money, although I am annoyed. I tried so hard to instil the value of money in her but like seeds on stony ground nothing I say ever takes root. She's always rather listen to her father, and he's always been a spender rather than a saver. Mainly wasting his money on the latest gadgets but also late-night kebabs. I'm worried how she'll manage to look after the puppy. I don't think she's thought it through--the reality of owning a dog, the responsibility. Probably acted on a whim.

I get up to make a coffee, still gobsmacked by her news. It's come out of the blue. Since when did she even like dogs? The only pet we had when she was little was a hamster, and she wasn't very interested in him. I can't remember her holding or feeding him. What I'd really love is for her to find a boyfriend. She's only been out with a couple of guys, and they didn't last long. She should be the one searching for love, not me. She has her whole life ahead of her, I don't want her to miss out on having a family because she's left it too late, having devoted herself to a high-flying career. She'll end up a lonely spinster.

I call her back, pleading with her not to buy the puppy.

'Okay then, keep your hair on. I won't then. I was only ringing to see what you thought of the idea, and you made that very clear. You don't want me to get one.'

Exasperated I ask, 'Why couldn't you have told me it was just an idea?'

After ending our rant, I curl up on the sofa, steaming mug in hand. Munching on a chocolate biscuit, I hear my phone pings with a text. An unknown number.

'Hello sexy. You want it as much as I do. Can I send you a pic of my horny dick? That might get you in the mood.'

'Who is this?' Although I already know. I blocked him on the dating app but how the hell does he have my number?

'A mystery man.'

Maybe it isn't him. I don't like not knowing. This is freaking me out. I don't reply but wait to see if another message arrives.

'It's Richard. You've got a lovely pair of tits. I expect you already know that.'

I swipe to block, my heart hammering in my chest. He must have got my number from Janet's phone book. Shit, what am I going to do? He might not get the message and I don't want to find him at Janet's again. He creeps me out. Maybe Olivia was right, I should report it. As much as I like Janet, I don't feel as if I can go back there. I have plenty of other clients. I better ring my supervisor at the agency and tell her exactly what has happened. They need to know. After all, I have a duty of care to other carers. We are lone workers, and I don't want to risk anyone else's safety.

CHAPTER 8 - SLIMY MUSSELS

 onna

HOORAY, it's Freedom Day. Pubs, cafes, and restaurants have re-opened. I thought this day would never come. Boris, the Prime Minister has released us from our shackles. I punch the air and pull back my bedroom curtains, smiling up at the acid blue sky. It's like being a teenager all over again, allowed out after being grounded for coming home drunk. I wonder how many other singletons are feeling this way today––fired up and ready for a proper date, as opposed to traipsing round a muddy field, or getting a numb bum sitting on a park bench with a takeaway latte.

I connected with a guy called Adrian a few days ago. He's slim, has blue eyes and a friendly face, although his glasses making him look officious like a civil servant and super geeky.

I suggest meeting. 'If you fancy a drink, pubs are open again. Be nice to meet you!' I'm curious to see the post-lockdown pub environment with the raft of measures and rules now in place to ensure they are Covid-safe.

'That would be good. How about lunch? I'm off all next week. Only day I can't do is Thursday because my car will be in the garage.'

'Only day I can do is Thursday! But I don't mind meeting at a pub near you. Will check diary later.'

'Cool. Get your people to contact my people.' I love his jokey style.

'My secretary, Mr WH Smith diary says I'm free Wednesday, daytime.'

'I've run it past my people, and they say that's fine.'

Olivia thinks I'm mad. 'You make it too easy for these men,' she said. 'You should have waited for him to ask you out.' What codswallop. I like to think I'm a modern woman and I go Dutch––many of my friends don't. They are firm believers that the man should always pay.

The evening before we meet, Adrian asks me, 'What do you miss most about a relationship if anything?'

Here we go. Only interested in one thing. I prepare to block him.

'Whole package,' I reply.

'So just everything then,' he replies with a smiley face emoji.

'What you'd like me to say is intimacy, isn't it?'

I'm embarrassed when his reply pings through. The experience with Janet's son has made me cynical. 'I was going to say that moment you wake up and put your arms round someone and go back to sleep. Amongst other things.' I was quick to judge, he seems a lovely guy.

'Let me give it some thought while I put some washing in the machine.'

'It's okay,' he replies. 'It was a hugely insightful question. No right or wrong answer.'

'Sorry for being blunt. It's just that so many men I meet online are one-track minded.'

'I like blunt. But I'm not most men. I really miss cuddling and holding hands. So pathetic.' He adds a sad emoji.

'Washing in machine. Still thinking.'

'You can just say any old nonsense. I'm not judging you or asking deal-breaking questions. Unless you say burying under a patio.'

'1. Sitting in a coffee shop on a Sunday reading the papers together. 2. Reading books together holding hands and occasionally sharing things we've read. 3. Kissing while watching a sunset. 4. Looking at a problem that's occurred and saying what shall WE do about it. 5. Throwing my legs over someone and snuggling in together to watch Netflix. 6. Long walks in the snow or autumn leaves.

'All sounds rather nice. Is rubbing legs allowed?'

What can I say to that? I reply with a laughing emoji––it's a good cop out.

'Go on, just ignore me,' he jests. 'Women tend to do that!'

Adrian and I share a love of photography. It's always good to share at least one interest––makes conversation easier when there's common ground. 'Moving swiftly on, what about a walk after lunch with our cameras. See what piccies we can take?'

'Great idea. I'll bring my Nikon and show you what lenses I've got.'

'I'll bring my Canon.'

HERE I AM, a few minutes early, standing outside The Cricketers, shoes I've not worn in months cutting into my feet and my skirt threatening to burst at the seams with all that belly fat I've amassed in quarantine. Wicked Wagon Wheels and heavenly Hobnobs are to blame. Although M&S Yum Yums must take some of the responsibility for the extra pounds.

I remember how things were at this quaint, beamed establishment before lockdown. Getting jostled by people struggling to carry a round of three pints in two hands. And before the smoking ban, standing in a cloud of smoke, swerving my hips to avoid getting burned by cigarettes as smokers squeezed past, holding their fags at dangerous angles. Now look at the place—— it's unrecognisable. A member of staff in an apron and mask is standing next to a trestle table at the entrance holding a clipboard. He stops people as they head into the pub, taking their names, phone numbers and time of entry for the NHS Test and Trace before asking them to spray their hands with sanitiser. Busy watching, I don't notice Adrian sneak up behind me until he says 'boo,' in my ear.

'Hi, sorry, didn't see you.'

'You were miles away. Shall we?' He sweeps his hand towards the door, and I follow him to the Gestapo officer guarding Fort Knox who takes our particulars and explains how the new pub experience works before allowing entry and forewarning us not to leave by this entrance as there is a separate exit at the back of the pub. It's hardly an 'experience' and feels more like entering a danger zone where landmines or hazardous chemicals lurk. We follow the large yellow arrows marked out on the floor to the bar. There are arrows in other directions leading to the toilets and exit. They make me think of the yellow brick road in the Wizard of Oz and I'm tempted to start singing Elton John's Goodbye Yellow Brick Road. The staff are waiting behind tall Perspex screens, and this reminds me of what banks looked like back in the 1970s.

Sniffing the air, I realise that something else has changed. It doesn't smell like a pub, there are none of the usual aromas of beer mixed with body odour. With everyone drenched in hand sanitiser there's a nasty chemical whiff tickling my nostrils.

'It's table service, sir,' the barman says polishing a glass. A waitress steps forward to show us to a table.

'What's up with your car?' I ask Adrian when we're seated and half glancing at our menus. And from that point on it feels as if I'm interviewing him for a job. I try not to be interrogatory but I'm literally asking all the questions while he asks me nothing. I manage to slip into the conversation small snippets about my own life because this has become so centred on him. It's hard going.

On several occasions while I'm speaking, he pulls out his phone and says, 'Sorry, just checking to see if my car's ready.' I stop talking and after he puts his phone back on the table, he looks at me as if he's about to give me his undivided attention and says, 'Sorry, what were you saying?'

I'm struggling. It's not just his complete lack of interest, it's his dry, cutting sense of humour too. He's trying to be witty, but I find his comments mildly insulting.

While we're waiting for our food, he asks to see some of my best photos. Scrolling through the library on my phone, I come across one of my favourites––a black and white picture of Olivia dancing in a launderette wearing earmuffs and a long coat.

'You're stalking your daughter. I'd get arrested for that.'

No praise––this is one of my best shots. 'I'm always looking for that elusive, unique shot. Wherever I go, my eye sweeps round people and landscapes and out my phone comes. Maybe you're the same? I take after my dad; he was a professional photographer.'

'Everyone is a photographer these days,' he says dismissively.

Still scrolling, I come across a picture he'll love. A lighthouse with a dramatic sky.

'And that's when the good Lord appeared.' He's laughing and sounds like Moses preaching from the mountain. 'Did you Photoshop the sky?'

'No.' I did but don't want to admit it.

Maybe the picture I took of three women standing next to Quadrophenia Alley in Brighton might impress him.

He studies it and by the look on his face he's trying to think of a wisecrack. 'Looks like they're wearing Christmas hats. Did you get their permission before taking it?'

I consider showing him a few of my dad's pictures, but if he dismisses those, I know I'll be upset. Dad's death, coming so suddenly after a short illness a couple of years ago is still raw. I was very close to him and have fond memories of watching him develop photos in his darkroom, as well as all the places we visited because of his hobby, which invariably became my hobby too. Memories anchor me to the past and to the future. A five a.m. photo shoot in Brightling churchyard in the mist dressed in my nightie. Sunsets in Hastings. A group of old men lined up in the cricket club after a match. Standing on an old defunct railway wearing a Victorian costume. Fun times, all too brief. Each memory is like a thread I struggle to keep hold of-- balloons that float in the sky.

He shows me some of his pictures, taken around the National Trust property, Sheffield Park. The clarity is stunning, such sharp images and vibrant colour and I can't help but gasp. He's brilliant. 'Wow, they're excellent.'

He waves me away. 'There was no skill involved.' He looks at me with a frown as if I'm dumb. 'They're just point and click.' He picks up his beer glass, immediately thudding it back on the table. 'There's a spider trying to abseil into my glass.'

'I don't think I've ever seen a drunk spider.'

And for the first time we laugh but it's short-lived because the food has arrived.

'Is it safe to eat those?' he asks, peering at my bowl of mussels in garlic butter.

'Maybe not as safe as your lasagne.' I smile and for the first time I feel relaxed.

'You don't like those pesky little things, surely? Shellfish are plain wrong. Slippery little suckers'

'Why would I order something I don't like?'

He's looking at my mussels in a strange way, as if they've just landed in a spaceship. 'You do realise what they look like?'

My face is going pink. I don't want to lift my fork, I'm so embarrassed. We are talking body parts. And I'm about to eat.

'But there's a big difference.' He winks. 'I don't like eating mussels. You're a very discreet person, Donna.'

'I try to be, don't want to be offensive.' I smile.

'And I've noticed something about you. Not sure it's appropriate to mention on a first date.'

Oh God, what's coming? 'Try me.'

'I love your feet.'

'My feet?' Not my hair, my bottom, which always makes a statement, or my boobs? Just my feet.

'Sparkly shoes, pretty.'

'I hope you don't have a foot fetish.'

'I might do.' He gives me a cheeky grin. How have we gone from a stilted conversation to flirting, in five easy steps?

'I like to be walked all over, makes me feel wanted.'

'Do you now?' I hope he doesn't go into detail. Luckily he just gives me another cheeky grin and tucks into his lasagne. It's time to move on, before this banter leads onto dodgy grounds.

'What do you think about this new set-up in here? It's a bit Orwellian and controlled. It feels unnatural and over-the-top.'

He puts his fork down and glances round before staring at me. I feel uncomfortable under his gaze and already know that he disagrees with me. 'They had to do something. They've got to protect their customers and staff. It gives people some reassurance.'

'It's superficial reassurance. It's unwelcoming. And I don't want to wear a mask to the toilet.'

'This isn't just about you. It's about protecting and being

kind to others. Basic humility. I suggest you speak to one of the nurses on the frontline or a family who've lost someone to Covid. I'm amazed at your views. Good luck with that.'

I flinch at the animosity in his voice which has taken me by surprise. His harsh words still rankle even after the conversation has moved on and a part of me wants to walk out. I've seen a side to him that I shouldn't see on a first date and that bothers me.

I won't be seeing him again. At the end of the meal, he checks his phone for the umpteenth time, and declaring his car is ready to be picked up from the garage, he scrapes his chair back and waves at the waitress for the bill.

With the bill paid, we head outside. 'Didn't you say you might go for a swim in the sea this afternoon?' he asks. 'Although why you'd want to. You don't know what's lurking in that filthy water. Jellyfish, floating turds, who knows.'

'Nothing will ever put me off swimming in the sea.' Not even you, I want to add. 'I might not go down today; I'm doing a twelve-hour shift tomorrow.'

And when he asks, 'Sorry, what is it you do, again?' it's confirmed he's not interested. I've learned a lot about him over our meal--how he feels about work, his kids' names, and ages, yet he knows very little about me other than my shoe size.

CHAPTER 9 - LUXURY TEABAGS

onna

'OH, MOTHER.' The granitelike sternness is back in Olivia's voice. 'I don't have the time to see you.'

She sounds like the CEO of a large corporation. Always too busy to see her old mother. No surprises there. Since the easing of lockdown she's found plenty of excuses why I can't come up to Leicester. Too many post-lockdown parties and catching up with friends she hasn't seen. It's been weeks since I last saw her. And now, as if things aren't difficult enough, the Prime Minister has put the boot in. He's only gone and announced that new local restrictions will be necessary in Leicester following a high number of people testing positive for Covid. It would be Leicester of all places. The city where my daughter lives. This has got to be the start of a slippery slope; I can see more of these northern cities tumbling like dominoes and then bang, we'll be back in another lockdown before we know it.

'Please, Liv. You're going back into lockdown. I can book a

hotel in the city centre for tomorrow night and take you out for a nice meal. This could be our last chance for a while.'

'Oh, all right,' she says like a moody teenager. I'm glad I can't see her rolling eyes.

All parents need to feel wanted. It's only natural. If a friend or a boyfriend made me feel unwanted, I'd dump them. I'd go to the ends of the earth for Olivia, but I must live with the fact that I am a nuisance to my daughter and a hindrance in her life. Children aren't always loving and warm, even adult children. They can be cold like a stone in the palm.

I BOOK a hotel in the city centre and a three-course meal in a swanky restaurant. I want to treat her; she works hard, and we need quality time together. As we head towards autumn, I have a strong feeling that we will be locked down once again, but I hope I'm proved wrong.

About to sling my bag into the car, Olivia phones. Oh God, I hope she isn't about to ply me with excuses and pull out. Despite her grumpiness on the phone yesterday, I'm looking forward to seeing her. I bet her dad wouldn't rush up the M1 to see her, let alone treat her to a night in a hotel. Sometimes, the way she talks you'd think the sun shines out of his backside, but in practice he makes little effort. He's stopped giving her birthday and Christmas presents, would you believe? Told her he couldn't afford it because the divorce lawyers had screwed him for every last penny. Now if I'd pulled that stunt, I wouldn't hear the last of it, but he can never do wrong--she worships the ground he walks on.

'Just wanted to warn you, it's nothing to worry about, but I've got a slight cold brewing.'

'I'm not bothered about a cold, darling.' I'm in the car, the key in the ignition, ready to go. Her nose sounds a bit blocked, but everything is booked, and nothing will deter me. Maybe I'll come home with a cold, but it will have been worth it to see her.

The roads aren't busy, and I glide up the M1, turning off the motorway near Glenfield and head into the city centre. I drive the car into the concrete tomb of the multi-storey carpark, drumming the heel of my hand on the steering wheel as I sing to the latest Ed Sheeran song, my excitement mounting. I haven't seen my daughter since March. It feels like ages. How will she be? Will she look the same? I glide into a space and kill the engine. I'm glad I've come here. It was the right thing to do. I get the impression that sometimes Olivia doesn't think I care about her and that breaks my heart. Maybe there was a time when I put my love life ahead of her needs. I was so consumed with finding a man. I bitterly regret that now but at the time all I could see was her growing up fast. She'd leave home and I'd be alone, and I couldn't bear that thought. That crushing loneliness, the meals for one, the silence, buying a budgie and a bungalow and slipping quietly into old age. And here I am, years later and that thought still scares me, but back then I wish I'd just relaxed and not worried so much about the future and just enjoyed her company. I'll never get those times back again. It's too late. They're gone, like autumn leaves on a tree. I'm sure she's punishing me now for how I was. That undercurrent to her words, the digs, the snide comments.

Still pondering these thoughts, I make a beeline for the food section in M&S. Into a metal basket I put some pretty paper napkins, a bottle of her favourite wine, Rioja, a box of Luxury Gold Teabags and a selection of chunky, freshly baked cookies that smell divine, and I carry my basket to the tills. She's meeting me at the hotel at five. We can have cookies and tea and take our time to get ready for the evening and I'm sure she'll love a glass of Rioja beside the bath while she pampers herself. I've even bought a bottle of bubbles because she only has a shower where she lives, and I know how much she misses a tub.

Throughout her teens she'd spend ages in the bath, the water laced with frothy foam that came right up to the taps.

In the hotel room, I take two plates from my bag and put a folded napkin and three cookies on each. I'm just arranging a teapot between the plates when I realise she's late. It's already 5.15. That's a quarter of an hour less time with her. Never mind, I mustn't fret, we're not due at the restaurant until seven. There's plenty of time. I've already texted her the room number. Any minute now, her feet will come pounding along the corridor. She has a distinct walk I'd recognise anywhere. Like her father, she takes long strides and bounces on the balls of her feet as she walks, her bottom rising. I kick my shoes off and sit on the bed to wait. Ten minutes disappears. I check my phone, but there's no message from her. Maybe she's late finishing her Zoom lesson.

There's just one thing I've forgotten to do. Jumping up from the bed, I rummage in my bag for the Manuka honey pamper peel-off face mask and prop it against her pillow before checking my phone again. She's now forty minutes late. This is getting ridiculous. What the hell's keeping her?

Stop fretting, I tell myself. *Does it matter she's late?* It could be worse. Imagine if I'd come all this way only for her to cancel me.

Something niggles at the back of my mind. It wouldn't surprise me if she does cancel. I wouldn't put anything past her these days, not after she called me a loser. Picking up the remote, I flick the telly on and watch the local news which is all about the rise in Covid cases in the city. A gym owner and a café owner are complaining about the forthcoming lockdown, telling the interviewer that it's not fair that Leicester has been targeted for these restrictions when other cities have rising cases too. The gym owner is cross and says that the city's immigrant and ethnic minority population are being blamed for the spike in cases.

I'm so engrossed in the news, that when I next check my

phone, it's gone six. My heart sinks. This isn't fair. She should have told me she'd be late. I fire off a message asking where she is and several minutes later, she pings back, 'Running a bit late, soz.'

'Restaurant is booked for 7.'

'I know.'

I glance at the cookies. It's too late for tea and biscuits even if she arrives now. I'd better get changed and wait.

Just when I decide to call the restaurant to alter the booking to 7.30, Olivia calls.

'Liv, where are you?' I can hear music and laughter in the background.

'I'm at a party. I'm having so much fun.' Sounds like it—there's excitement in her voice. I feel flat, disappointed, and cross with her, because this is selfish and thoughtless of her, but a part of me envies her. She's young and she's enjoying life. I'm just her mum, I don't play the big part in her life that I used to. She's left me behind to live my remaining days.

I know I mustn't be like this, but I can't help that feeling of rejection. 'I've come all this way, Liv. If I'd known...' And hang on a minute, yesterday she told me she had the sniffles and thought a cold was brewing. Her cold must have conveniently gone away.

'It was organised last minute, because of lockdown. I won't see my friends after tonight. I hate these lockdowns. It's going to be horrible.

'You want me to cancel the restaurant?'

She doesn't immediately reply, and I hear more laughter and shouting in the background. It's some party.

'I'm really sorry. I will stay with you tonight though. I'll get there around ten.'

What does ten even mean? She'll probably roll in at midnight, flop onto the bed drunk and go fast asleep. Then morning will arrive, and she'll nurse a hangover and it'll be time for me to head home.

My stomach growls. I was looking forward to eating out. I could do with a bowl of pasta or a risotto or some other substantial meal. But sitting in a restaurant all by myself, feeling conspicuous like a goldfish in a bowl; it's not going to happen. That would be grim, so I call the restaurant to cancel the booking, before easing myself back onto the bed and scoffing all the cookies as I scroll through the TV channels to find something to watch.

TRUE TO HER WORD, Olivia turns up at ten. Just as I'm nodding off, her sharp rap at the door jolts me awake.

'Sorry Mum,' she says giving me a hug and kicking her shoes off. 'That was such a good party. I couldn't not go.'

Batting away sadness, I sweep her into another hug, her warmth comforting and reassuring. Her hair, the colour of champagne smells of apricot. There's something different about her and I realise what it is. She has a blunt fringe, the ones you spot in glossy magazines. She's not had a fringe since she was at school. It looks too severe.

At least she's not tipsy, I'd see it in her eyes, and she'd be swaying, but there's an odour of cheap lager on her breath which reminds me of when her father used to come home from the pub reeking of beer. This party has highlighted one thing. I'm not important in her life, her friends come first. It feels as if my role as Mum is effectively over; I've been relegated to the side-lines, like an MP who's been demoted to the backbenches.

I pull away, my hands resting on her shoulders. 'You look a bit peaky, darling.' I will always care, always be concerned, no matter what missiles she throws at me. Parents rarely let go of their children, but children let go of their parents. They move on, move away. My approval used to define her. Now it doesn't matter. My opinion is sneered at and no longer valued.

'Don't fuss. I'm just a bit under the weather, that's all.' She moves away from me and slings her handbag on the bed, opens it and pulls out a nightie and toothbrush. 'You're annoyed with me, aren't you? I can tell.'

'You're here now.' I keep my voice upbeat. 'Come on, sit.' I pat the bed. 'I want to know everything that's going on in your life, I've not seen you for so long. Zoom isn't the same.'

'This is lovely, Mum.' She glances round the room, peeping into the bathroom before heading over to the kettle. She spots the discarded M&S patisserie bag, crumbs spilling out over the table. 'What have you been eating? Shouldn't you be watching the calories? You're not going to hook a guy by piling on the weight.'

'I like to think there's a man out there who will love me for my personality.'

Absentmindedly, I flick the kettle on.

'What planet are you on, Mum?' she mocks. 'All men are shallow. You should know that by now.' She laughs, swings round and pinches my waist. 'You should go to the gym.'

Having changed into my nightie an hour ago, I throw my dressing gown on and tie it around my waist defensively, not wanting her to see my bulging belly.

'How's the dating going?' She plunges onto the bed laughing, as if I'm a prize comedy act. I'm glad she finds my life so amusing––I don't. 'Dad's life is so normal compared to yours.'

I stifle a sigh. We're on well-trodden territory––does this comparison of parents by adult children go on in every broken home across Britain? It's soul-destroying.

'What's he up to these days?' I can't help being curious about Nick's life even though I'm torturing myself by asking. I want to know if he's drinking again, but I don't think she has any inkling that he used to have a drink problem. It's as if that part of his life has been erased from the history books and forgotten about.

'He came up last week, with Pamela. We had lunch out and wandered round the shopping centre, then they went home.' She makes the three-hour journey up to Leicester sound like a breeze. Nick likes driving on motorways and he's got a faster car than me. I'm miffed though. She always makes excuses as to why she can't see me, but she'll happily invite her dad up, dropping everything to fit him into her busy routine.

Her eyes light up and she says excitedly, 'He's decorated a room for me, so that I can stay whenever I want. I'm thinking of heading down tomorrow and spending lockdown there. Not as if I can see my friends with all this going on.'

My heart plummets. I may as well be invisible. She obviously prefers going there because they offer a semblance of normality––they are a Hallmark couple straight out of vomitsville. But I'm a frazzled single mother living with a motley crew who queue for the bathroom each morning and jostle for space in the tiny kitchen. Plus, he has a much bigger telly than me and a Sky package. Whatever I can't afford, the chances are, he can.

I can't help wondering why his second marriage is going so well. I was always told that leopards don't change their spots, so why hasn't their marriage fallen apart? How does she put up with his behaviour, or does he act like a reasonable human being around her? I have a theory. It's not a complex one, it isn't rocket science. They don't have stress in their marriage. They haven't had children for starters. Tiredness, hormones, the huge pressure that comes with raising little people, all put a strain on relationships and shrink the hours left to enjoy quality time as a couple, as well as putting pressure on the purse strings. Not to mention the shell of sleep deprivation, existing day-to-day in a fog.

After chatting we climb into bed, switching the bedside lights off. Trying to find sleep amid my thoughts, I turn to watch Olivia fall into a heavy slumber, her hand resting under her head, a dribble forming at the side of her mouth. She's so close, I can feel her hot breath on my face. She snuffles and occasionally snorts. It's cute, she looks so peaceful and innocent, no longer angst-ridden with a spine of steel running through her. I'm reminded of when she was little, tucked up in bed with her favourite Teletubby, Laa-Laa, under her arm after storytime. I doubt she remembers now, all the hours we spent snuggled up in her little bed with its princess duvet cover, reading stories by authors such as Julia Donaldson and David Walliams.

She's on the cusp of becoming someone, doesn't yet know who she is but one thing is certain. She'll make mistakes like I have because we remain children despite the advancing years. We spend our whole life growing emotionally. For now, Olivia is blissfully ignorant; she doesn't believe she will make mistakes.

CHAPTER 10 - THE DREADED LURGY

onna

DESPITE THE RUINED EVENING, I'm glad I made it to Leicester. I am constantly trying to make amends for the damages of the past: divorce, and the string of dating disasters that followed which ate into the time and energy I should have expended on Olivia. The simple truth is I put my own happiness and well-being ahead of hers. A hard and painful lesson. Being a mother is an attitude, a state of mind, and my attitude and approach was wrong. I cannot go back and be the mother I should have been. I'll never regain those wasted years. It's too late. I'm no longer needed. I barely exist as Mother. She has flown the nest, is carving a future for herself and I must fit in around her and snatch whatever morsels she throws me.

THREE DAYS AFTER VISITING OLIVIA, it's the middle of the night and I jerk awake in the pitch-black darkness of my bedroom. I feel dreadful. My head is pounding. It's as if a clamp is squeezing my skull—the headache from hell. Switching on the bedside light and reaching for a packet of paracetamol, I realise this is more than just a headache. Sweat saturates my face, pooling in the hollow of my neck and my nightie is clinging to my back. My body aches with the effort of lifting the glass of water to my lips to swallow the tablets. I inch up the bed but it's too painful to move. It's as if a poison has seeped into my bones. I lie there waiting for the painkillers to take effect and for daylight to carve patterns through my thin curtains.

When grey morning light floods my room, I adjust my head on the pillow and when I cough to clear my throat, there's a tightness across my chest. My first thought is that I'm having a heart attack. I could die here. How long would it take my lodgers to notice my absence? They'd just assume I was away and had forgotten to tell them. I am alone. With the ticking clock on my wall. The hum of traffic outside.

Stop it, Donna. I mustn't sink down the rabbit hole of self-pity. What will that achieve? I am alone—it's a fact. Lots of people are and they cope. There's nothing that a few hours rest won't cure, then I'll be fit for my night shift. I slip back to sleep, waking sometime later to my phone ringing.

'Mum, I feel awful. I think I'm dying.' As she lets out a sob, my heart silently breaks. My baby needs me and I'm miles away. She can't leave the city, can't even take the train home. I should be there, helping her, proving my love for her. That she comes first and always will.

'I think it's Covid. All my friends are ill, and one friend, Alfie, was rushed to hospital last night. He was gasping for breath. What if I end up in hospital too?'

I do the mother-hen routine and tell her to keep her fluids up, take regular painkillers, get plenty of rest. She's an adult; she knows all this. But I'm worried sick, I don't care that I'm ill, that I went to Leicester and probably came back with the virus.

Miles away and lying here in bed; I feel so helpless. That same old feeling of being a useless mother.

After our phone call, I ease myself out of bed, every limb and every muscle aching, and I stagger downstairs to make a cuppa. It's now eleven but I don't feel like eating. I should eat, I need to keep my strength up so that I can beat this and get back to work. Unless I work, I won't get paid.

Olivia and all her friends have Covid, but without a test to confirm it, I won't know I have it. I don't want to get a test and be a government statistic. Every positive result leads to further lockdowns. Another case, another notch on the graph. I won't break any rules though; I'll stay at home and keep away from others until I'm better.

I delve into the biscuit barrel and tear open a packet of Custard Creams. I don't feel like one but nibbling on a biscuit might revive me. Yuk, it tastes awful, like soggy bread. There's no flavour. Maybe I'd be better having a satsuma. More thirst-quenching and refreshing, it will stop me feeling queasy. After peeling one, I bite into the zesty segment but cannot taste it. Like the Custard Cream, it may as well be soggy bread. I've never experienced a loss of taste before––this must be Covid; it's a symptom that's been widely talked about.

I SPEND the next few days languishing on the sofa, cat-napping. At times I'm barely able to pick up the remote because I feel so ill. It's an effort even scrolling through Netflix or Amazon Prime deciding what to watch and as for online dating, I don't have the energy or the inclination. Messages are piling up in my inbox like snow on the driveway. These men can wait. Chances are they are timewasters, either looking for casual sex or a pen pal. It's like wading through a river of porridge––it's a hard slog, a chore I don't miss.

I've spoken to Olivia several times and each time we

compare notes on how we're feeling. I imagine her sitting in bed in her tiny room in Leicester, cut off from friends, but when she next calls, there's a voice in the background I recognise.

It can't be. What hell is *he* doing there? Breaking lockdown rules. Risking catching the virus and passing it on. 'That's not your father, surely?'

'Yes,' she says sheepishly. 'Dad drove up to Leicester to bring me home.'

Home? This is her home. Her base. With me. Where she grew up. A desire to vent my jealousy rises inside me—– a slick of anger that's hard to tap down. He's given her a nicely decorated room with a large TV on the wall. Fast internet. Cola on tap. Crisps in the cupboard. No wonder he's the go-to parent. That used to be my title. I carried her, gave birth to her. I was the one day care rang when she was sick. I took her to birthday parties. I juggled several jobs. I did it all. And yet he has climbed the parental ladder; he is the favoured one. Kids are mercenary, they sniff out the parent with the money and he has pots of it.

'But he'll catch the virus from you?'

'We drove home in his convertible.' I'm always hearing about Nick's Mazda MX5. 'It was bloody freezing with the roof down, but I wore two hats and a scarf. We're all wearing masks round the house and being super careful.' All—–meaning his wife too. I visualise their cosy household. They have each other even if they are confined to different rooms because of the virus. Something flares inside me—–I'm sick of internet dating, but as soon as I feel up to it, I must try again. I bet the three of them are secretly laughing at me—–,Mum, the hopeless relationship failure.

Living fractured, busy lives, internet dating is the only way to meet someone. I cannot give up hope. I cannot be labelled a disaster zone. I am too young to accept a life alone. Internet dating is like doing the lottery. You must be in it to win it and the more swiping I do, the more chance I have of meeting Mr Right.

I'd like to think though that I could meet someone outside of my computer screen. In that place we call the real world. But where? In the fish aisle of Sainsburys, or at the gym? But I don't work out. I'm too knackered for that. I wouldn't want to be approached by a man in a gym when I'm red-faced and sweating. What about the park? I've spent enough time there during lockdown. I can't randomly strike up a conversation with a stranger, however hunky he might be. It would be too weird. I'd have to own a dog and be prepared to walk in all weathers and exchange canine-related chat with other dog owners.

Sometimes love appears in the most unlikely of places when you least expect it. I mustn't give up hope.

CHAPTER 11 - LAUNDRY MAN

onna

NUDGING the glass door with my basket of washing, I feel the steamy air hit me as I enter the launderette. It's so humid, it feels as if I've stepped off a plane in Singapore or some other sticky climate. I don't have a dryer at home and the lodgers create so much washing that I need to come here to dry it.

There are a couple of children clamouring along the wooden bench and when they see me, they shriek and jostle, 'Can I put your coins in the machine, please?'

It's as if they're in an amusement arcade, but without the prize toys. 'Off,' a woman orders. 'Leave the lady alone.'

A man further along the bench has a laptop balanced on his knee and it looks as if he's working. He glances up at me, smiles and raises his eyebrows as if to say, *kids, who'd have 'em?*

'Sit down on the floor with your colouring books,' the woman orders, waving her finger at the kids with a frown.

'Colouring is boring,' one of the children complains before

turning to the other child and with eyes lit up and saying, 'Let's pretend the machines are rockets, shall we?' He goes over to a row of washers and begins slamming the doors.

'Excuse me, lad, you shouldn't be doing that, you might break the doors,' the man says glancing up from his laptop, an exasperated look on his face. I'm guessing he's never had kids. Doesn't have the patience. God knows how he can work in a steamy launderette--it's not the most ideal of workspaces. I'm wondering if he commuted to London before the pandemic but is now working from home and trying to multitask with household chores.

After loading my machine, I slam the door and feed coins into the slot before sitting back on the bench. It'll be a half-hour wait, so I watch the children causing havoc. The boy is encouraging the little girl--probably his sister-- to climb on to his shoulders and get on top of one of the washing machines opposite me. The mother is outside bringing more laundry from her car. 'When you're on top you're safe,' the boy says to the girl. 'No monsters can get you up there. I'll fit my special tracking device to my back, to detect aliens. The machines are special interceptors.' He's screeching and flinging his arms around. I've got to get out of here. They're giving me a headache. Can't hear myself think. The last time I was in here there was a weirdo doing yoga on a mat, now this.

Tucking my laundry basket under the bench I head over the road to Costa where I can watch my knickers doing somersaults from a vantage point by the window. Joining the queue, I glance behind me. Laptop man has followed me in. I smile. 'We had the same idea.'

He shakes his head. 'That mother, she had no control over her kids.' His face relaxes now that we are away from the screaming brats. He laughs. 'I'm getting too old to deal with kids.'

'No lively grandkids then?'

'Huh, I'm not old enough.' He looks at me straight on. Piercing blue eyes, a wide grin like the Cheshire cat in *Alice in Wonderland*, full set of teeth. Teeth that are too perfect given his age--in his late fifties like me, I'd guess. Must be falsies. Glass of Steradent by the bed at night. Lovely.

After paying, I step aside to wait for my latte, watching him glance at the menu and speak to the barista. Despite owning a Mac, he's not city slick and is sporting the old man, grungy look: baggy brown cords and a crumpled brown shirt--the type made of itchy fabric. He's also wearing a green tweed jacket and chunky brown lace-ups which are a real turn-. If I came across him in a forest, I might mistake him for a moss-covered log. He certainly doesn't look like your average Canary Wharf banker or accountant.

I carry my steaming mug to the window table and am just taking the first sip when he pops up in front of me. 'Mind if I join you?' he asks, before plonking himself down regardless.

'I'm surprised you could work over there.' I nod in the direction of the launderette. Looked a bit tricky, laptop perched on knee.'

He laughs, a sexy, throaty laugh and I see right inside his mouth. 'I wasn't working, I was on a dating site.'

That's one thing we have in common. Along with half the adult population, also on dating sites. I best skate around that thorny subject. 'There's me imagining you worked in the city, but now work from home.'

'Ah no,' he says slowly, raising his eyebrows as if he's coaxing me to keep guessing. 'I'm a carer.'

'For an elderly relative?' I should stop. I'm being nosey.

'In a care home.'

'No way.'

'Someone has to.' He laughs and speaks in equal measure. Unusual for a bloke. But it's infectious and I reach for my asthma spray.

'I've never met a male carer. I'm in care work too. But I work for an agency visiting people in their homes.'

'I wondered about that, until I discovered they don't pay travel time between clients.'

'Yeah, that's one of the drawbacks, but I take in lodgers and Airbnb guests to supplement my wages, while I wait for a rich man to ride into my life and rescue me.' I laugh hard and nervously. Why the hell did I go and say that? It's so not true. Am I flirting with him?

I hope he realises I'm joking. I'm an independent, modern woman. Like to think of myself as enterprising. I don't believe in the nonsense of fairy-tales. Maybe there is a small voice at the back of my head that would like to be rescued. Somebody to share household bills with and the burden of life.

'And I'm looking for a rich lady to rescue me.' Laughing, he glances across the road. 'Your washing's ready.' Is he trying to get rid of me?

I drain the rest of my latte and get up.

'Want to swap phone numbers?'

I'm not expecting this. I'm flattered he'd like to meet again. At the very least, I've made a friend. A friend called Simon. To me he's Laundry Man.

LAUNDRY MAN'S grungy appearance and grubby fingernails don't make him a suitable contender and I don't fancy him. But in my quiet moments I find myself thinking about him and wondering if he'll call, or whether we just exchanged numbers out of politeness. Maybe I'm just getting desperate. But it would be nice to see him again--for coffee, a glass of wine, a stroll round the park. Anything. It's company.

I drop into the launderette from time to time to dry the Airbnb sheets and towels--but in the past fortnight I've been lots of times. Washing duvets, net curtains, rugs. Anything I can find to wash or dry, in the hope that I'll bump into him.

Alas, there's no sign of Laundry Man. And then one evening out of the blue, he rings.

'I meant to call you,' he says, 'but it's been so busy at work and emotionally draining. One of our oldest residents died last week, aged 110. I was with her when she passed away. Old wartime songs were playing in the background.'

'I'm sorry, that is sad. But such a privilege to have cared for her.'

'I knew you'd understand. I had that feeling about you. To be honest I'm having a hard time coming to terms with it. Such a dear old lady, she was the only one in the home that didn't wear a pad at night.'

Only a carer would share that. 'Amazing.'

'She'd sit on the loo and tell you about the day news broke of the end of the First World War.'

'Incredible.'

'She got very muddled though. Thought the Nazis were coming for her.'

'It's hard when they pass away. You get attached to them.' I'm not comfortable sharing information about my work; I don't know him but at the same time it's easy banter.

'It was so nice to meet you the other week,' he gushes.

'You too.'

'If you're free, would you like to come out for lunch on Saturday? We've got to make the most of the Eat Out to Help Out scheme while it lasts.'

Cheapskate. What if the government weren't giving us all generous discounts on meals out to help the hospitality industry after lockdown? Would he still ask me to dinner?

· · ·

ON THE JOURNEY over to the Duck and Bucket, it occurs to me that seating inside will be limited to comply with social distancing rules. Maybe we should have booked. I park in a nearby road and head to the entrance where Simon, aka Laundry Man, is already waiting, hands in pockets staring at the roof of the pub as if that is where all the action is.

He turns and beams at me. 'All right?'

'Hi, and what's this?' At the door, next to a bulldog-sized bottle of hand sanitiser on a trestle table, there's an off-putting notice warning customers not to enter. We are to find a table in the carpark where a waitress will take our order.

'Come on,' he says, linking my arm, 'car park it is.'

At the back of the pub a huge marquee has been erected over pot-holed tarmac and metal tables and chairs have been arranged on the uneven ground.

'Looks a tad grim. How about we find somewhere else?' I suggest.

'Let's give them a chance.' He's positive, the type of person that would make the best of any situation, a compromiser. I bet he had a good divorce. One of those rare, neat, amicable settlements cobbled together over the kitchen sink.

He pulls out a rickety and uneven chair for me and nods in the waiter's direction. 'This is great, it's safer than everyone breathing in Covid particles. You've got to hand it them; they're doing their best to stay open.'

I glance down at the waterlogged potholes and sling my handbag over the chair. It's August, the sky was blue when I left home, but it rained heavily in the night, and more is expected, judging by the dark clouds gathering. The metal seat connects with my buttocks, a cold chill seeping through my body.

The waiter comes over with menus and asks what we'd like to drink. Before I've had the chance to peruse the wines and spirits, Simon jumps in and asks for two glasses of tap water. As soon as the waiter disappears, he leans towards me and whispers conspiratorially. 'There's no discount on the drinks. I rang the pub earlier to check what the scheme covers.'

After this, I decide he's just a friend. Partner material no, I hate cheapskates. He's totally unashamed of his frugality. I should have realised when I first clapped eyes on his clothes. Today he's just as frumpy and is wearing a faded rainbow coloured t-shirt that's frayed around the collar. It's got to be at least twenty years old. Surely, he can afford to update his wardrobe rather than hanging on to clothes he's clearly owned since the Dark Ages. I can imagine him going to great lengths to save a penny or two. He's the type to reuse teabags and only flush the loo once a day.

'It's so nice to see you,' he gushes, taking my hand and squeezing it. In that moment I forget about his stinginess, his dated wardrobe and enjoy the warmth of this new person in my life. 'This is my first day off in a month.'

'I'll have to call you, Saint Simon.' I laugh.

'They're so short-staffed. Some of that is down to Brexit. The Poles, Romanians and Hungarians didn't stick around, and it's been hard to fill the vacancies ever since and several people have been self-isolating with Covid. I'm always offering to do extra shifts.' Showing me how exhausted he is, he flops his head theatrically and expels air through puffed cheeks.

'A glutton for punishment by the sounds of it. How long have you worked there?'

'Getting on for ten years.'

'No way.'

'In a weird way, I love it.'

'I know what you mean. Physically it's hard, but the people are delightful. Mainly.' I give a little laugh. Some can be a pain in the bum. But they can't help it. They're in pain and they've lost their independence.

The waiter comes over to take our order. We've barely

looked at the menu. Before I have the chance to decide, Simon looks at me, 'Macaroni cheese? Sausage and mash?'

I glance at the choices. Macaroni cheese and sausage and mash are both £8. Everything else is over £15. Dear oh dear, he really is tight. But I'm not expecting him to foot the bill. He can't be earning much. And I don't want to be constrained, I'd rather we split the bill, or I pay for myself. This is mega awkward. There are no rules in the Wild West of dating.

'Are we going Dutch? I fancy the salmon.' It's the most expensive meal on the menu.

The waiter is poised with his iPad. 'Shall I give you a few more moments?'

Simon looks at me horrified. 'You're not paying a penny.' I've offended him. Bruised his male ego.

'Okay,' I concede, 'I'll have macaroni,' even though it gives me indigestion.

'I love old people,' Simon says as soon as the waiter disappears. Forgetting the question of the bill, he ploughs on with our earlier conversation. 'Their stories, their wisdom, everything they've been through, it's awe-inspiring. And they're funny too.' And then he's off, painting a picture of their characters, one by one. 'There's Cybil Smith. She takes my arm and starts singing 'Onward, Christian Soldiers' as I lead her down the corridor to her room. "What are we to do, what are we to do," she says when we've reached her room. And there's George Oliver, he's in his late nineties. He stands at his bedroom window and tells me, "We need to get going, we'll be late for bowling," then he asks me, "how long have you been a member of the bowling club?"'

I visualise these people in their tan pop-socks tight like bands, and pilloried cardigans, their minds having reaching the end, ravaged by dementia, their bodies just shells rattling on.

'What about you? What are your clients like?'

'Yesterday I went to see a lady who's hard of hearing. I asked her if she wanted tuna salad for lunch. "Tulips?" she asked, "why do I want to eat tulips?"' We both laugh.

'Bless her,' he says.

As lunch arrives, out of nowhere the skies have darkened like a bruise. The heavens look fit to burst.

The conversation is stuck on work, so I ask, 'What do you do in your spare time?'

'Camping. I love it. Any free time I get I escape.'

'Oh my God, we're in for a downpour.' The wind is whipping up. We're close to the edge of the marquee and half exposed to the elements. Within minutes rain is drumming on the canvas, and the roof of the marquee sags as pools of water form. Cold droplets nail me, and I move my chair further in.

'It's just a drop of rain,' Simon laughs, moving his chair too. 'You wouldn't survive a night in a tent.'

'It's a bit more than just a drop. Shall we pay and go?'

He looks at his plate as if it's the last supper. 'But I've got loads left.' Hardly. Three or four large mouthfuls at the most. 'I'm not rushing,' he says bluntly.

CHAPTER 12 - BILLY NO-MATES

onna

As AUTUMN APPROACHES, to suppress Covid, the government, on the advice of its cranky scientists and cronies, prohibits social gatherings of more than six people. What a test of friendship this will be. Squabbles will break out across the nation, fisticuffs, and bust-ups as we are left to self-navigate the loss of our liberty. It's a social minefield––a return to the playground. There will always be one unlucky friend. No room at the inn. A legitimate reason to exclude the most unpopular of any friendship circle. The rule makes no sense. A gathering of six doesn't spread Covid, but seven does. I thought seven was supposed to be a lucky number and six the mark of the beast.

Olivia spent the summer holiday at her father's house and didn't miss the opportunity to remind me why. 'There's nowhere for me to sleep at yours, Mother. Can't remember when I last slept in my room.' She's always persecuting me for the cardinal sin of using the house to make money. I refuse to let guilt drown me and remind myself the lodgers help with the bills.

In October, on a whim, I book a surprise holiday for two to the Canary Islands for Christmas. Quarantine restrictions have been lifted and after the crap year we've had, it will be good to get away. Olivia will be so excited. There's an ulterior motive to my plan––I'll have her all to myself. No galivanting off to see friends. And as for her father––he'll just have to see her after Christmas instead.

Donning my mask, I go into the travel agent. The two ladies sitting behind their desks immediately put their masks on even though they're sitting behind a Perspex screen. I book a six-day trip to Tenerife for a great all-in-one price of £600. A bargain.

Pushing all thoughts of Olivia spending the six days either glued to Instagram or making TikToks of me sunbathing by the pool, I ring to tell her about the trip. I'm like a kid in a candy store, I'm that excited. It feels like an eternity since I last went abroad, but it's only been one missed summer.

'Mother, I was about to ring you.' Oh dear, I'm in the doghouse. Now what have I done?

'What's up? I was ringing with some exciting news.'

'Don't say, you've met the man of your dreams? Oh, there goes another flying pig.'

'Very funny,' I say flatly.

Before I have the chance to tell her about the holiday, she interrupts. 'We had a party last night and the police raided it and we've all been fined, a hundred pounds.'

'Oh no. But you know the rule of six. You could have had a dinner party instead.'

She bursts into a cackling laugh. 'Oh Mother, we're students, we don't have dinner parties.'

'Don't you watch the news? There was a party last week at some university or other. A hundred people attended, and the hosts, having just tested positive for Covid were fined £10,000 each. That's more than a year's tuition fees.'

'What's the point of going to university if you can't party? That's what it's all about.'

'You're there to study of course.'

'Bore... ring. Anyway, Mother, these stupid rules, most lectures are on Zoom but sometimes we're in class. Only ten people per class, all spread out, wearing masks and windows open so that we freeze and catch the cold from hell. Then when the lesson ends everyone takes their mask off and rushes to the door and we chat in the corridor. There's no social distancing there.'

To stop her sinking further into a gloomy moan fest, I tell her about the holiday.

'Wow, thank you, Mum, sounds amazing. But I was wondering, could you pay this fine for me? I can't afford it.'

'No, I can't. A fine is a fine, to teach you a lesson.'

'Please.' She stretches the word out as if it's elastic. 'That's three weeks' food you've deprived me of.'

'No.'

OCTOBER EXTINGUISHES itself in a flurry of gales and driving rain, but when November arrives the news is once again gloomy, and the threat of lockdown becomes yet again a grim reality. Shut away inside their homes, people take to Facebook and Twitter to talk about the Covid vaccine which will be rolled out in the spring. Every Tom, Dick and Harry has an opinion, and every idiot is suddenly a scientist because they've being watching YouTube and have learned a few new fancy words and terms like Messenger RNA. I try to stay out of the arguments floating around, the twats that are saying the vaccine is poison and they wouldn't want to "put that shit in their bodies."

Just as I'm thinking I should reschedule our trip to Tenerife, the travel agent rings on the first day of lockdown to cancel the holiday. I'll get a refund, but it's still disappointing. I'd been looking forward to it. My disappointment is made worse when I find out Olivia is spending this next lockdown with her dad.

'Well, Mother, if a weirdo lodger wasn't occupying my room, I'd be able to stay with you. And I'm not sharing the settee with one of your creepy men.'

'I'm not dating any creepy men. There's nobody on the scene.'

'Yeah right, am I supposed to believe that?'

Now that it's winter and we're also in lockdown, dating has lost its appeal. On my days off, I meet a friend for a few laps round the park, now the highlight of my now non-existent social life. It's a grim outing, the paths are slippery with wet leaves and our conversation is depressing and always about the virus. 'The economy has contracted by 11% and isn't expected to recover until 2025,' she laments. And 'Honestly, Donna, when I had Covid, you can't have a sensible conversation with NHS Track and Trace staff. They just read from a script. They're robotic. And if you get pinged to say you must self-isolate because you've been near someone with Covid, they don't care if it's someone who lives in the next flat to you, because as far as they are concerned, you've been near someone with Covid.' I must admit, these rules have become as daft and pointless as avoiding ladders and black cats. 'The problem is, people just aren't sticking to the rules,' we overhear a haughty, woman say to her friend. There are many sanctimonious people like her.

After our regular walks, we shelter from the drizzle under the canopy of the little kiosk, warming our hands on our disposable cups of delicious hot chocolate. I miss going in cafes. The buzz, the friendly staff, the noisy coffee machines, the random chats with strangers. I'm an avid reader, one of those simply-can't put-a-book-down type of people. When I'm not contorted at the kitchen table fighting off dead leg or propped up in bed reading, my local Caffé Nero is my hideout. The ambient murmur, exotic coffee aroma and dare I say, sumptuously satisfying cake––the perfect partner for my escape into the world of fiction. I miss the cosy corner or the window seat where I watch the world and his dog go by as I dig my nose further into my chosen adventure. It's my indulgent time. Me time, and it's important to me. As the days go by, I find myself worrying about the future of cafes and restaurants. How can they withstand these lockdowns, even with government help? Many will go out of business, especially the independents. Worrying about the economy is good in one respect––it takes my mind off being single and whole days now go by when I forget to go on the dating site.

My job keeps me focused on what really matters right now––keeping vulnerable people safe and spreading my cheer. Isolated as they are from friends and family, I'm often the only contact they have with another human being. Mostly, their days pass in front of the TV watching soaps and quiz shows. Their day centres are closed. Routine activities are on hold. I have my favourites––all carers do. Sometimes I stay longer with Kim if she's my last call. She makes me laugh because she has funny names for her body parts. Her boobs are called Larry and Betty, after her late budgerigars. We'll watch *Tipping Point* together and then she'll drift off in her wheelchair, wake with a start and ask me to re-wind the episode because she's missed the dream prize. 'What did they win?' I make up holiday destinations I've long dreamt of. The Maldives, Thailand, Borneo. After winding the programme back several times, I'm frustrated and that is my cue to go.

I have a favourite man too. He's placid, kind and only seventy-one. Poor chap has diabetes and Parkinson's. Classic FM plays in the corner of his bedroom, day and night and he wears a happy smile as I arrive, making me feel valued and wanted. 'Hello, love, oh I have missed you.'

'Do you need a wee?' He's always ready for a wee.

'Yes, love, I need the bottle.'

Picking up the plastic urine bottle from his bedside table, I put his shrivelled willy in the opening, waiting for him to pee, while longing for him to engage in a meaningful conversation about the book he's reading, *The God Delusion*. Sadly, he has nothing to say.

'It's coming, love.'

'It's not.'

'In a minute, love.'

Pee, the colour of amber nectar fills the bottle.

And this is my life.

BY THE END of the year there's further panic and fear about soaring Covid cases. On the advice of a panel of mad, unelected scientists, and our scarecrow Prime Minister, who doesn't know how to brush his hair, let alone steer the country through a viral soup, casts another spell of solitary confinement over the nation turning my Christmas into a damp squib. It's okay for Olivia, she's holed up at her dad's house in London with his geranium-loving wife. That's my fault, I guess. Her bedroom here is occupied by a batty woman in her sixties who keeps leaving the hob on.

So much emotion is wrapped around Christmas. It's heralded as the most wonderful time of year. That only applies if you're surrounded by loved ones. I'm sure some of you would call me the Grinch or Scrooge, but there's so much pressure to put up a bright and merry façade. I'm just not feeling it this year. The spicy odour of fruit cake, the tang of alcohol and even the pine smell of bog cleaner, are all reminders that I will be spending this year alone. I zap the TV off when John Lewis adverts fill the screen. I avoid takeaway coffee from Starbucks because they're served in red cups during the month of December.

The answer to this malaise is to sign up for all the anti-social shifts: Christmas Eve, Christmas Day, Boxing Day and even New Year's Eve. The agency must think I'm desperate for money. Truth is I'm Billy no-mates.

On Christmas Eve I watch *Emmerdale* with ninety-year-old, Cybil, and polish off the unwanted toffees in the tub of Quality Street, marked, 'for the carers.' On Christmas Day I drive Jan to her brother's house because he is in her 'support bubble.' Half the day is wasted though, driving back and forth between his house and hers because I've forgotten essential items like her slipper pan and sanitary towels. Boxing Day is spent with Kim. Easter is now underway in her house. It's a mammoth operation. She gets me to write fifty Easter cards and wrap twenty Easter presents. The list of recipients includes the taxi driver, the staff at the Halifax and the 'nice girl' on the customer service desk in Waitrose.

I'm glad when 2020 comes to an end. That rollercoaster of a year is now behind me. I'm so looking forward to getting my life back on track. The prospect of meeting someone becomes an exciting thought once more. I'm feeling hopeful. And there's been good news, a breakthrough on the long-awaited vaccine. Once this is approved and rolled out across the country, normal life will be resumed.

CHAPTER 13 - THE URN

onna

I'm glad we've wrapped up 2020, but the start of 2021 doesn't conjure much hope. Boris-the-Buffoon warns that restrictions will get tougher and on the 6th of January the guillotine of lockdown once again falls, slaying our freedoms and dashing all hope for a brighter year.

The 6th is a day off for me before the painful slog of a twelve-hour shift. With cafes and shops now closed, I get up early and wander the empty streets, saddened by the thought that this draconian method of battling the virus will cause businesses to fail and many ruined lives.

I do like a girls' day out round the shops. There's a certain buzz to shopping: bright lights, the delight of a bargain and the launch of next season's fashion. But lockdown has axed all that. The thought of shoppers going online, destroying retail units forever, fills me with dismay.

It's early morning and I'm peering in the window of Robert

Dyas looking at a sale on kettles, when a white lorry pulling up onto the pavement beside me, is reflected in the glass.

Someone shouts, 'You don't need a new kettle.'

I keep my eyes on the kettles because, a) I'm not quite sure who the person is talking to, it's probably not me because I don't know anyone with a lorry, and b) even if it is me they're talking to, I figure that maybe if I ignore them there's always the hope they will go away.

I recognise the voice when I hear my name being called. Takes me a few seconds to process who it is.

Laundry Man.

I spin round. 'What on earth are you doing in a lorry?'

I'm glad to see him. I'm surprised by that. He's leaning across the passenger seat speaking to me through the open window.

'Jump in.'

When I hesitate, he nudges the door. 'Come on, we're going on an adventure.'

Curious, I step over and climb aboard, giggling. 'What kind of an adventure? Have you got illegal goods in the back?'

'Only my worldly goods.'

He pulls away from the kerb and stops at the traffic lights.

'And what might they be?' I chuckle. He's going to amuse me with some story or other.

'I'm going up to London to scatter my parents' ashes at Teddington Lock.'

'That's sad.' I frown at him, unsure what else to say. Have I missed something? Have they died recently? 'I'm not being funny or anything but why would you need to hire a lorry for an urn?'

'My push bike wouldn't get me far. And I don't have a car.'

I'm confused as hell.

He glances at me sheepishly. 'This lorry is my home.'

It takes me a few moments to process. There must be a bed in the back. Surely he's kidding me.

He works full-time and yet he lives in a lorry. 'How come you never mentioned it before?' We've met several times since the meal at the Duck and Bucket and he's never talked about where he lives. For some reason I imagined him living in a poky one-bed apartment in a block of flats. I never thought to ask.

'I thought it might put you off me if I told you too soon. Women usually run a mile. People judge.'

'But we aren't going out.' Even if he lived in a palace, I still wouldn't want to go out with him.

He looks disappointed. Why do men make assumptions? Look at them for two seconds, go out for an innocent meal and they automatically think you're into them. My "how's your day?" texts must have given him the wrong idea.

'How come you live in a lorry?' He went to a private school. His parents must have been loaded. I'm sure he told me his dad was a stockbroker. He must have inherited money to buy somewhere. Now it's me making assumptions.

'I kip on a friend's sofa when the weather turns cold.'

What a sad way to live.

'I was fed up of living in a house. I prefer this nomadic existence. It's fun.'

Really? Unconvinced one jot. I conjure up a gamut of possible scenarios: he lost his home in divorce, he gambles, he overspends, he gave all his money to his children. He's on the minimum wage––can't afford to rent or buy. House prices are soaring, so is rent. And as time's gone by, his struggle has worsened. Poor guy.

If I liked him enough, it wouldn't put me off. What would put me off is Olivia's reaction. She'd say he was a loser, and I'd be a loser for dating a homeless guy.

I'm not sure I want to go all the way to London, not in lockdown. We might get stopped.

He glances at me as he negotiates a roundabout and it's as if he's guessed what I'm thinking. 'Trust me, we won't get stopped, not in a lorry. The coppers will assume we're out on business.'

Sounds dubious but I like the idea of a walk along the Thames after scattering the ashes. I'm surprised he's asked me to join him on such a personal mission. I'm not sure whether I feel honoured or awkward. If it were me, I'd want to be alone, reflecting on the past and my memories. I definitely wouldn't want somebody with me, not unless it was a sibling or a loved one. But he seems upbeat, as if this is a regular occurrence.

It's something he should have done ten years ago, he explains. He doesn't want to keep hold of their ashes any longer having reached the tenth anniversary of their deaths. It's as if he needs to declutter now it's the New Year.

'They left no instructions, but over Christmas I had the idea to send them down the river. Together. Because it's where they met. Along the towpath at Teddington. I had my reservations though because Mum couldn't swim. But hiding them in an urn in the footwell for so long seemed inhospitable.'

I glance down at the footwell. There's a Tesco's sandwich wrapper and an apple core next to the urn. Can't imagine my own mum being happy sloshing about in a lorry, judging by how particular she was.

We find plenty to chat about and the journey passes quickly. I'm curious to know how he lives in a lorry.

'Where do you wash?'

'In The Caffé Nero or the leisure centre.'

'How do you heat the lorry?'

'I've made radiators--tin cans with a tea light in and there are solar panels on the roof.'

'Why's the bed not jolting around in the back?'

'It's chained down.'

'Very kinky.'

We're on the M23 and as I glance out of the window, I have a sudden thought.

'What I'd really love is to go into Central London, to see it in lockdown. I've seen pictures of London in the first lockdown. It looked eerie. Deserted streets, like a ghost town.'

'We're don't go anywhere near Central London. We're heading to the south-west of the city.'

A wave of disappointment washes over me. 'Shame. I would have loved that.'

He glances at me and smiles. 'Go on then, just for you. It's a day out after all.'

The fields disappear and we reach the urban jungle of South London and on into central London. As we reach the Thames, the Houses of Parliament loom ahead. That ancient seat of power that has been controlling every minutia of our lives for the past year from how many people we can meet to how long we can spend outside on a humble bench. It's passed laws and regulations so draconian it may as well be the Reichstag in Nazi Germany. I just want it all to end, but it feels as if we will be under the boot of restrictions for months to come.

Westminster Bridge is busy; a few groups are clustered at intervals. Some are carrying placards, banners, most are wearing woolly hats, for it's a chilly day.

'What's going on?' I ask Simon.

'I'm guessing there's a protest ahead of this afternoon's vote on lockdown.'

'But we're already in lockdown, as of midnight.'

'It's a retrospective vote.'

'It might not go through then?'

'It will. Boris has a huge majority and Labour support lockdown. There are a few stragglers against lockdowns, like Sir Desmond Swayne and Charles Walker, but in the main, most MPs support it.'

'That's a shame.'

'They just want to protect the NHS, stop it from being overwhelmed.'

'I suppose.'

'That guy, Chris Whitty, the one with the fancy title, Chief Medical Officer, who thinks he's now running the country, I heard him say that we might need another lockdown next winter too.'

'Over my dead body.'

'Protests don't do a lot. If you look back in history, people have tried every tactic to change the course of government. Petitions, vandalism, sitting on motorways, hunger strikes. None of it works.'

'The suffragettes got us the vote.'

It's then that I see her. Huddled in a small group. Standing next to someone with a placard which says, 'No more lock-downs.' And a banner with words painted in red. 'The vaccine wasn't brought in for Covid, Covid was brought in for the vaccine.'

Olivia.

What the hell is she doing here?

CHAPTER 14 - LOCKDOWN PROTEST

 onna

OLIVIA IS SUPPOSED to be at her dad's house, in Fulham, studying.

Please God, she can't be embroiled in this commotion. Mixed up with anti-vaxxers. She told me off for kissing on a first date. Said I should be careful, that I could catch the virus and die. She's had Covid, knows the dangers. Little hypocrite.

'Simon, stop, I've got to get out, it's Olivia.'

'I can't stop on the bridge.'

'Quick, just let me out, I'll be okay, I'll get the train back.'

I unclip my seat belt, my heart hammering. I must stop Olivia, get her to go home. There are police gathering at the end of the bridge and if they stop her, they might even arrest her for being out.

'Text me,' Simon says before I slam the door and hurry away.

Simon toots as he passes, a worried expression on his face as I rush over to Olivia.

She breaks away from the group. 'Mother, what the hell are you doing here?'

'I was going to ask you the same thing.' I'm out of breath and in shock.

Her friends are glued to their phones and one of them is making a call.

'Someone's just put this message up,' one of Olivia's friends shouts. 'It's on a Facebook group, *Protests Everywhere*.'

Olivia sweeps her hand towards me. It's a rude gesture, she's batting me away. It feels like she is fourteen all over again and I've just come home to find she's had a party, and everyone is high on drugs and alcohol. 'What are they saying? What shall we do?'

'Urgent message,' a woman says. 'Get out of London, you are walking into a trap.'

'Ignore it,' one of the friends says. 'You can't trust these Facebook groups. There are plants policing them.'

'I think we should quit; something doesn't feel right. Where is everyone? They said they'd be here. There are more police than protesters,' a good-looking guy with dark olive skin says. 'It's not safe.'

'We shouldn't have got here so early. Gives the Filth time to sweep us from the streets,' Olivia says.

Grabbing her arm, I yank her away. 'Don't get mixed up in all this, Liv, please.' But no amount of begging and pleading convinces her.

'Mother, please, just go home, I'm an adult now, I can do what I like.'

'If you go with them, I'm coming too.' The row of police officers dressed in yellow high-vis jackets and helmets standing on guard at the end of the bridge look ominous. I'd rather head in the opposite direction, away from Parliament and find the nearest tube station but at the same time I don't want to leave my daughter here. Anything could happen.

'Do what you like, Mother, I'm going with them.' She's extra stroppy.

One of the protesters, a woman in her forties, has the good sense to warn the group not to walk in a group and to remember that we aren't supposed to be mixing with other households. She tells us to head over the bridge in pairs but at a two-metre distance and to avoid eye contact with the police officers. Where did Olivia meet all these people? They aren't students. They vary in age and are all much older than her. I'm completely baffled.

We head towards the line of police officers. I'm terrified they will stop us but to my relief, they stare through us as we skirt them. We hurry across the road and towards Caffé Nero. I could murder a coffee and I will buy one, but it will go straight through me, I'll be bursting, and I doubt there are any public toilets open. I order a hot chocolate--it's too tempting not to. I enjoy the warmth and delicious sweetness as it slides down my throat. It's good to be inside; I was getting cold out there and I feel safer in here, away from the police. Once we've all been served, we gather in the corner of the tiny café. Olivia's friends are trying to work out what to do when the assistant calls over, 'you need to drink it outside, sorry, but we're in Tier Four.' A tiered system of local restrictions has been in force in recent weeks. Four is the highest level--effectively a lockdown.

'Why aren't there more people?' one of group says as we leave the café.

'They chickened out,' Olivia says.

'Which is what you should have done,' I snap. 'Come on, Liv, let's get the tube.'

'They're ruining our future,' she shouts, pointing her finger at Parliament. 'Go home, Mum.'

I'm not leaving her, so I wander behind her, crossing White-hall at the traffic lights, glancing at the Cenotaph as I mount the pavement of Great George Street before crossing over to Parliament Square. Strewth, there even police officers on horseback. What are they intending to do, charge into the innocent crowd causing mayhem and accidents? It's hard to keep up with Olivia and her group--they are walking so fast.

There aren't many protesters in the square--maybe fifty tops. But there are plenty of police officers swelling the pavements. I've never seen so many in one place. It's a total overkill. Police sirens fill the air, squad cars rush by. The northern perimeter of the square is lined with police vans. At least twenty of them. Is this necessary given the low numbers of protesters? We live in an era of angry and aggressive policing; who is policing the police? I'm scared, unnerved by the sight. I don't want to hang around a moment longer than I must.

In Parliament Square I look up at the bronze statue of Millicent Fawcett, erected to commemorate her life as a suffragist leader and social campaigner. She's holding a banner with the words, 'Courage calls to courage everywhere.' What an amazing woman--campaigning for women's right to vote. A true feminist. Standing up against male pigs. Lost in thought, I don't notice the female police officer standing next to me, asking me a question. Glancing round, I can't see Olivia. I'm panicked, ignore the officer, and walk away.

'Can you clear the square,' the officer calls after me.

'I'm looking for my daughter, she's here somewhere.'

'Where do you live?' I wish she'd leave me alone. I don't need her help.

'Haywards Heath.'

'You're a long way from home.'

'And it's a long story how I ended up here.' I spin round hoping to spot Olivia. Hoping the officer will buzz off and catch a criminal. There are no criminals here. Just a few people standing around with placards.

'What's your name?' It feels like an intrusive question. I don't understand why she's asking me.

'Why do you need to know?'

'So that I can issue you with a ticket.'

I stare at her. 'A ticket? What ticket?'

'You can either give me your name and I'll issue you with a ticket or I'll arrest you.'

This is too stupid for words.

'I haven't done anything, I told you, I'm looking for my daughter.'

She doesn't believe me. 'Unless you give me your name so that I can issue you with a penalty notice for breaching Coronavirus laws, I'll arrest you.'

Something inside me snaps. This isn't fair, doesn't make sense. The police wouldn't waste time arresting somebody like me. 'Do what you like, here's my wrists, go on, put me in handcuffs.' Her superior will come along any minute now and tell her to leave me alone or at least help me to find Olivia and encourage her to go home. Somebody is bound to realise how ridiculous this is and come to my rescue.

She links my arm through hers and walks me towards the row of vans. 'What are you doing?' I ask in bewilderment.

'I'm arresting you.' She cautions me. 'You do not have to say anything. But it may harm your defence if you do not mention when questioned something which you later rely on in court. Anything you do say may be given in evidence.'

CHAPTER 15 - LEYTON POLICE STATION

onna

THIS CAN'T BE HAPPENING. Frantically I look round, hoping that Olivia will rush to my rescue. Where the hell is she?

A thought slices through me.

Shit, she must also be under arrest too–– in a police van, waiting to be processed. I can't see inside any of the waiting vehicles.

Her future––ruined by a criminal record. They can do what they like with me, but not my baby. About to blurt Olivia's name to the police officer, I tap down the emotions that threaten to overwhelm me. It's best to say as little as possible, that's what I've been led to believe watching crime dramas on TV. All those hours spent watching *The Bill* in the 90's has paid off.

'Can you just let me walk to Victoria? I'll go straight home. I wasn't meant to come to London today.'

'You're now under arrest, the less you say the better, for your sake. Let me take your bag.' She removes my bag from my shoulder--politely, but it feels like theft.

I'm taken to one of the police vans. The sliding door is open, and I'm asked to get onboard. There's an officer in the driving seat and he turns to look at me. He's carrying a few extra pounds as well as the weight of dealing with everything wrong with the world. He has a kind face, he's about my age so maybe he'll be reasonable and let me go home. They don't want to waste their time; the police are always complaining about unnecessary paperwork.

'I'm happy to head home if you'll just let me go.' May as well be polite, that's bound to work in my favour.

His voice is firm, authoritative. 'You have a choice, you give your name, we issue you with a penalty notice or you come with us to the police station.' Why's he speaking in such a loud voice? It's as if he thinks I have a hearing problem.

I feel like a child on an incredibly naughty step. Their attitude is making me stubborn. I'm not budging. I won't give my name. This is supposed to be a free country. I have the right to speak with a duty solicitor once we arrive at the police station--he or she will sort out this mess and then I'll be free to go. I hope this doesn't take long. It's a waste of my day off.

I sit down and the female officer stands next to me, still holding my bag. She's white, blonde hair tied up in a bun. She's shorter than me. I think of all the jobs she could have done, but she chose to join the police, a dangerous, thankless profession. People don't respect coppers, not like they used to when I was young.

'Can I look at my phone, my daughter might be worried?'

'No,' she says, a cool expression on her face. This is just a job to her, there is no human side to these men and women in uniform. They are robots.

'How long will this take? What's happening?'

'We're just waiting to find out which station to take you all to,' she says matter-of-factly.

'All?' I glance round at the other seats even though there's nobody else in the van and then I realise they're waiting for more arrested protesters to board. Bloody hell, no wonder the place is teeming with coppers. They've come here just to make arrests. The small number of protesters in the square aren't a problem to anyone and surely, they have the right to object to another lockdown. My emotions suddenly perform a crunchy gear change from exasperation to anger. What's happened to our right to peaceful protest? We live in a democracy. The government has no right to order us to stay indoors, to close our businesses, to intrude on our lives to this extent. I know they are trying to contain a virus, but we are adults, we can make our own health decisions. This is tyranny. What a great word. Just saying it in my head stokes my fires.

She doesn't answer me but as I peer out of the open door, I can see a couple of people in handcuffs arguing with officers. Olivia isn't one of them. I close my eyes for a moment. *Please God, help her to get away.* If I see my daughter arrested, handcuffs slammed around her tiny pale wrists, I think I'll throw up.

I feel so cold, so alone, swallowed by the system.

A few people walking dogs or jogging turn to stare at me, disgust written across their faces. I'm an animal in a cage. I'm despised, they hate me. London hates me. Perhaps London has always excluded me for I rarely come here. It's a hard city, unforgiving. Now all its hardness is against me. A mob of bitter faces––they know that I am guilty of something. There's no one in this vast city who will defend me.

The driver is talking on his radio and turns to speak to the female officer who hasn't moved from my side in all this time. She's still clutching my bag as if it's her bag not mine. 'We're going to Leyton.'

'Where's that?' I ask. Nobody answers. They're taking me

away, to a place I do not know, and I have no control. I don't know London well. Leyton sounds like the back of beyond. I've been sitting here for ages, maybe an hour. I can't just glance at the time. It's been years since I wore a wristwatch. The officer won't let me look at my phone or anything in my bag. If I ask the time, they might not tell me. They might get stroppy. Quash my questions, order me to be silent.

And despite my nerves––I'm hungry. It must be way past lunchtime. I've just remembered, I've not had breakfast. I never skip breakfast. When can I eat?

Moments later, three people––all handcuffed––board: a woman about my age and a couple of men, one black, one Asian. The woman smiles at me and asks, 'how come you're not in handcuffs?'

'Don't talk to each other,' the blonde officer snaps.

The Asian man tuts. 'Not allowed to talk to each other now. It's like we're school kids.'

A male officer in his forties approaches the van and gets on. 'Shut up, the lot of you.' He reminds me of the maths teacher at my secondary school. Like this guy, he was a harsh disciplinarian and barked every order. His classes were always well-behaved; nobody dared step out of line.

'She's got a point though, why are they in handcuffs and I'm not?' I ask.

'It can be arranged.' The male officer looks at me through cold, cruel eyes but I refuse to be scared.

'It's up to each officer,' the blonde officer explains. Maybe they were being arsey. I've been polite. And I haven't tried to run away.

The Asian man under arrest nods at a dirty mask and plastic glove on the floor. 'It's such a deadly virus,' he says with sarcasm dripping from his voice, 'shouldn't they be in a bio-hazard bin?'

The male officer doesn't rise to the bait but looks thoughtful. 'Yeah, maybe they should.'

The van moves away from the kerb, and we begin the journey across London. As everything disappears in a blur, I don't notice the buildings or the route we take. Today I'm not a tourist and this is not one of those red open-top, hop-on, hop-off sightseeing buses. But as we pass over a bridge in the heart of Canary Wharf London Docklands, I can't help but look up in awe and wonder at the skyscrapers jammed together. Like silver trees reaching heavenward in a futuristic forest, beaming light across the city on this dull January day. A bustling financial district before the pandemic––huge office space now a waste ground, abandoned like derelict, decaying Victorian workhouses and northern factories. Desks eerily empty. Silence. When will the workers return, will they ever?

I'm glad we're not allowed to talk. I need this space to think. Now is not the time to get emotional––I need my wits about me. In my head I make a list of everything I know: 1. They can hold me for twenty-four hours. 2. I'm entitled to a duty solicitor. 3. I can make one phone call.

Shit. The clock was ticking back in Parliament Square the minute that blonde woman took my arm and cautioned me. Twenty-four hours takes me to about lunchtime tomorrow afternoon. I can't imagine I'll be at the police station long, but if they have lots of people to process, maybe it will take ages, like it can take in A&E at busy periods. The police probably work like a slow cog.

Who will I phone? One precious phone call; I must choose wisely. It's my lifeline and reminds me of Chris Tarrant's quiz show, *Who Wants to Be a Millionaire?* But this isn't a game and it's anything but entertaining.

No point in phoning Olivia, she might be under arrest. God, I do hope not. Can't phone her dad, useless waste of space he is. He'd call me a dozy bitch and tell me I deserve what's coming. I could phone a good friend, but what use would they be? None of my girlfriends would drive up to East London to pick me up.

And then I think of all the men I've dated in the past few years, some of whom are now my friends. What a complete bunch of good-for-nothings they are. And then it hits me, like a sledge-hammer to the skull. So much time I've wasted on different men and look where it's got me. I could ring Milk Tray Man. He'd come to pick me up, but he'd expect a shag in return and he'd start sending me boxes of those ghastly chocolates that were popular in the '70s because he's under some illusion that women like to be constantly treated and pampered and show-ered with gifts.

There's only one man of use in this instance. Jeremy, a crim-inal defence lawyer. We dated several years ago and have remained friends––thank goodness––because I really need him right now. But he now lives in Scotland. He could offer advice but couldn't pick me up.

I think of Laundry Man. He'll be back in Haywards Heath soon. He won't want to drive all the way back up here to pick me up. I can't blame him for the plight I'm in, but I wouldn't be here if it wasn't for him.

The thought of being released in the middle of the night, walking the streets of East London trying to find the nearest tube station and discovering trains aren't running, fills me with abject horror. It's common knowledge that parts of London are dangerous places and that knife crime is out of control. And shootings and gang violence are on the increase. I shudder at the thought of getting raped, mugged. I'm a country mouse out of my comfort zone.

My mind is awash with worry. 'If we're released late evening, can we leave as a group? I don't know East London and it's not safe to be on the streets alone.'

'No,' the female officer snaps. 'You're in different households.'

The woman in handcuffs turns round with a scowl on her face. 'That's bang out of order, that is.'

The male officer is quick to defend the blonde officer's decision. He's enjoying this, the power-hungry weasel. 'You should have thought about that before you left home this morning. You've been told to stay at home. We're in lockdown.' I flinch at the animosity in his voice. He's such a smart alec--very few brain cells in that head of his.

Everything is out of my control. I always used to look up to the police--guardians of the peace and protecting members of the public. But right now, I loathe them. I can taste a million angry words on my tongue, but I hold them back knowing retaliation would only make things worse. A whole string of swear words rattles around my head. It feels like I've been thrown down a dark chute. I'm careering forward, trying not to bang myself on the sides and at some point, a hole is waiting for me to plunge into.

CHAPTER 16 - PLEASE, SIR, I NEED A WEE

onna

My most important issue is work. If only I wasn't due at my first client's house at six in the morning. I might not make work and if I don't turn up without ringing in sick, I'll be sacked. If I can speak to Jeremy, I could ask him for legal advice and get him to call in sick on my behalf.

I'm calmer now I have a plan.

The van sweeps into the police station, pulling up under a brick-built carport next to a side entrance. The driver gets out and goes inside the building. With a strong and persistent urge to wee, my bladder is about to burst. I just want to get out of this van, dash to a loo. He's gone a while; why are we just sitting here? Will someone tell me what's going on? I'm about to wet myself.

'When can we use the loo?' I ask. It's a reasonable question. Peeing is a basic bodily function. Something we all need to do.

'Yes, I need the loo too,' the woman says.

'We're women of a certain age,' I jest, for the first time seeing the funny side to all this.

The answer I receive shocks me to the core.

'You're all under arrest,' the male officer barks. Nazi. He's power-hungry, testosterone-driven, thinks he's so important, so high and mighty. 'I'll say when you can use the toilet and if you wet yourselves, you'll be charged for that.'

I don't know whether to laugh or cry. He's insane, a total prick. I refuse to be intimidated by him and besides, he's half my age and probably has half my life experience. I turn away and fix my gaze on the entrance door to the building as I keep the expression on my face neutral so that I look unconcerned. Inside though I'm laughing at his bullying arrogance. It's types like him who should be weeded from the force.

'Charming,' the woman in handcuffs mutters with a snigger, but I stay silent––I'd rather not give him the satisfaction to slam me down again.

We file into the custody suite, my nose wrinkling at the fetid sweaty odours: a mixture of gym bag, old boots, and stale alcohol. There are no windows, and the walls are covered with posters for the missing and the wanted. There's a raised area, a semi-circle where custody officers are entering information onto computers. Countertop screens provide a physical barrier against face-to-face interactions. It looks like a customs and immigration desk at an airport. But this is anything but a sunny destination.

We are guided into bays to stand in front of an officer at a computer who is holding a black mug with steam coming off it. Screens divide each bay––there is no privacy. The blonde officer orders me to stand on a set of footprints marked on the floor. She frisks me, and puts my Radley handbag on the counter. She's wearing gloves just in case my belongings are contaminated with Polonium or a deadly virus, because obviously I'm to be treated like a dirty dangerous criminal.

The contents of my handbag are scattered across the desk. My lipstick, diary, mask exemption lanyard, pen, tissue, asthma inhaler are now items on a database. It's a personal assault––as if they've just delved into my knickers. My life exposed, every dark corner illuminated. My purse is opened and between them they examine my five bank cards, my driving licence, three café loyalty cards.

They've pawed everything. Even a dirty tissue and a scrunched-up Kit-Kat wrapper. There's no hiding. In seconds they have what I could have given them two hours ago, saving myself this aggro, this humiliation.

My name and address.

I'm now on their system.

The desk officer takes a slurp of his drink. 'Any medical conditions?' His auburn moustache is wet.

'Asthma.'

He taps away at his computer. I'm a number, an entry on the Police National Computer. All the thousands of crimes that go unrecorded each year; all the burglaries, the violent assaults, the fraud and yet here I am, a middle-aged woman who's worked hard caring for the sick and elderly during this crisis and now I have a stain against my name. I was in the wrong place at the wrong time.

Relief washes over me when my phone is handed back. I can make a call, anyone I like. I can find out what's happened to Olivia, go on social media. Check emails for tomorrow's shift pattern. Thank God. Tension seeps out of my body like a balloon deflating.

'Unlock your phone.'

A prickling sensation spreads over my scalp. What's happening?

I cross my legs. Tap my feet. Anything to distract me. To relieve the pressure on my groaning bladder. I'm seconds from an accident. I'm in agony. I'm trying like buggery to hold on, clenching my internal muscles, squirming.

'I really need the loo.'

'In a minute.'

After entering the passcode, he takes the phone. I can't see what he's doing, but suddenly the screen turns white and there are three sets of bar codes, and the screen says 'Driver.'

A cold eddy of fear rises inside me. 'What are you doing?' He passes the phone over a scanner. Have they cloned my phone?

'We have to check if it's stolen.'

I should feel relief, but I don't trust them one jot. They could be lying, planning to spy on me, monitor my activity. It's surveillance. I've read about this happening. What the hell have they done to my phone?

They turn their attention to my body. 'Remove your rings.'

A fist of panic squeezes my insides.

My mum's rings.

I've never taken them off. Not in the ten years since she's been gone. They are my link to her and part of me. They might not even come off because over the years my fingers have swollen. I can't, I won't. They're worth thousands. Will they even bother to lock them away? I don't trust them or this place––they'll get lost or stolen.

Something inside me cracks. This place, these little Hitlers, they are a battering ram to my fragile emotions. That's when I surrender myself.

Tears.

Great gulping sobs.

And then the unimaginable happens. Warm urine floods my pants, my jeans.

Neither officer appear to be surprised. I guess it happens in all the time. But it's never happened to me before.

I stare down. Even my socks are wet.

This is the ultimate humiliation. They've beaten me to

submission, wormed their way into my head, pummelled me into this weak and pitiful state.

The female officer appears unconcerned.

'I need some tissues. I've wet myself.'

'I'll arrange it.'

Is this what I want--for them to win? Sniffing, pulling my shoulders back, I feel an inner voice urging me to compose myself, to regain my strength. I will not be beaten. I am not a criminal and will not be made to feel like a criminal.

The desk sergeant nods at my hands. 'Your rings.'

'You better lock them away,' I snap, wiping my eyes with my sleeve.

'Everything gets locked away.'

I hand them over, those small pieces of my mum, sparkly reminders of her beautiful soul and try not to shed more tears.

He's still entering information on the computer. 'What do you do?'

'Why?'

'We need to know in case you are a danger to a vulnerable person.'

Shock ricochets through me as my brain stutters for a moment.

'I'm a cleaner.' Even though it's a half-truth--because all care work involves some cleaning--I'm left feeling dirty and ashamed of myself. I hate lying but unless I do, this could be the end of my career in adult social care. Everything I've worked hard for. All the hours of training. The relationships I've built, the people who know and trust me.

He's satisfied with my answer. Thank God, but, jeez, I hope there won't be any repercussions.

'I'm authorising your detention.' The rest of his words disappear in a blur as the realisation that I will be locked away smacks me into me. 'Would you like me to phone anyone?'

'You phone? Why can't I?' A pang of anguish hits as this last fragment of control is seized. The clock is ticking; I might need to phone in sick. No way am I letting him ring my employer. I'll have to make up some dreadful story if I don't show up for work. Like what? A car accident, my phone broke. More lies. I can't do it. If it comes to it, I'll just have to face the music.

'Would you like to speak with a duty solicitor?'

'Yes, please.' This is my only saving grace and I hold on to it.

'I'll arrange it.'

'What's happening now?'

'You'll be put in a holding cell.'

I shudder. My body goes hot then cold, the feeling my grandma would have described as someone walking over your grave. 'And then?'

'It depends on what the sergeant says.'

I expect to have fingerprints and DNA taken but I'm led away by the blonde officer along a corridor and to my cell.

CHAPTER 17 - PRISON CELL

*D*onna

I stare at the metal door, heat rising all over my chest as though I'm standing in front of a fire. She opens the door.

'Pop yourself on the bed. Might as well take a rest. Could be here a while.' She hands me a bunch of tissues.

This is no bed. It's a blue rubber mat about two inches thick and it sits on a bench that's bolted to the wall. Reminds me of a school P.E mat. Over the bench there's a window but it's been blacked out. In the corner of the cell, there's a metal toilet.

'Give me your belt,' she says.

I take it off, give it to her.

'Now get in,' she says.

'I don't belong in here; I've done nothing wrong.'

'Get in.'

I go in, sit on the bench with my back to the white wall.

'Would you like a tea, coffee?' As if this is going to make my stay more comfortable.

'Tea, milk no sugar.'

She nods, leaves the cell, shutting the door on me.

I feel completely wretched. I pull my trousers and knickers down and dry myself, but I'll be soaking for the rest of the day. This is utterly miserable. I probably stink. Like a homeless person. That's what I've been reduced to. And I have lost my freedom, a freedom I always took for granted. Having never been in trouble with the police, I'm now a prisoner, detained at Her Majesty's pleasure.

Myra Hindley was locked away. She was a serial killer.

Rosemary West was locked away. She was a serial killer.

Great people have also been locked away. Nelson Mandela fighting to topple South Africa's racist system of apartheid. And special envoy to the Archbishop of Canterbury, Terry Waite, for his humanitarian work.

I am not a killer, or a great humanitarian. My only crime is that I broke Covid rules. I left my town and travelled the thirty miles to London.

I will be in here for a few hours. It's not long, yet without a phone, a book, a TV or anything to do, it will drag. Alone with my thoughts, I know that the hours ahead will shape and define me, might even change who I am, because there are no distractions––I can face my demons head on. Time is all I have, and my body will be my compass. Until now, time has been in short supply. I've been a busy mother, a full-time care assistant, rushing around, beating the clock, never a moment to do just this––sit and think.

Right now, there is nothing I can do to control the situation so I may as well resign myself to being here, go with the flow–– like so many difficult situations I've found myself in over the years. I close my eyes and it's then that I realise––I'm not good at waiting, particularly in long queues. In fact, everything I do is impulsive and badly planned. I go on dating sites to speed up the process of finding love. I must learn to step away, chill, let things happen naturally. I cannot control love any more than I can control the here and now. Love is as fine and fragile as the morning dew, but my problem is that I set myself goals. I'm constantly trying to prove something to Olivia. Does she really care if I find someone? Probably not. People don't care. They might laugh at my serial dating and offer advice, but it doesn't matter what they think. It's my life.

I don't need a man for validation. Why have I fallen into this toxic pattern? I'm fine on my own. I jump up from the bench, lifting my arms above my head, breathing deeply, standing on my tiptoes, flexing my feet, and feeling what it is to be human.

I swivel my head releasing the tension. I'm so sick of being caught in the relationship trap. The past few years have felt like Groundhog Day, an endless loop of first dates. Life is passing me by. I want to travel, take up new hobbies.

All these thoughts are slamming into me at once and they are empowering, hard-hitting, yet refreshing. I am strong, I can survive as Donna the divorced, single woman. Alone––no, I'll never be alone because I have my inner core. I have faith in myself.

I get up and walk over to the toilet pull my trousers and knickers down and have another wee. I only do a trickle this time. I glance up to the corner of the room and realise there's a small camera. My every action is being watched. I am here alone and yet this is not a private place. There is no such thing as privacy, only my private thoughts.

Back at the bench, time ticks by. I press the button by the door at intervals to ask the desk sergeant what the time is. This is like being in a casino in Las Vegas, where gamblers don't know if it's day or night because there are no windows or clocks.

The walls feel like they're crowding in on me. It's like being stuck in a broken lift––that feeling that you will suffocate. Trapped, unable to break free. I could easily get stressed and hyperventilate. I must stop myself from letting the room swallow me whole.

I don't normally notice the detail of a room, not even when I'm viewing a house as a prospective buyer. But I know that I'll never forget this room. It's committed to memory. Every inch of it indelibly printed on my mind: the river of rust in the toilet bowl, the web of cracks in the flooring, the peeling posters on the ceiling, the finger-marks on the metal door. It will haunt me in my sleep. Return to me on my death bed. This is an important day in my life, on a par with my wedding day. It's a bizarre thought that makes me smile.

Someone comes to unlock the door and I'm taken to a tiny room so that I can speak on the phone to the duty solicitor. I can't hear her very well; the line is crackly, and she has a thick accent, but I get the gist of what she is saying. I have been arrested for allegedly breaching the restriction of movement during lockdown and that I will be released under investigation without interview whilst the police continue their investigations. I won't be subject to any bail conditions or restrictions.

I return to the cell to await a decision. Hours roll by. My only company are my life regrets. Endless time to ponder them.

My only concern right now is work. I need to get out of here; I can't skip tomorrow's shift. If I'm not released soon, there's no hope of my getting to work in the morning.

I could lose my job.

Someone brings me food although my appetite has gone. It's chilli con carne in a cardboard container and there's a cardboard spoon to eat it with. It's like trying to battle rain with a cocktail parasol. When it goes all soggy and disintegrates, I end up having to tip the food into my mouth instead.

CHAPTER 18 - FREEDOM

onna

I HEAR a bolt being slide across and the cell door opens. A friendly sergeant casually tells me I'm free to go. Is he just expecting me to step outside into the night air, all alone in an unfamiliar part of London, long after the trains have stopped running?

'What time is it?'

'Two in the morning.'

We walk along the corridor and at the custody desk my belongings are handed back. He explains that I'll be issued with a Fixed Penalty Notice in due course which I can pay or challenge in court.

'I might take it to court.' Part of me wants to show the world how ridiculous the Covid laws are, but really, what is the point? Best just pay it and move on.

'I wouldn't bother. It is what it is.'

He walks me to the entrance, but I don't want to step

outside, not until I know how I'm getting home, so I sit on a plastic chair in the foyer and switch on my phone. A whole string of messages immediately pings through. Thirty missed calls from Olivia and a single message from Laundry Man asking if I'm all right. I hit dial-back and am relieved to hear my daughter's voice.

She sounds all squawky and breathless. 'I was arrested. They took me to Hammersmith. Dad picked me up. He was so angry. Oh my God. What's wrong with him? His eyes, they went all evil-looking. I've never seen him so angry.'

I have. More times than I care to remember. Which is why I left him.

'He was literally pathetic. He shouted at me all the way home, said I'll get a criminal record which is actually crap, I'm getting one of those stupid fixed penalty notices which I'll use to wipe my bum with.'

'Olivia,' I snap, exasperated.

'I'm not paying it, Mum. We've all said we'd rather take it to court. The judge will throw it out.'

'Pay it and be done with it.'

'You sound like Dad.'

For once he's talking sense. She's so wound up she doesn't ask about me. 'I got arrested too. I'm about to ring for a taxi. But I stink of piss.'

'I'm really sorry, Mum. Are you okay?'

'It was an experience.' I let out a much-needed laugh. Sometimes crying or laughing are the only options and right now laughing feels better. 'I'll survive. Promise me you won't go on any more protests? Just keep your head down now. We'll get through this. Lockdown won't last forever. That's what you told me, remember?'

'And let them get away with it?'

No point in arguing with her, and besides, I must ring for a taxi.

CHAPTER 19 - THE HYPODERMIC NEEDLE

onna

I'M NOT sure how I muddle through the following day, all bleary-eyed and groggy through lack of sleep and with yesterday's events hanging over me like a dark and ominous cloud. I pull up at my first client's house, Mrs Garton. Sitting here in this quiet cul-de-sac of bungalows, each with perfect manicured lawns and where nothing of note ever happens, it's hard to believe that just a few hours ago I was locked away, a danger to society. Today I'm wearing a carer's badge on my blue uniform and people will smile at me in that sycophantic way they do, open doors for me and lavish me with praise. I am an 'essential' or 'key' worker, a frontline, critical health worker in this pandemic. Makes it sound as if we are at war and I'm about to head into battle. When I turn on the BBC news where these terms are banded about all the time, I'm made to feel very important as if I am part of a Covid army. The fact is, we're all key workers, every one of us. Without the dustmen, the bakers and even the candlestick makers life and the economy would soon grind to a halt.

I get out of the car and reaching Mrs Garton's front door I squirt my hands with sanitiser before putting on a mask. I'll give my hands a thorough wash once I'm inside, take my temperature and do a quick lateral flow test before going in to say good morning to Mrs Garton. It's all part of the pandemic routine to keep our clients safe.

Eight hours in a cell has shifted my mindset. It's as if my brain has been reprogrammed. I'm looking through a kaleidoscope and all the floating pieces of my world have been reassembled. I glance round at the dull little bungalows seeing them differently for the first time. Life is colourful, beautiful and I'm alive and well and free and I'm going to embrace it, enjoy every moment. I'm going to live in the here and now and stop fretting about all the regrets of the past and the worries of the future. Wow, I haven't felt this positive in a long time.

A fixed penalty notice will soon be landing on my doormat and yet I'm feeling happy. My shift flies as I smile my way through the morning routine: meds, toilet, teeth, bath, hair wash, hearing aids. I even sing to Mrs Garton while I'm soaping her in the bath, *Rub a dub dub, three men in a tub.*

THE DAY FINISHES in a flush of euphoria as I pull onto my driveway and spot the huge box sitting next to my front door. It's obvious what it is by the picture on the side. A bouquet of flowers. I love surprises and it's extra exciting because I've no idea who has sent them. Olivia's dad, Nick sent me flowers once. It wasn't my birthday or our anniversary or any other special occasion. They were sent to cheer me up after the bruise he'd delivered when I dared to challenge him for staying in the pub till three in the morning.

Impatient to find out who's treated me, I hurry into the

house and through to the kitchen where I slash the cardboard with a bread knife to reveal a huge spray of red roses.

A declaration of love?

Whoever has sent these wants to make an impression and although I'm touched by this extravagance, I'd be thrilled with a few garden sprigs. Sending flowers of any kind is such a wonderful gesture and lifts my spirits. I dip my nose to inhale the perfume before easing them out of the box, keen to discover the sender. There's a bulky envelope and it feels as if there's a present inside it. I tear it open and before reading the card inside, I open a small box which has been wrapped in pink tissue paper.

A surge of horror sweeps through me.

I am staring at a hypodermic syringe and needle.

My body goes rigid and all I can do is stand and stare at my reflection in the patio window, my heart banging in my chest; I'm too scared to read the card.

Who the hell would send this and what is the significance?

This must have something to do with the protest outside Parliament. It wasn't just about the lockdown. There were anti-vaxxers at the event too. I visualise their placards. 'No vaccine needed; I have an immune system.' 'Vaccines can cause injury and death.'

Someone is targeting me--they've labelled me anti-vax.

With shaking hands, I slip the card from the envelope and read the message.

Scum.

You should not be working in healthcare. You deserve what's coming.

A horrible sickness rises from my stomach. I'm trying to think who would do this. Other than Laundry Man and Olivia, no one else knows that I was in Parliament Square. This is completely bizarre. It's not as if I have a strong opinion about the vaccine and if I did, I wouldn't broadcast it. Those creepy-looking scientists that appear on the BBC every day bang on about the vaccine being the route out of the pandemic. Who am I to question a scientist?

My lodger works at the new vaccine centre in the town and every evening last week she came home with a funny story. She's been ringing everyone in their nineties to book them in for their vaccine. They're half-deaf and shout back, 'pardon dear what was that? I don't know a Maxine.' She's had to explain, multiple times that her name's not Maxine––she's ringing to book them in for their vaccine. They're all stoical and hardy, queuing outside in the freezing cold, with smiles on their faces as if they are waiting for wartime rations, turning to chat to all the other old folk without a care in the world for social distancing. As far as they are concerned, getting the vaccine is an afternoon out. Poor old dears, they've been cooped in for months.

I don't want the flowers now I realise their intent. To shock. Scare. I decide it's wise to keep the card as evidence in case I get something else through the post, but everything else I chuck. Standing in my slippers on the driveway, ramming it all into an already full bin under the glare of the streetlight, I glance up and down the road hovering for a moment or two. Is someone watching me, or am I becoming paranoid? The cars along the street are empty and there is nothing out of the ordinary. It's a quiet road. The biggest thing to happen is cats going missing. They garden-hop and attach themselves to new families.

I LIE awake listening to the house click and settle into that odd way it does like it's a living breathing beast just pretending to be bricks and mortar. I toss and turn, shift the pillow, tug at the duvet trying to get comfortable, but one question plays in my mind and stops me sleeping.

Who sent the parcel?

I fall into a disturbed sleep, jerking awake when my phone

vibrates on my bedside table. The sun is pushing through the crack in my curtain, so it must be around eight. I reach to answer it, my breath catching in my chest when I hear Olivia's frantic voice.

'Oh my actual God, Mother, you're on *You Tube*. There's a clip of you being arrested and someone's posted it on the town's Facebook page.'

A prickling sensation spreads over my scalp as I inch up the bed into a sitting position. The flowers and parcel were bad enough; this is much worse. A drumbeat of fear plays in my head as I process the enormity of this news.

Everyone will soon know that a local healthcare worker whose clients are elderly and vulnerable has broken Covid rules.

The whole town will hate me.

I am ruined.

'I'm not in that Facebook group. Message admin, tell them to take it down. Do it now, Olivia, before anyone else sees it.'

'Several hundred already have,' she says flatly. 'But I will do. I'm so sorry, Mum, this is all my fault.' She's practically crying. 'You should see the comments. They think you're a Covid-denier, an anti-vaxxer, a rule breaker. My mum, branded a criminal.' Vicious lot. The pandemic has turned people nasty. 'They say you're putting people's lives at risk.'

After the call I immediately go onto *You Tube*. It's doesn't take me long to find the clip and when I do, I gasp. I'm being led out of Parliament Square by the female officer and behind me people are waving anti-vax and anti-lockdown banners. It's only a matter of time before people from work see the video clip.

CHAPTER 20 - INFAMOUS

onna

THE FOLLOWING evening I'm in my kitchen throwing a healthy dinner together when my manager calls.

'Hi Donna. Can you tell me where you were on Wednesday?'

My heart leaps to my throat and my breathing goes all ragged. It feels like a trick question and puts me on heightened alert. I know she must have seen the video by now, but she doesn't know for certain that I was arrested. I didn't give the police my work details.

'I didn't work on Wednesday. Is there a problem?' *Shit, have I missed an appointment?* I rush to my desk to check my rota. *Phew, I've not made a mistake.*

'A video of you being arrested in Parliament Square, has been brought to my attention.'

My voice goes all wobbly like a toy that needs batteries. My brain refuses to engage with what she is telling me as shock and disbelief hit.

'Unfortunately, Mrs Garton's son, Richard, has seen this video and he's put in a strongly worded complaint.'

I feel disembodied as if I might float off like smoke at any moment. There's a ringing sound in my ears. It gets louder, louder.

'It was posted onto *YouTube*.'

A huge howling sob rips through me. 'I can explain.'

'What happened?' Her voice is suddenly kind and soft.

'I didn't do anything wrong.' Apart from leave town in lockdown--hardly a crime and I'm certainly no danger to my clients. 'I went up to London with a friend, another carer, to help scatter his parents' ashes. It was a difficult day for him, I was trying to be supportive.'

'You're a kind person, but maybe that wasn't such a great idea.'

'Mrs Garton's son is always causing trouble for the team. You know that.' I want to tell her about what happened the other week in the kitchen, but I can't bring myself to. I had intended to report him but didn't get around to it.

'I'm really sorry, Donna, but you're being suspended on full pay pending a disciplinary investigation.'

'Suspend me? What do you think I'm going to do to my clients, rob them, beat them up?' I blink back tears of anger.

'There's a risk to our clients, having you continue to go into their homes when there is evidence that you are not following the government's health and safety legislation put in place to control the spread of Covid.' She sounds like a robot and it's as if she's reading from a script.

This is surreal. I'm crushed, defeated, as if a great heavy iron is bearing down on my chest sucking all power from my being. Now the knives are out, I fear they will destroy me. What's happened to our civil liberties? We are living in the dystopian setting of Oceania in George Orwell's book, *1984*.

'Good luck, Donna, you'll be hearing from HR by email in the next few days.'

HOW DID it come to this? I could lose my job. My home. Everything I've worked for. Thank God I have lodgers. Their rent helps, but if I'm out of work, I'm going to notice the squeeze. There won't be much spare cash. This is not just about survival though. It's as much about reputation and that's more valuable than money. It's taken twenty years to build my reputation as a good care worker. Integrity is everything--mine's destroyed. Everyone thinks I have a callous disregard for the health and safety of the vulnerable and that my behaviour is an insult to the efforts of all the other frontline workers.

Standing at my lounge window, I glance up the street.

Is he out there, watching me, waiting?

That horrible weasel, Richard.

Shuddering, I pull the curtains across even though it's not yet dark, suddenly feeling the need to hide away like a murderer about to be discovered and hounded out of his home.

I retreat to bed earlier than usual, the worries chasing around my head, snowballing until I feel immobilised and unable to think, a panic-induced brain freeze. I clutch my hot water bottle, taking comfort from its warmth, and curl into a foetal position. Cocooned under the duvet, I could easily sink into an everlasting sleep.

Even after all these years alone, I still sleep on the left side of the bed, force of habit, one foot over the edge and every night I glance at the empty pillow beside me and wonder if the day will ever come when I'll share my bed with someone else again. Sleeping is one of the most intimate things we can do with another person. It's primal. I miss that togetherness. My cold feet on his legs, nuzzling into the crook of his back. As drowsiness signals, a nocturnal voyage commences, the boat pushing away from shore, sails furled, limbs tangled, drifting into a heavy slumber side by side.

Rapturous lovemaking to forget the day's worries is what I most need right now, even if it's workmanlike, like the aerobic classes I attend each week. My fluffy dressing gown is no substitute for a husband. Sex would be good therapy, a distraction, a release. I grip the hot water bottle tighter, pull my legs up to my chest.

I SPEND the next couple of days researching the coronavirus regulations and writing notes for my disciplinary meeting which is in two weeks' time. I narrate the story of how I came to be arrested to my union rep, who is based in Manchester. I leave no stone unturned. I tell him about Richard––the vulgar texts and the ghastly delivery.

'It sounds like harassment, and you shouldn't have to put up with it.'

Except that I did. To save the embarrassment of my manager finding out that I was on a dating site. Meeting men in lockdown––it would be another strike against my name. I feel ashamed of myself.

'I've blocked his number and until this, he hasn't been a problem. It's obvious he only reported me to get his own back because I wasn't interested in him.'

'Do you have a copy of the workplace policy on sexual harassment?'

'I don't want it brought up at the meeting, I'd rather forget it, it might just add ammunition to their case.'

'I think you need to. You could consider putting in a formal grievance. His actions could be investigated.' I'm sick of the police––can't face more interrogation. 'It's not acceptable behaviour, but if you decide not to, then keep the text messages and a record of events in case you change your mind.'

He continues. 'We need to stick to facts. They're alleging that the health and lives of the vulnerable people in your care are being put at risk by your behaviour because you're not following the government's emergency health and safety legislation.'

I'm Winston Smith in *1984.* Jeez, it'll be spyware in houses next to check we're not breaking rules. Our every action watched, judged, scrutinised. I'm aware of the despair in my voice, the pleading. 'I wear a mask and plastic gloves at work. What more am I supposed to do?' Life's crap right now. My every last vestige of freedom is being questioned. As if I'm living the life of Riley. My social calendar for the week ahead consists of a virtual dinner, a *YouTube* yoga class and freezing my tits off on a cold bench with a friend in the park. Yippee. Better than staying in with my houseplant. Not much conversation there.

'They're saying it's gross misconduct.'

Strong words--to scare me.

'Serious negligence.'

More strong words. And reinforced in writing. I've read their letter that many times, I know it off by heart.

'I never put my clients in jeopardy. I've been doing this job for years.' How dare they question my integrity. 'My record is unblemished. Not a single complaint on file.'

'That's what we'll focus on at the meeting. We'll be humble. You were perhaps naïve, driving up to London to help a friend in need because you're a kind-hearted person. Unfortunately, you unknowingly walked into a trap to rescue your daughter. You weren't breaking the rules, your daughter was. You were doing what any mother would do, protecting her.'

CHAPTER 21 - CAREER ON THE LINE

onna

THE MEETING CAN'T COME SOON ENOUGH. I just want it to be over. I'm in limbo, don't know what to do with myself each day. I can't settle, even to watch a movie. I should relax and enjoy this paid break and do some decorating or chores I've put off. But it's the uncertainty. It's hanging over me like a dark cloud. I can't sleep and I have zero motivation to start the search for a new job. It could be a waste of time if they drop the allegation, and if they don't, will I be struck off, unable to return to care work or any job involving vulnerable people? I can't think about anything else until this is resolved. It's doing my head in.

My heart bangs away as I fire up Zoom on my desktop computer, enter the meeting passcode with shaky fingers and wait for the meeting to begin. I slurp my coffee and fiddle with the notes in front of me as three people appear on the screen: my immediate manager, the HR man and my union rep. They are working from home. The union rep' is sitting in what appears to be a loft room. A shaft of brash morning light streams through a Velux window creating a halo around his head, a divine appearance. I hope he's a miracle-worker.

The HR guy is in a bedroom; a black dog is curled on a bed behind him. Above the bed, a magnolia wall is crammed with tired-looking wedding photos––1970s I'd say judging by his hideous brown suit and long sideburns.

My manager is wearing a bright smile, to put me at ease, or to give me false confidence? She's sitting in a cramped messy room with washing hanging on a clothes rack and stuff piled on every available surface.

The HR guy introduces the meeting and after outlining the allegations, describes the purpose of today as 'fact-finding.' Addressing me, he asks, 'In your own words can you tell us what happened on Wednesday 6th September?'

The union guy steps in before I'm given the chance to present my well-rehearsed case. 'This is unfair. She's being singled out. This lady wasn't at work on that day. Have you asked all your staff what they were doing on that particular day?'

My manager raises an eyebrow. There's a hint of an amused smile playing on her lips. He's made a good point. She doesn't reply and the HR man shrugs.

The HR man rubs his bristly chin and shifts in his seat uncomfortably. 'We received a complaint which we must investigate. By leaving your hometown, and travelling to London to attend a protest you have breached the Skills for Care Code Conduct. It states that you must be accountable by making sure you can answer for your actions or omissions, behave and present yourself in a way that does not call into question your suitability to work in a health and social care environment.'

'The social care document doesn't apply to this lady's private life. Also, the words in the document are wholly, arbitrary and can be interpreted in whatever way you like.'

'Your behaviour is putting our clients at risk.'

'Behaviour?' This whole thing is absurd.

The HR guy peers into the screen. I don't like his eyes. They're raven-like and intimidating. 'You were in a crowd of people. A mass gathering.'

My blood is boiling. I was outside. Where Covid is less likely to transmit. This makes me think of last year's outcry following pictures in the news of crowded beaches, mass hysteria and dire warnings of a spike in Covid cases and that crowds were super-spreaders. The warnings turned out to be complete codswallop. And what is the difference between the crowd I was in, at a protest and a crowded supermarket?

'Again, I'm going to reiterate that this lady has a right to a private life. And you cannot accuse her of putting other people's lives at risk. Where's your proof? What exactly has she breached? How did she endanger the lives of others?'

I add, 'The proof's in the pudding. None of my clients have caught Covid.'

The HR guy, floundering, furnishes his answer with waffle, then asks me, 'Could you outline what happened on the 6th? Why were you seen with a police officer?'

The union rep laces his fingers together on his table. 'This lady doesn't have to answer. She was seen with a police officer but that doesn't mean she has a criminal record. You have no proof of anything or why she was in London. If you were to do a DBS check on her, you would find she has a clean record.' He's right. I wasn't charged with a crime. I received a Fixed Penalty Notice. These notices are being issued like confetti for silly minor breaches of Covid rules. Two women were on the news the other day because they were fined £200 each after driving a mere five miles to take a walk. They were told the hot drinks they'd brought along were not allowed as they were "classed as a picnic." God help us if we can no longer picnic. These rules are bonkers. Fixed penalty notices are fines--like a parking ticket, which we've all received in our time and not lost our jobs over. A pernicious way of raking money in--a tax on our liberty and freedom. Soon, we'll be too scared to leave our homes. And to think how my day had begun--eyeing up kettles in Robert Dyas.

This won't go away. I need to tell them what happened that day. I also need to tell them about Richard's move on me. I remind myself that I'm an asset, they don't want to lose me and there's a staff shortage, so despite the union rep's advice, I explain everything.

When I'm finished, there's silence. I watch their minds ticking over. The union rep' is first to speak. 'She didn't go to London to attend a protest. She was not a willing participant on a protest. Her actions were motivated by a need to help and support others.' Under his breath he adds looking at me, 'you didn't need to explain your actions.' Then directed at my manager he adds,' If we make judgements about people's private lives and what they get up to in their own time, it's a slippery slope, where will it all end? You're setting a very dangerous precedent.'

'Why didn't you report Richard's behaviour to us?' the HR guy asks.

'I don't know. I did intend to. I was embarrassed. Ashamed of myself for going on a dating site.'

'As your union rep I'd advise you to contact the police if you're uncomfortable with his behaviour. They can issue him with a warning.'

'You should have filled out an incident report.' My manager is only interested in procedures and paperwork. There's not an ounce of sympathy and concern for my well-being and by the look of horror on her face she doesn't want me to contact the police.

'Is there anything else you'd like to say, Donna, before we close the meeting?' she adds.

'I've worked here for twenty years. I'm up to date with my training, I follow all the work practices, Covid procedures, I go above and beyond.' Tears are threatening because I'm starting to feel sorry for myself, but I sniff them away. 'Last week I baked Mrs Garton a cake and sometimes I do the odd bits of shopping for my clients in my own time. And I stayed with Mr Oliver an extra hour the last time I was with him, because his asthma was so bad.'

'I didn't know that, Donna,' my manager says with a sympathetic smile.

'And I've done extra shifts in lockdown to ease the pressure on the team.'

Without acknowledging my efforts, in a curt voice the HR guy says, 'We'll let you know our decision in the next seven days.'

CHAPTER 22 - HASHTAG METOO, MOTHER

onna

THE NEXT FEW days are stressful while I wait for their decision. I feel hopeful but in limbo. I don't hear any more from Richard which makes me think I won't, but there are times when I'm nervy and on edge, as if I'm waiting for his next move. Something shivers down my spine when I draw the curtains on the dark, foreboding night or when I open the door to the postman, fearing the next package.

Olivia calls to find out how the meeting went and after I've filled her in, she asks if I've contacted the police about Richard.

'Why not, Mother?' Her tone is angry. 'You have to.'

'I don't want to make a fuss.'

She groans. 'God, you sound like a 1950s woman.'

'I just want to keep my job.'

'Hashtag MeToo, Mother. Women like you aren't helping.'

I'm being personally blamed for the woes of the entire planet. I've only been on the phone with her for two minutes and already she's given me a headache. 'Sexual harassment percolates like a poison into every woman's life. It's the white noise we can't drown out, it's encroaching into our very existence. It's got to stop.' Wow. Sounds as if she's been fighting the cause of women's lib'. It's as if her words have been pulled from a famous speech.

'Seems like a lot of effort.'

'Effort?' she snaps, giving me earache. 'Now you're being lazy. Get off your backside and get down to the police station. If I was there, I'd march you down myself.'

I sigh heavily. Maybe I should contact the police, but I still don't want to. 'I'll think about it.' I sound unconvincing.

'Well don't think too long. He shouldn't get away with it. He'll try it on with someone else next time and might even rape her. You wouldn't want that on your conscience.' She's cross with me and has a clever way of making me feel guilty.

Ending the call, I go to stand at the window to think. I can't shake the nagging feeling that I'm letting other women down by not reporting him. Turning to the kitchen to put the kettle on, I make a snap decision and ring the police even though I'm terrified of making things worse at work. A few hours later a female officer arrives on my doorstep and when I open the door, she's fiddling with the radio clipped to her chest and the radio chatter quietens as she goes to introduce herself and shows me her warrant card before coming in.

I invite her through to my lounge where she perches on the edge of the settee. She taps away at an iPad on her lap as she asks questions and I give answers. I feel a weight begin to lift from my shoulders as I tell her everything. Maybe this was the right thing to do after all.

'We can issue him with a harassment warning. This is a formal written notice and is designed to make it clear that his behaviour has caused you harassment. It's also designed to deter him from carrying out further acts. If he does do anything else that causes you alarm or distress we can charge and arrest him for the offence of harassment. Are you happy to go ahead with us issuing a warning?'

'I don't want to cause trouble. What do you think I should do?'

'I think we should issue a warning. It's not a conviction or a caution. It's just the first stage. Hopefully he will back off and won't bother you anymore. That's the intention.'

I show her Richard's text messages which she takes photos of and I give her the card that was attached to the roses. I glance at the mantel clock and can't believe this has taken a whole hour. I'm glad when she leaves but all alone in the house, I start to feel scared. I hope he won't find a way of paying me back for contacting the police.

A COUPLE OF DAYS LATER, an email from HR pings into my inbox. From its title, 'lifting of suspension' I know it's good news and feel my spirits soar. What a relief. I've won. I open it and read. 'I am pleased to confirm that you are no longer suspended from your role.' Thank God. 'The care team will be in touch to confirm your next shifts.' I'm about to close the email without reading to the bottom when I notice a final, contradictory sentence. 'I will be putting together a report following my investigation and the outcome of this will decide whether the case needs to be referred to a disciplinary hearing or if no further action is needed.'

I thought I'd already been through a disciplinary hearing–– now I'm totally confused. I've told them everything I can. I don't want to repeat the whole grisly experience. What will it achieve? They know I'm a good carer, I don't know what more I can prove. I'm beginning to think the care industry doesn't deserve people like me. The ones who go above and beyond, who do their job diligently and try their best. It's getting difficult enough, without this sort of aggro. Take holiday leave for instance. Since Brexit it's been tough filling care posts and there are gaps in the rota and sometimes my manager turns down our leave requests. It's outrageous after our efforts this past year.

I don't have to wait long for the next email with a final decision. It comes two days later after I've already returned to work. It reads, 'I can confirm that I will not be referring the matter on to a disciplinary hearing.' So daft, why did they threaten me with a hearing but allow me to work? It doesn't make sense. If I am a health and safety risk to my clients, they'd have kept me away. They must realise their own stupidity. The letter states that this is an informal warning and will be kept on my personal file. A permanent stain on my name and all because I ventured up to London and stood in a crowd. 'All risks to our clients must be kept to a minimum,' the letter says. That will never happen, can never happen. There will always be illnesses. We cannot wrap our elderly and vulnerable in bubble wrap. We cannot eliminate illness or risk. It's time we learned to live with this virus.

One thing I will have to learn to live with--no Mrs Garton. My supervisor changed my rota and I'm no longer visiting her. I'll miss her but I can't risk contact with Richard, especially now that the police have issued him with a harassment warning. I've not heard anything from him since it was served, but I didn't expect to.

CHAPTER 23 - DELETE

 onna

ONE OF THE first things I did on release from Leyton police station was delete my dating app. After the events of that day, my love life should have been the last thing on my mind––but being locked up in a cell was a sobering experience and made me realise what a waste of time these apps are. Deleting the app was somehow symbolic, as if I'd reached a turning point, a new beginning. I didn't know what that new beginning would involve and still don't but using the app had become worse than pounding away on a treadmill; the experience was repetitive, monotonous and I was going nowhere fast. It's time to take a break. I feel worn out and tattered. I think I've reached dating burnout––I can't tolerate another mind-numbing text. These men, they communicate in drivel. It was worse than chit-chat at a party. 'Hi, how are you? What are you up to?' Those annoying texts made me want to scream, throw my phone on the floor and stamp on it in utter frustration. And as for meeting up; no more dodgy dates.

I'm done.

But as a Cistercian abbot once said, 'the road to hell is paved with good intentions.' I don't go back on the app, but I do reply to a message on WhatsApp late one night in March.

'Hi, how are you?' it begins in that grating and predictable way.

It can't be from anyone I wanted to stay in touch with otherwise I'd have saved the number. Scrolling up the thread I discover it's from someone on the dating app from weeks ago. It's obvious he's been blown out by his list of hopefuls, and I'm tempted to tell him. I'm last on his list, the bottom of the barrel. Great, that's really encouraging.

My finger hovers over the screen. What have I got to lose by replying? If the conversation is crap, I'll block.

'I'm fine, you?' No point wasting my energy by writing reams when he clearly can't be arsed. Men like him are what I call 'masquerades', they play at dating, like actors on a stage. Their communication is Neanderthal-like. Has nobody heard of the art of building up a meaningful connection first and a reason to start a conversation?

'Great thank you. I wondered if you'd like to meet at the weekend for a walk. It's been a while since we last chatted on here. We seemed to have a few things in common and I thought it would be nice to meet.'

I'm flummoxed. This wasn't what I was expecting. I thought it would be another dead-end chat. Someone looking to simply pass the time by text bombing. This is hopeful. Looks like this guy isn't too tired to put his shoes on and come out, and like me doesn't want a pen pal.

After arranging to meet on the bridge at Arundel on Easter Saturday, I prep by whizzing up the thread to read the chat history and all the things we are supposed to have in common.

Be good to have a picture of this mystery man, but I've deleted the dating app, and his WhatsApp doesn't have a picture. But I find his name. Always a good start.

Colton.

Surely, I'd have remembered such an unusual name. Either I'm developing dementia, or I've messaged so many men, I've lost track. I'll go for the latter. There have been several men with ridiculous names. He must have been one of them.

It's a great name though. American I'd guess. I roll it around my tongue. It has a cowboy feel about it. As I conjure images of him in my mind, arriving on Arundel bridge on horseback, his feet in fancy spurs and a Stetson on his head, a warm glow rushes through me because with a name like that he'll have a Wild West edge to him. He's bound to be rugged, sexy, and clad in brown leather. He must shorten it to Colt, the term for a frisky young horse.

Why am I even considering meeting this guy without knowing what he looks like? I must be mad. But I'm not asking him to send me a picture because that would look dumb on my part, like turning up for a job interview without knowing what the job is for. I'll just have to take that leap of faith. Afterall, it's just one day out of my life and I've got nothing else planned over Easter.

After arranging a time, I circumnavigate the thorny issue by asking him what he'll be wearing so that I can easily spot him. 'A brown leather jacket,' he replies. Wow, he's certainly living up to my image of him. I'm already looking forward to meeting this guy.

SATURDAY ARRIVES. It's a beautiful day. A light frost sparkling on the lawn soon clears and the welcoming arms of spring reach out. Flinging my wardrobe doors open, I riffle through my clothes wondering what to wear. Once upon a time, my date-night look was a dress with a V-neck to show off a little cleavage, hair long and curled. A pair of high-heeled black velvet boots. This tried and tested ensemble was perfect for drinks or dinner. A show. The theatre. But it's not 2019 anymore, when pubs, bars and restaurants existed. This is 2021 and everything is shut up. Dating is alfresco, weather-dependent and bugger, it's chilly out. I slide into my tightest jeans hoping he'll notice my best asset––,my bum, and pull a comfy jumper over my head before turning to my reflection in the mirror. This is the Rambler's Association look, but it will have to do.

With butterflies skittering across my stomach, I realise how important this date is to me. This time I really want to make an impression. He could be the one. I cringe. Why am I even thinking about the concept of 'the one'? It's so antiquated. And then I realise it's a goal that's been programmed into me from way back in my teen years when I used to pour over articles in *Jackie* magazine––the 1970s teenage girl's bible on everything to do with love, romance, clothes, and make-up.

A part of me is chilled because this will most definitely be my very last date. I know I keep saying this and maybe it won't be. But I'm a great believer in everything in life having a natural end; it's important to recognise when to move on. I can't go through this again; dating has taken its toll on me, and I don't have the resilience to bounce back from another crappy date.

At the door I ease into my filthy walking boots after slamming them hard against the outside wall to loosen the mud. How I long for the end of this prolonged lockdown when I can finally step into a pair of heels and feel like a million dollars.

It's a pleasant drive to Arundel. The sun is bright and puffy clouds snail across a baby-blue sky. The grass verges are bursting to life and there's a splash of yellow in many gardens––daffodils in full bloom. I park near the cathedral at the town's summit which dominates the town's skyline and walk towards the castle. Perched on an outcrop of land it's the centrepiece of this picturesque and historic town. A town dating back to Roman and Saxon times. I'm forever in awe of this imposing and formidable stone edifice. Parts of the castle date back to 1068 but it was once the breathing heart of the community centuries ago, now a tourist attraction for hordes of day-trippers descending on the town in the summer months clogging the roads but bringing income to the town. From the castle an assortment of antique shops and pretty cafes tumble down the hill. I stop to admire the amazing display of hand-crafted Easter eggs in Pallants, the town's rustic and earthy deli. Catching my reflection in the window I realise I've put my woolly hat on. It's become second nature to wear a hat and I'll be cold without it, but I've got to ditch it. I pull it off and tuck it into my bag. I don't want him to see me in a hat. Not on date number one.

I'm five minutes early but am bursting for a wee so I walk beside the ruins of the old friary next to the River Arun to the row of toilets in the carpark. The town has been mobbed. I'm glad I didn't attempt to park here. My pulse skips a beat when I see the long queue snaking around the car park. Everyone's diligently following government advice, standing two metres apart and looking like dominoes. One nudge and they'll tumble.

I fire off a quick text warning Colton I'll be a few minutes late and I get chatting to the woman in front of me as I wait.

Hurrying back to the bridge, I round the corner and catch my first glimpse of him. Impressions are formed in seconds. It's the same as buying a house. Wow. He's good-looking. But good-looking men are womanisers, cocky and full of themselves.

I love his hair–– a full head of wayward chestnut curls is sticking out in funny directions making him look like a chinchilla. At least he's not playing at being a wizard or a druid. There's no facial hair. Beards, moustaches or heavy stubble are most off-putting. His hands are deep in the pockets of his leather jacket, and he's gazing out at the river and hasn't yet noticed me. My boss used to say hands in the pockets murder rapport and make you come across as unconfident and is the mark of a liar and that showing your hands builds trust. This guy looks cool, sexy, relaxed.

He's thin, but not weedy. Thin is tons better than the weighty men with distended bellies and man boobs I'm all too familiar with. Crushing me in bed, snoring heavily and eating all the time. Turning, he says 'hi.' He grins but it's not an awkward grin, more a warm and welcoming one.

'I'm so sorry I'm late.' I'm all out of breath and flushed.

'Hey, don't apologise, I was bursting too, soon as I arrived.' He's a far-cry from the cowboy figure I'd imagined. His voice is not dissimilar to my own––a BBC voice. It's as if he's crafting each word into perfect shape like a potter. I like a poshly spoken distinguished man. They effuse success and class. A good education, confidence, sociability. He's a modern-day Jane Austen character. Darcy or George Wickham in *Pride and Prejudice*. It's as if he's stepped out of his stately home for the day to mingle with the riff-raff. I know it's wrong of me to make judgements and that I'm being superficial and downright snobby, but I can't help it. There are certain accents and ways of speaking that really grate on me.

'I've a confession.' I laugh. 'I googled the toilets to check they were open.'

'Good thinking. When you've gotta go, you've gotta go.'

'It's a barrier to going out. Shall we head down to the riverbank?'

Our chat is polite as we make our way through the car park, past the boatyard and onto the towpath, the weather and other trivia offering easy conversational fodder.

'Your name's unusual. Are your parents American?' I ask him.

He looks embarrassed. 'No. I suppose it is.'

I don't plan to, but I find myself confessing that on the

journey down here I decided this was to be my last date. 'Whole thing's too stressful, so many time wasters out there.'

'Yes, yes, it is,' he agrees. 'I'm tired of all that swiping. Women are so cautious, so reluctant to meet up. There's no point in days or even weeks of texting. You've got to meet.'

'Have you been on the dating site long?' I'm conscious not to pepper him with too many questions and this is certainly a dull one, but it's a good fallback and is the main thing we have in common otherwise we wouldn't be here.

'Not long. This is only my second date. I was married for thirty-eight years.' Sounds like a prison sentence. He doesn't elaborate and when he thrusts his hands deeper into his pockets, dipping his head to the pavement, I wonder if he's widowed. Now I wish I hadn't asked; I've put my foot in it. 'A few weeks ago, I drove all the way down to Portsmouth for a date, to be told I was too gentle, and she had no respect for nice men.'

'That's mental.'

'You?' Now that it's my turn, I feel embarrassed, a shameless hussy compared to his seemingly unblemished history.

'I got divorced years ago, but I've had a few relationships since.' All ending in disaster, but I don't tell him this.

We step aside to let people pass and for a moment we watch a couple of people kayaking on the river, battling against the current. 'I used to kayak when I was in my teens,' I tell him. 'We had a river at the bottom of our field. It got heavy lugging it down there.'

'I used to canoe too, until I had kids.'

'How wonderful. I'd love to take it up again; it's been years since I sat in a boat and pootled down a river.' I don't know where the years have gone. 'Time's a cruel thief to rob us of all the pastimes we enjoyed in youth.'

'So would I.' He turns to face me. 'We should do it.'

'What, now?' I'm not wearing the right clothes.

'No, silly. Just sometime.' He smiles and beckons me on. 'Hey, don't be hard on yourself, you were busy working, paying bills, and raising a family. Life gets put on hold.'

Climbing over a stile, we stop to gaze at the castle on the hill.

'Life's full of regrets, isn't it?'

'Tell me about it,' he says raising his eyebrows. 'I wish I'd spent more time with my three kids, but I was always working. It wasn't easy running a business.' He explains that he had a property maintenance company but now works in B&Q as a sales assistant. 'I'd come home knackered long after the kids were in bed and for many years, we could only afford a week away in Ramsgate.'

'My biggest regret is all the men I've been out with.'

'Should you be telling me that on a first date?' He smiles and gives me a friendly nudge.

'God knows what you think of me.' I laugh. 'Olivia was young when we divorced, and I was lonely and wanted company. I wish I'd waited until she was eighteen and left home before I started dating. It wouldn't have been a waste of time because look where it's got me. Precisely nowhere. I should have been a better mother and put her first. She holds it against me, I know she does.' I can't believe how easy he is to talk to. I don't usually pour out deep thoughts like this until I know someone well. This is the type of conversation I'd have with a girlfriend.

'If it had worked out with someone, you wouldn't be harbouring regrets.'

'I guess not.'

Already I like him, a lot. There's something deeply seductive about him. Maybe it's the tone of his voice, soft, confident, well-spoken or the way every word sounds carefully considered. He's relaxing, easy-going. There's compassion in his words, his eyes. He's a listener. But it's more than that. Something intangible. This feels different. It's to do with the way we are--together, in sync like two dancers on stage as we stop every so often at the same moment to look at the sky, a bird in a hedge, the water, a flower. Making simple comments. Breathing the air. Appreciating. Content in the here and now. The landscape is not background wallpaper, it's a part of us. We're experiencing it with a real sense of togetherness. There's synergy. He doesn't fill silences with weird noises like diddly diddly dee or make crass comments about the countryside, like oh man this is so cool. He doesn't rattle on about work, or brag about his educational achievements and career ladder. He's open and honest, self-deprecating. He tells me he hasn't a single O-level, left school at the first opportunity and only sold his business when he developed arthritis. He doesn't talk at me. He talks with me. Doesn't blather and crucially, he picks up on cues and body language. We find a rhythm between talking and listening. It's asymmetry in the conversational 'give and take'. Rare and refreshing. Neither does he regale me with boring tales or explain the key features of his car. Or educate me on the different varieties of seagull or letterboxes or other inconsequential random entities. I do seem to have dated a disproportionate string of very dull men in my time. It's no wonder Olivia calls me a loser.

We reach The Black Rabbit on the banks of the River Arun. The views are stunning across to the wetlands in one direction and Arundel Castle in the other. It's a popular spot, a honeypot, attracting hordes of walkers and tourists especially from this time of year onwards.

We stand in disbelief.

It's all closed-up. Forlorn. Abandoned. Like an establishment that's had its heyday. Reminds me of an abandoned ghost town after a gold rush. By now there'd be flower baskets hanging from the black beams of the wraparound veranda, waiters and waitresses dashing in and out, serving food to customers seated along the length of the veranda and outside at one of the benches on the wooden jetty.

'This is terrible.' My heart quietly breaks as I think about the

plight-- not just of this pub now facing an uncertain future--
but every other pub, café, restaurant, and business up and down
the land, forced to close. 'Lockdown is too brutal; this place
could go bust. It's success down the toilet, people out of work.'

He shakes his head. 'And the worst of it is, all I want is a
bloody pint.'

'I'd pay over the odds for a G and T.'

We briefly laugh, but there's nothing funny about the situation. This is not about us, thirsty on a warm day deprived of a
drink--it's about a whole livelihood in jeopardy, everything its
owners have worked for.

As we sit down at one of the tables it feels strange because
it's often hard to find an empty table at this pub and now there
are at least twenty to choose from.

He pulls a water bottle from his rucksack and offers me
a sip.

I take a glug. 'Ironic isn't it, here we are exchanging saliva,
but if the pub was open, we'd be drinking from our own glasses.'

'The rules make little sense. I don't want to be wrapped in
cotton wool. I can make my own decisions on safety like I
always have. This is an extreme form of nanny-state. And if
businesses like this one fail, that's less tax coming in to support
the NHS. It's a Catch-22.'

'I bet there are plenty of people breaking the rules.' I don't
tell him about being detained at Her Majesty's pleasure. That's a
story for a future date. 'I bet the politicians are laughing at us
plebs. I bet they break the rules on the sly.'

'They made the rules, they're hardly going to break them.' He
looks at me incredulous. This is the first time we've disagreed.
It's better than him agreeing with me out of politeness and not
wanting to offend. He sighs and stares out over the river.
'Without lockdowns we don't know how many would have
died.'

I rattle out something Olivia keeps telling me. 'But lives will be lost because of lockdown. Missed cancer treatment, suicide, domestic abuse.'

'I'm glad I'm not a politician. So many tough decisions. Must keep them awake all night. And there was me thinking it was bad enough being kept awake with arthritic pain.'

'That sounds nasty. I'm sorry you're suffering.'

'It's not your fault.' He gets up and in a bright tone closes the subject. 'Come on, what about walking to Swanbourne Lake?'

Strolling along the road that runs parallel to the river, we soon reach the lake, and follow the trail around it, taking us through a wood and round to a kiosk serving ice creams and takeaway drinks.

'I'll have...' A black tea or a hot chocolate with soya milk. I can't decide.

He smiles and winks at me. 'You look like you need a hot chocolate with soya milk.'

It's as if he's read my mind. 'That's exactly what I need.' I can't remember telling him I don't drink dairy, but I'm impressed he's remembered and is listening. Full Brownie points to this one.

We continue to notice the same things as if we are doing so with fresh new eyes, commenting on the beauty around us. The lake is reflective blues and greens, a canvas of grass and blue sky bringing its own artistic watercolour effect. It's lovely to sit and watch children playing beside the lake and the seagulls swooping to pick at the overflowing bin. And the way the tethered boats catch the sunlight every bit as much as the water.

'I so miss foreign holidays,' I say looking up at the sun through closed eyes.

'Me too. I can't wait to travel again. I've got money saved and ready.'

I glance at him. 'Same. It's just sitting in the bank. So frustrating.'

'I just want to get on a plane.'

'Tell me about it.'

'Where shall we go?' *We?* Bit forward—he's making me blush.

He's dreaming. Just being hypothetical but I can't help hoping that he likes me and sees this going somewhere but he'd go with anyone if it meant sun. 'Literally anywhere abroad. Greece, Spain, the Canaries, Caribbean. Just not bloody Bognor Regis.'

'No, definitely not Bognor Regis.'

We laugh. The desire to jet off is something we have in common. Soon we're sharing crazy stories of road trips and disaster camping escapades.

'When the kids were little, we could only afford to go camping, but it was fun.' Deep in thought, he stares out across the lake, giving me the chance to study his face. He's well-groomed and chisel-jawed. Soft lines around his eyes and mouth are shadowed with fatigue. His skin is slightly leathery, a faded brown. The souvenir of a holiday long committed to memory, or many hours spent outdoors. 'At Pevensey Bay it rained for eleven days. We were flooded out.'

'Sounds like our boat trip on the River Shannon when I was a kid. Didn't stop raining. My parents argued the entire time, then we got marooned on a rock.'

He laughs. 'I can see a book here. One hundred and one camping stories. One time, at Selsey, our tent took off into the sea it was that windy.'

I don't ever want to camp again and I'm pretty sure he feels the same. 'I fell asleep under a tree on one holiday and woke to an army of ants marching over me and up the tree as if my body was the M25.'

He chuckles. The sharing of our stories is like tennis. I'm loving it.

'In Holland my dad drove on a one-way bridge in the wrong direction. There was a lot of beeping and shouting out of car windows but my dad, pig-headed as usual, insisted he was in the right and everyone else was wrong.'

It doesn't sound as if he had a good relationship with his dad. 'Are your parents still alive?' I ask.

'Yes, but I've not seen them in years.' There's an awkward beat of silence as I wait for him to elaborate. I'm not going to pry as this is only our first date. It would be too intrusive.

He gets up and stretches his arms as if to indicate closure to the conversation and heads to the bin to dispose of our empty cups. When he returns, we wander back towards town.

'You hungry?' he asks brightly. 'I'm starving. I could murder some fish and chips.'

'Big fat greasy chips, yes please.' Not great for the figure though. I'm bulging in my size fourteen clothes; at some point I must start dieting.

The hours have rolled by. I can't believe it's early evening. There's a long queue outside the fish and chip shop and it's snaking round the corner. Looks as if they're feeding the nation, which collectively this humble simple quintessentially English fare probably is. Let's face it, there's a dearth of takeaways open in lockdown. I bet they've soared to the top of the hospitality ladder. There's something comforting and safe about this return to a bygone era and I find myself thinking that I could easily settle into a way of life that resembles a time warp.

'It's always good to taste the seaside.' It's getting chilly so I rub my hands to keep warm while Colton puts on a surgical mask. I don't see the point; we're standing outside.

The windows are steaming, and inside the glass-chrome cabinets gleam. My stomach growls when I see the golden battered fish and a jar of bobbing pickled eggs. Right now, I'm loving the nostalgia of this experience, it's like living in the 1950s. But tomorrow is another day and I'll be back to missing my favourite cocktail bar.

'They tasted better when they were wrapped in newspaper,'

Colton says, laughing, as we make our way to a bench by the river, our hands carrying the warm bundles.

'They were. I can picture them wrapped in the *Daily Mail*, Harold Wilson's face peeping out from between the chips.'

Sitting on the bench; we unwrap our parcels. 'Hot fat, vinegar mixed with dirt and carcinogens. Made them tasty.'

'Perhaps with Brexit we can restore that fine tradition of poisoning ourselves with food.' I laugh and nibble at my first chip. It's too hot but tastes deliciously fluffy.

'I'd move abroad if it wasn't for bloody Brexit.'

'So would I.'

'We've got so much in common, Donna.' He smiles at me, his lips shiny with grease. 'I don't want to leave you; I've had such a lovely day.'

'Aw. Me too. It's been great.' There's fondness in his eyes—— he's making me blush.

'You free tomorrow? I'd like to see you again.'

So soon——he's surprised me, but I've nothing planned and although we've not yet parted, I'm missing him already. This feels like the start of something.

After eating, he walks me up the hill to my car and this is when I say the crassest, most embarrassing thing ever. 'It's a shame my dad's not still alive. He would have really liked you.' I don't know why I say it; it wasn't planned. I sound way too serious, as if I'm relaying the message that he's the one. *Eek*. He must think I'm a right ha'p'orth.

One person who does accuse me of being one sandwich short of a picnic is Olivia. I rush to ring her as soon as I step through my front door. I really should learn to hold back. I don't need to tell her everything, especially where my love life is concerned. It constitutes a parent-child boundary violation, but I never learn; I'm always itching to share my news. I'm too excited to keep it to myself.

Her seagull laugh is a knife to my eardrums, and I wince,

immediately regretting telling her. 'Oh, Mother, I suppose you think he's the one. If he asks you to marry him, say no.'

'I've only had one date and who said anything about marriage. I'm not getting married again. Not in a million years.'

'Good, glad to hear it,' she says, sounding like a headteacher reprimanding a student.

'You're only bothered about your inheritance,' I say glumly.

'Of course.' The seagull laugh is back and slamming into my ear. She shows not an ounce of shame and embarrassment. The brazen little cow.

CHAPTER 24 - QUACKERS

 onna

I'M SITTING in the car overlooking Piltdown Pond waiting for
Colton to arrive. After such a lovely day in Arundel, I could
barely sleep. I glance in my car's mirror. There are bags under
my eyes and my face looks bloated and puffy. Looks like I've
been out on the lash. I'm a mess of nervous butterflies. An infat-
uated teenager. *Pull yourself together, Donna.* Every single little
thing I like about him. I can't even deny that fact to myself.
Heck, I know we've only just met and that my heart is ruling the
show. I'm behaving in a desperate and maybe deluded state, but
I can't help it.

There's a tap on the window and I jump when I see Colton
standing by my car.

'Didn't you hear me? I tapped a couple of times,' he says after
I get out and lock the door.

'I must have zoned out.'

'This is beautiful. I'm glad you suggested it.'

Walking towards the pond, I see there's a young family feeding the gaggle of mallards, moorhens, and coots. Looking round at the tranquil setting, I tell him it's a retreat I only discovered in lockdown, but it's become my favourite place. Secluded, peaceful, it's a perfect place to contemplate, read a book, or catch up with a friend. The pond is surrounded by reed, gorse, and heathland. A golf course to the east and north orbits the pond. It was closed as part of lockdown measures and became a well-trodden path for walkers. It's only recently reopened––annoyingly. I'll miss my walks across the lush emerald lawn admiring the view over heather and Scots pines. It's as special and magnificent to me as grand parks like Richmond in Surrey. I bet the club are glad us riffraff are no longer trampling their playing surfaces. They will have had their work cut out, repairing the turf.

For a few moments we watch the ducks go into a series of plunging, diving, and bathing routines. It's a spectacular show. Several ducks waddle onto the bank, indulging in vigorous preening and body shaking.

Skirting the pond, we brush past spiky gorse bushes. In full bloom, they are a hue of yellow and give off a faint coconut smell. The mud in places is thick and we laugh as we take great strides to avoid getting our feet dirty. Reaching the bench under a tree and about to sit, we are distracted by two Canada geese in flight. Graceful and smooth, they glide through the air with such ease and self-assurance–– a pure delight to watch.

'Wow.' Tilting his head to the sun, he shields his eyes. 'Just incredible.'

'Such beautiful birds. They have a pride about them, as if they're aware of their own magnificence.' Sitting down, I unscrew my flask and pour coffee into a mug. He joins me and does the same, before offering me a slice of raspberry jam Swiss roll he's bought from M&S. 'You rarely see them alone. Once they find a mate, they stay with them for life.'

'Unlike us humans,' he says, taking a bite of his cake.

'Most people want to pair for life. But things don't always work out that way. Your relationship history is way more stable than mine. I'm slightly envious.'

'Don't be. I got married too young. I didn't know what I was doing. I wish I hadn't rushed into it, but marriage was my escape route from home.'

I turn to look at him. 'I thought you went to boarding school.'

'My mum walked out on us when I was eight. I didn't have a good relationship with my dad even at that age. Shortly after she left, he packed me off to boarding school.'

My head is full of questions. What sort of mother would leave her children? Did Colton's father abuse her? Was she having an affair? There's something profoundly shocking about a mother deserting her children.

'We never saw her again. I barely remember her. What memories I have, I've tried to blank.' He takes a bite of cake and stares out at the pond.

'That's awful, I'm really sorry.'

'My dad was hoping I'd go on to university, but I hated schoolwork, didn't get any O levels, so I went to live back at home at sixteen. I was a massive disappointment to him, a huge embarrassment and I never lived it down. As far as the old man was concerned, I'd wasted thousands of pounds of his hard-earned money. I'd humiliated him. He'd tease me, call me a dunce, a dummy, the village idiot. I hate him, haven't seen him in years. I don't want anything to do with him.'

'I'm really shocked.' I feel privileged that he's told me. This is a big thing to tell a stranger.

For a moment we sit in silence, our gaze following a robin as it hops over the damp wands of grass as if it has springs in its delicate feet and the grass is a trampoline.

'This really is such a peaceful place.' He wipes his hands on a serviette and leans back.

'Yummy cake.'

'Like some more?'

'I shouldn't.'

'Here's a question for you.' He looks suddenly thoughtful. God knows what he's about to ask. 'I asked the guys at work the same question. Has lockdown changed you?'

'Interesting question.' I stare at the beautiful plumage of a nearby blue tit. He's like a clockwork toy hopping on the grass searching for worms. I watch him fly to a branch in a tree a couple of metres from where we are sitting and break into a joyous melody. Moments like this have become special. 'I didn't take much notice of wildlife before lockdowns. Now I find myself stopping to watch little creatures. Birds, ducks, squirrels. They seem to be everywhere. It's as if all the cars and the people and the human noise have chased them away and they've come out to play and entertain us.'

He smiles, tilts his head towards me, and touches his lips with a single finger before pointing to a tall branch in the tree. 'Up there,' he whispers.

A robin is sitting on a branch, his head switching from side to side. He peals into song before rising aloft into the blue sky.

'Yeah, I'm the same,' he says. 'I never used to be so fascinated by the flutter of small wings. Now I find myself stopping at every hedge. Sometimes I wonder what it would be like to skip work and join the birds in the hedge. I'm sure they talk more sense than the guys at work.'

'I've saved so much money in lockdowns. It's made me realise I probably don't need half the things I buy.'

He laughs. 'I'm the opposite. It's so easy to order stuff on online. I'm always on Amazon.'

The light shifts and changes, a yellow warmth spreading

across the trees as the sun sinks and melts across the sky. There's companionable silence between us, like the kind that grows like a vine through the long years of friendship. He seems as unbothered by quiet as I am. It's as if neither of us feels the need to speak unless it's to comment on the view before us. Some people fear silence and will do anything to fill it, talking about trivia, asking endless questions, as if silence indicates failure.

We watch a trail of ducks gliding across the pond seemingly effortlessly. 'They make it look so easy, don't they?' he comments.

'Underneath the water their feet will be going like the clappers. The effort never shows on their faces.'

'They make me think of unsung heroes. The strongest people are not those who show strength in front of us but those who win battles we know nothing about.'

'That's very profound, but true.'

'Life's a bit like a pond, don't you think?'

I turn to him and frown. 'How do you mean?'

'Every decision we make is a pebble flung into water.'

We watch a male mallard splash into the water making a long wake, the ripples spreading out like those behind a speed boat. The sun catches its head-- green and iridescent, it's so beautiful. 'Every decision we make has consequences and impacts so many lives, like ripples that spread from a tiny stone.'

'Do you have a big decision you need to make?'

'I'd like to retire,' he says. 'Every day is a slog. I'd like to make a decent income from my buy-to-lets but they all have mortgages on them. I don't make enough.'

I think of my own slog to earn a living, taking in lodgers and Airbnb guests to supplement my income. It's tough on my own, always has been. 'We both make an income from property. One day I'd like to sell up and move to a cheaper area and maybe do bed and breakfast.'

'Me too. I've always wanted to run a bed and breakfast. But

I'm also a bit lazy. Really I'd just like the income but not have to do very much.'

I laugh. 'Wouldn't we all?'

APRICOT and red bleeds across the sky making the branches of the trees surrounding the pond form jagged shapes and appear charred like used matchsticks. It's getting cold––time to go. We amble back to the carpark, surprised by how long we've been here and how much we've enjoyed such a simple afternoon. A bench, a pond, and a flask of tea.

We reach his car. It matches his character. It's not flashy or posy. Wasn't bought to show off or make a statement. It's just a small, cheap, no-frills Panda. It strikes me then––he's the most unobtrusive man I think I've ever met.

Before saying goodbye, he invites me down to his house in Durrington, near Worthing, for lunch and a walk the following Saturday. Of course, I say yes––I can't wait to see him again. When he asks me what I eat, I tell him nothing that attacks. He'll make an omelette and toss in plenty of mushrooms and peppers and hold the chilli.

Before turning to go, I think he's going to hug me. I'd welcome a hug right now. My body is crying out for human comfort and if he reached out to embrace me, maybe it would indicate that he likes me. Although he's asked to see me again, I don't know for sure what his feelings are, and I'm always rubbish at reading the signals. But I know I wasn't imagining that unspoken undercurrent, that tiny jolt you get when an attraction is reciprocated. The waiting itself feels charged and sensual, a kind of silent foreplay.

When he grins and gives me an awkward wave, I know that a hug isn't likely. Disappointment slams into me as I watch him unlock his car before I head over to my own.

CHAPTER 25 - PASSION

onna

I'M curious to see where he lives, though a part of me is wary to be alone with him in his house. Afterall, this is only our third date. The last time I accepted a similar invitation, I ended up in bed and regretted it. It was too soon and maybe because we'd been too hasty, it didn't lead to a lasting relationship. I might be an outdated dinosaur, but human nature doesn't change. Best to keep men keen, give them something to look forward to. I don't want them thinking I'm easy. What's the rush? Sex too soon destroys the mystique and sense of anticipation.

It's all very well having convictions, but not so easy sticking to them. When I'm caught up in the moment, feel a tingling wave of longing, a throbbing in the undercarriage region, kissing leads to other things. But I don't think I need to worry today--heck, we've not kissed yet.

I pull up outside a row of bland 1970s semis on a housing estate. Cars are parked haphazardly over kerbs, but I find a space in the next road. Colton is smiling in the open doorway, his arms folded as I approach the house. He's dressed in jeans and a sexy tight-fitting black t-shirt that makes my heart skip a beat. On his feet are a vintage pair of leather flipflops--making him look as if he drives a VW campervan. Thank God he doesn't appear to own a pair of slippers, otherwise I'd use them to fuel a bonfire.

I follow him through to a very clean and tidy kitchen, glancing briefly into the lounge where I can see a wood burner and flooring that looks to be real oak. He's clearly someone who takes great pride in his home.

'I've built our omelette; it's just waiting to go in the pan.'

A bizarre choice of words. 'Built it? It's not Lego.' I snigger.

'It's liquid till it goes in the frying pan.'

On the kitchen worktop are ramekin dishes containing various ingredients--or building blocks as Colton might say. Basil, mushroom, red onion, peppers, sweetcorn, cubed bacon. It reminds me of the counter in Pizza Express.

'What do you drink?' He presents a chilled bottle of wine to me, but I remind him I'm driving.

'Water's fine.'

'You hungry?'

His over-preparedness makes me giggle. 'Not really. It's only eleven. Are you then?'

'Not really.' He beams at me. 'Shall we go for a walk first then, that way we can work up an appetite? You'll need some room for the lemon cheesecake I've made.'

'Wow, one of my favourites.'

'Me too.'

I had been hoping we'd stroll along the pathway beside the River Adur in Shoreham. We'd talked about doing that. There's a village of about fifty crazy-looking houseboats and they're fun to see. But Colton has other ideas for today. We drive a few miles from his home in Durrington, along the main road to

Highdown Hill where there are remains of an ancient hill fort on the summit. I've not been here before, but Olivia's grandparents used to take her kiting on windy days when she visited their home in nearby Worthing.

Parking at the base of the hill, we take the bridlepath and begin the steady climb to the top, following the line of the chalk ridge, stopping to look at a converted windmill and on beside a vineyard. The sun is coming up over the hill, fingers of light spreading across the grass and pretty chalkland flowers bursting to life––buttercups, cowslip, crosswort. The air is cool, and I think how beautiful it is. At the summit, gazing around us, he slips his hand into mine. The gesture is so simple, so intimate. It would go unnoticed if we'd been together for ages, but this is the first time we have touched, and it feels as if something has flowed from him to me. I'm aware of my heart beating faster, it's the thought that we are becoming a pair, a sign of togetherness, a statement.

'I wanted to bring you up here because you shared your special place with me, well this is mine.'

I catch my breath; it's been a steep walk. 'I'm honoured. Can't believe I've never been up here before. The view, it's just wow.' I tuck a few strands of hair behind my ear that have escaped my velvet scrunchie. 'Just incredible.' It's getting warmer––it's that time of year when you don't know if you'll need a coat or not. I take mine off and sling it over my shoulder.

'It's the whole of the South Coast––maybe a hundred-mile stretch? You can see everything. It's like looking down over a model village.'

I'm so excited to discover a view I've not seen before. To our left are the gentle slopes of the Seven Sisters and to our far right, Butlin's at Bognor and beyond, the Spinnaker Tower at Portsmouth. We can even see the Isle of Wight.

He points to the industrial estate where he works. Being orange, the B&Q is easy to spot. I, in turn, point out the places that are connected to my life. So much of our pasts are here in this view. It is a visual aid to a potted history of our lives. Where we were married, where we worked, happy days out on different beaches. Days of bliss, much too brief, our memories have become the pages that define us and anchor us to the past, for better, for worse. Twenty minutes, maybe more passes and in that short time we've powered through a fast-track course in getting to know each other. We share the pain of divorce, the events that led to the crucial moment when we knew our marriages were dead. And we comb the string of regrets that still haunt us. But above all, there's the devastation to our children––like a wildfire raging through a forest, the scars are still visible years on.

'If only marriage came with an instruction manual.' Turning away from the view, we amble back along the path towards the car. 'Maybe all love is finite, like reading a book. There's nothing deader than dead love. I know that for sure; I've been there, got the t-shirt,' I say with sadness.

'I wish I hadn't married so young,' he says. 'I've always felt that I don't have my own identity. I was somebody's kid, someone's classmate, someone's brother, someone's dad, someone's husband. After I got divorced, I didn't really know who I was on my own. I'd never been on my own. Everything I did was for somebody else.'

I stop and frown at him, my heart quietly sinking. 'Maybe a relationship is the last thing you need right now.'

'No––I'm really enjoying your company and I've come off the dating site. I'd like to get to know you. I know it's early days, but I'm really looking forward to some nice days out with you. There's so much we have in common. I'd like to walk the Downs with you, swim in the sea, have lazy beach days.'

'But have you given yourself enough space? It's not good to go straight from one relationship to the next. Maybe you need to be alone for a bit to discover yourself again.'

'I'm more than ready to move on. It's been a couple of years since we divorced.'

'Okay.' I look away, unconvinced and wonder at the pain he's carrying. A mother who walked out on him, an abusive dad, a controlling wife. It's a lot of emotional baggage. How's all that affected him?

'Hey, come here.' He's holding out his arms and I sink into a tight hug. It's a cocoon, and just what I need; it feels like it's the glue connecting us and forging a link. But all I'm thinking is that he's so painfully thin as if he's been on a starvation diet, or in his case burning more calories than consuming. I can feel his shoulder bones, his ribs, and I can even put my arms right round his back as if he was a mere teenager rather than a middle-aged man. I brush my disappointment aside because I fancy him like crazy. His posh voice––it's sensitive and gentle and beautiful. And those intense eyes, they are the colour of autumn leaves. Olive skin, chiselled features. Hair the tone of rich maple syrup. How I'd love to sweep my fingers through those curls. I bet they're soft, springy, and playful.

We pull apart, do a strange dance of not knowing what the other is intending. Were we supposed to kiss, or was that meant to be just a quick hug?

CHAPTER 26 - MICRO PANTS

onna

BACK AT HIS HOUSE, I lean against the kitchen door frame watching him add salt and pepper to a bowl of eggs and milk. With a vigorous whisk until they are fluffy, he then tosses the mixture into a hot pan before adding the ingredients. There's a mood of frenzy to the room as he opens cupboards and drawers, taking out plates and glasses and cutlery while tending to the bubbling omelette as it rises in the pan. Hot oil, bacon and fried mushrooms linger in the air. It's a comforting smell, the kind of smell that brings people home.

The omelette is delicious, one of the best I've tasted. He's added grated cheese making it extra yummy.

Glancing at the fence in his garden, I ask, 'What are your neighbours like?'

'They're great, a young family. They've had a stream of visitors throughout all three lockdowns.' He gives a little laugh and takes a sip of wine. 'If they weren't relaxed, it would have been hard to sneak you in.'

'Every road has a nosey neighbour. I've got one opposite my house. He stands at the window watching the goings on in our street. One day I'd been for a walk with a friend, and she gave me a quick hug on my driveway. I looked over her shoulder to see the idiot taking a photo of us. Was he seriously going to ring the police because I hugged someone who wasn't in my household?'

'I loathe these smug lockdown zealots, taking the moral high ground and rules to the extreme.'

'Bunch of hypocrites, some of them.'

After lunch, he asks if I'd like the grand guided tour of the house. 'It'll cost you a fiver,' he jokes.

Upstairs on the landing, he shows me the decorative light-bulbs he's planning to fit in every room.

'There's still plenty of work I want to do to the house before I put it on the market.' Picking a pile of laundry up from a basket, he puts it in on a shelf in the airing cupboard.

'Do you have to sell it?' I glance into the bathroom. 'It's such a lovely house. Fresh and modern. It's got a good feel about it. I love white walls by the way. Our taste is similar.'

'I need to let it go. It'll be mentally freeing. I didn't realise how it had become an invisible prison keeping me locked in the past, unable to move forward with my life. Walls talk and there are thirty years of memories here.' He puts his hand on the bannister. 'I've held on to it for the kids' sake. Thought I was giving them stability. They aren't bothered. They've got their own lives now. Katrina's in Australia, Tim's in Scotland. Becca's the only one who's still in Sussex.

'It's the guilt of divorce. It seeps right into the bones.' I glance up at the ceiling. 'This is just bricks and mortar. The beating heart that was, is gone.' I'd hate to have stayed in the marital home. Don't know how he's coped. 'Memories keep us rooted in the past; we mustn't let them.'

I was never precious about the family home. I quite enjoyed carving up the proceeds of the sale, gaining my independence and moving into a small flat on a council estate. I found it liberating. But Nick was a bit of a tit. Unlike Colton, he didn't re-mortgage our marital home. He moved into a rental and blew his share of the equity on a fast car.

Out of the marriage, a strong survival instinct kicked in. It was a case of sink or swim. Everything was now down to me. I couldn't rely on Nick for regular child maintenance. I had to knuckle down. I had a child to support, bills to pay. Having been a stay-at-home-mum for years, I needed to work and retrained as a nurse. Hard graft and several years later I'd moved to a bigger property, albeit with a huge mortgage. When I look back on those years, I see struggle and stress, but also satisfaction. I've achieved so much on my own.

I glance into the three empty bedrooms, once occupied by his children, and try to imagine toys and clutter and general kiddie crap. 'Every room has a different memory.'

'So true. Sometimes I have these déjà vu moments when I walk in the kitchen––the source of nasty arguments and they all begin with something really silly. Maybe one of you doesn't rinse the dishes or fills the kettle to the brim for one just cup of tea. And before you know it, it's escalated to World War Three.'

I smile. He's so right. 'The trivial stuff. My ex could never shut cupboard doors. First thing I'd do when I came back from work was shut them.'

He's leaning against the sink, arms folded. 'We took out a loan because she insisted on a new kitchen. I worked weekends to pay it off when I should have been playing with the kids. She didn't care, she refused to work. Said she needed to be at home for the kids. And the lounge; I have visions of watching *The X Factor* with the kids on a Saturday evening. She was always so jealous––hated me having special time with them and would storm out and go to the pub with her friends and come back drunk.'

'I know all about drunk partners.' The lounge was where I asked Nick for a divorce after he came home horribly drunk one day and collapsed into his beloved armchair. I've never seen somebody sober up so fast when I said those four words––I want a divorce.

We head downstairs and after making coffee, we take our cups into the lounge. I don't feel comfortable being here, I'd rather we were in a pub or a restaurant––neutral territory. Here, it feels as if I'm invading his personal space, his family history and I'm having to think about my every move. Do I take my shoes off, which end of the settee is his, shall I offer to clear the dining table? But he's plunging himself onto the settee, seemingly chilled in my company as I perch awkwardly on the edge wondering what we'll do next. Netflix, kiss or talk?

'We could watch a film,' he suggests. 'What sort of thing do you like?'

My head is full of us. It will be hard to concentrate. 'Anything. Apart from horror, sci-fi and war films.' What sort of answer is that? And he's a bloke, they're probably the only genres he does like. There has to be an overlap in our preferences. 'A romcom?'

He looks at me, remote in hand. '*Notting Hill*? It's my all-time favourite.'

'Yeah, that's good.'

Leaning forward, he points the remote at the TV and when it doesn't work, he rises to his feet, moving like a clockwork soldier, all stiff as if in pain. The TV bursts into life but a whimper escapes his lips. He presses his shoulder blade with two fingers and sits down.

'What's up?'

'I've got a painful shoulder,' he says, giving it a squeeze.

'How come, what have you been up to?' I nudge him, winking.

'It came on a few days after I had the Covid vaccine.'

'Oh, that's not good. My lodger works at the vaccine centre. She came home the other day saying that someone was blue-lighted down to Brighton and died within half an hour of the jab. They weren't old and had no underlying symptoms.'

'That must be rare. It'll be saving more lives than it harms.'

'I don't like what I'm reading about the vaccine.'

'Turn off social media. Best way.' From his facial expression, I can tell his shoulder still hurts. 'Physio said it's a lump of gristle in my shoulder.'

'Gristle? You make it sound like dog meat.' Despite the question feeling too forward, I ask anyway. 'Would you like me to give it a massage?'

'I'd love that.' He looks at me with raised eyebrows. 'Sure you don't mind?'

'If it helps. Sit on the floor, it'll be easier.'

He settles himself on the floor, knees bent, leaning forward over the coffee table where our empty mugs sit. Hell, this is weird. Feels seductive, flirtatious, a come-on. Except it's not meant to be. I just want to relieve his pain.

I pull his sweater down a few inches and press around the pain. I can feel something lumpy; it moves as I dig. His skin is smooth, youthful, unblemished and I take the opportunity to examine his neck. There's a stray curl. I bet his hair is soft. It looks soft. I want to take the curl between my fingers and play with it. Kiss his neck. His hair is a medley of colour––rust, henna, cedar, coffee. If we were outside, the sun would pick up even more tones.

My fingers begin to ache, and I apply less pressure. My heart skips a beat as he turns, looks up at me, slamming a hand over my tired fingers to still them. His lips part, his gaze is on my mouth, there's a playful glint in his eyes. It's seductive. Suggestive.

Oh God, he wants me. There's a charge in the air as my pulse quickens. I want him too.

Our moist lips meet, arms wrap around each other, fingers pressing each other's backs. He pulls me onto the floor, pushing the coffee table back to make room as our tongues sweep our lips. Soon we are playing tongue tango and I'm taken to a higher level––my body trancelike, as if I'm under hypnosis. I'm relaxed yet on fire.

Pulling away, he beams at me and whispers, 'Can I make love to you?'

My body is aching for him, but I'm caught in a moment of indecision. I am going down a bad road here. I should hit the brakes. Sex too soon is my repeated mistake. That's why men don't respect me. But if I say it's too soon, the magic will burst, awkwardness will descend. When is it ever the right time to have sex for the first time with someone? He'll think I'm a prude and that's the worst label possible, especially at my age when I want to be seen as still desirable. But equally I don't want to appear too eager––my pride is important to me. Because how will he treat me beyond today if I give my whole being to him? There'll be nothing left to look forward to. He could just consider me a conquest, another notch on the bedpost. Most guys think with their dicks. They can deny it all they like, but it's a fact.

'It's a bit soon, isn't it?'

The warmth between my legs overrules everything. I want him with a ferocity that terrifies me. He must be reading signals I wasn't even aware I was transmitting because he doesn't answer me; he can see the longing in my eyes. No further words are spoken, he takes my hand, and we get up. He leads me up the stairs and I am careful not to tread on carpet tacks sticking up from the bare floorboards and I don't touch his freshly painted walls even though I am giddy and need the support.

In his bedroom he pulls his sweater off. I clock the beautifully toned muscles, the smooth skin. He doesn't look nearly sixty. But my eyes fall on three things. And all I feel is revulsion.

I'm about to ride roughshod through my list of no nos. A list as important as my bucket list.

Number 1:

No body piercings.

Number 2:

No tattoos. Even tiny ones like a small circle.

I do not do body piercings of any kind, or tattoos. They are disgusting. Common. Cheap. Call me a snob, call me prejudiced. Judgemental. These are my personal standards, my barometer. Even if he does turn out to have a stupidly long word like Constantinople tattooed across a very large dick, it's a Simon Cowell no from me.

It's not just the tattoo of a sunflower and his silver belly ring that put me off.

He has black nipples.

Who on earth has black nipples, unless they are black or Asian? I'm not a racist, far from it. And when I think of it, black nipples are better than man boobs. It's just that black nipples on a white man don't look right. It's like acne on a baby, wrinkles on a child's face. It's not normal. But then again maybe he won't like my caesarean scar or the web of stretch lines across my sagging boobs that have been pointing south for several years now.

He may have a belly ring, a tattoo, *and* black nipples, but they are just body furniture––like trimmings on a Christmas dinner. Like walking in a room and disliking the swirly carpet or the net curtains. I like him. And until now he turned me on. I concentrate on everything else and my desire peaks. I want him. I will get over this. I'm being superficial, fickle.

Pulling my sweater off, I suddenly remember my ghastly underwear. When I dressed this morning, I wasn't preparing for sex. I'm in an old, greying white bra from M&S. And because my knickers are bright red and silky, by default they should be sexy, which they would be if they were small and skimpy, but unfortunately this pair are large and waist high. They are for middle-aged women who no longer have sex. They are so high that they even cover my belly button. In fact, they are probably a size too big for me. I'm like a badly-wrapped Christmas present.

But it's all off in seconds and our hands are all over each other. The Christmas trimmings don't matter. It's the meat he's after. When his eyes trail to my below, there's one saving grace. My lady garden is not wild, it's shaved.

My gaze falls to his tiny waist. His pants are black, shiny, tight. They feel divine. God knows what material they are made of and what genius invented them. What an improvement on the baggy boxers and gross Y-fronts, or even the cotton briefs I remember from a different era of dating. This is the difference between Waitrose and Asda, an android and a smart phone, leather and plastic. Just wow.

He seems to read my thoughts as I feel the material. 'D'you like them?' he asks. 'They're M&S micro pants.'

'Yes, I do like your micro pants.'

There's a bulge that interests me more than the material of his micro pants. Despite his teenage appearance, his bulge is big. I ease the pants down and his dick springs out like a jack-in-the-box. Oh my flipping God. It's bigger than I could ever have imagined. His small feet, small hands, tiny waist should all be reliable indicators of an undersized dick. How could my estimations have been so wrong? I always was bad at DIY and get inches mixed up with centimetres.

His body is like a Tardis. Or a house that's described by the estate agent as deceptively spacious. I'm blown away by my own misconceptions, by this man who fails to disappoint on every level.

I can't resist it, even though my instinct is to let him make the moves; I hold it in my hands and work it like a piece of clay. Before I know it, it's in my mouth and my tongue is flicking up and down and I am sucking hard. After a few moments, he pulls it out and bending his head towards my chest, takes each nipple in turn in his mouth. His touch is so gentle and the lighter his tongue skims, the more erotic it is. He's not rough, doesn't nibble or tug.

'I want to be inside you,' he says. His words spoken softly, make my below pulse like a second heartbeat and I lie back, my head on the pillow. He's kissing my neck, I'm breathing in his aroma, clenching his small, perfectly rounded buttocks, then wrapping my legs around them. Being so slim, it's easy to do this. He eases gently into me. I'm tight at first even though I'm moist. It's been so long, and my body is tensing with the anticipation that it might hurt. But as he goes deeper, it's sensational. I relax, and my stomach hardens as I struggle to fight the orgasm that threatens to ripple across my body because I don't want it to happen too soon. I want to pace myself, savour how delicious this is. But when we climax together it's just as sensational as I thought it would be. He's calling my name; he's telling me he's fallen in love and fancies me more than any woman he's ever been with.

I think I've died and gone to heaven.

CHAPTER 27 - DIRTY STOP-OUT

 onna

'STAY,' he says. We are languishing on his settee the following weekend, one of my legs resting over his. The film we've been watching has finished and the credits are rolling.

I check the time on my mobile. 'I should go home. It's getting late.'

'What have you got to get back for?'

'Nothing really. I'm not working tomorrow, but I've got nothing with me.' This is not strictly true. I always carry my work overnight bag in my car boot in case I'm asked to do a night shift.

'I'd really love you to stay.' He's beaming at me. 'I can't get enough of your company, Donna. I don't want this to end. I really love you. I'm also thinking about the hour's journey you've got in the dark. And it's tipping it down.'

We glance at the window behind us. He's not drawn the curtains and the rain is pelting against the glass. I remember that I've parked round the corner and don't relish the prospect of dashing to the car in the rain.

'I have got a few things in a bag, but it's in the car, so whatever I do, I'm going to have to brave that rain.'

'Give us your keys, I'll get it for you.'

He's persuasive and I relent.

WE SLEEP WRAPPED in each other's arms under his mustard-yellow Habitat duvet. I'm woken early by the sunlight streaming into the room because his bedroom faces south, and the curtains are thin and white. He's still asleep, his back to me.

Flicking my phone to silent mode, I switch it on and a flood of messages ping through. All from Olivia. The last one reads, 'it's now five in the morning, where the hell are you, Mother?'

I tiptoe to the bathroom and perch on the loo, scrolling up the thread, to discover she's at my house.

'You told me you weren't working this weekend. Where are you?' Now she's angry.

This is the first time I've stayed away in God knows how long, and she decides to pay me a surprise visit. All the way from Leicester, or has she been at her dad's?

I can't get my head round this. After the many occasions she's said she prefers to stay with her dad because he's more welcoming, has a fridge full of food and hasn't turned her room into a 'bloody Airbnb.'

I reply. 'In Handcuffs.'

'Mother, that's disgusting.'

'Sorry. Bloody predictive texts. I mean Handcross,' I lie. 'I stayed over with a friend. I can be home in an hour. Will you still be there?' I know what she's like; I'll arrive back to find she's gone.

Come on Liv, answer me.

While I'm waiting for her reply, I wee and wash. I'll have to go home. I must see Olivia. It's so rare for her to make the effort. I barely see her these days. I can't help feeling a stab of disappointment though. Colton suggested a walk along the beach from East to West Wittering today. It's one of the best beaches in the country––a large unspoilt expanse of sand and with views across Chichester harbour. We seem to be getting on so well; I hope my going doesn't break the spell. It's especially annoying as it looks like it will be a superb day. I bet when I get home, Olivia will have a quick coffee and catch-up with me, then dash off and the day will have been wasted. Her life is so hectic and I'm usually an afterthought.

Colton is awake and facing me when I return to the bedroom.

'Getting up already?' He pats the bed and lifting the duvet, throws me a seductive look. It would be so easy to slip back into bed. He's awakened something in me, a desire I thought had left my body years ago. I'm like a woodland creature waking after winter's hibernation, full of the joys of spring, ready to play and bounce and have fun.

We start kissing and his hands are on my breasts. His fingers trail down, and he circles my clitoris two, three times, then without warning one finger slides inside me. I go with the flow lying back as waves of pleasure wash over me.

'Do you want to go on top this time?' he asks.

'Do you want me to?'

'If you do.'

Sex isn't supposed to be polite. All these questions, it's destroying the rhythm, the spontaneity. And time's creeping on.

I guide him in, our body parts slot together like puzzle pieces. I feel him all the way through my body. He reaches up, flicks his tongue over my nipples. My phone is on the pillow, the screen lights up, another text from Olivia. 'I thought we could spend the day together, have a walk around Piltdown like we used to, but you aren't here.' She's sent a couple of sad faces.

He's pushing inside me, harder, deeper, but my mind's no longer on the job and he can see that. I need to reply to the text. I need to get going.

I roll off him. Grab my phone.

'I was about to cum.' He sweeps his fingers through his hair. He's crestfallen. My heart is racing, I mustn't miss Olivia.

'I'm sorry, Colton, but I woke to several texts from my daughter. She's at home and if I don't get going, she'll give up and leave.'

By the look on his face, he doesn't believe me. His features are flat and pallid like a clay mask. He thinks there's a husband in tow. And he'd be forgiven for thinking that, because let's face it, there are so many dodgy people on these dating sites, you can't trust half of them and how's he to know I'm not one of them?

The expression on his face mellows when I show him the texts. 'We can go for a walk anytime, that's really nice that she wants to spend time with you.'

'Thanks, Colton, you're very understanding.'

I give him a quick kiss on the lips and rush to dress, zipping my jeans as I hurry down the stairs and out of the door to the car. There's a heightened sense of importance to the day; this feels like dashing for an interview or a plane. There's that fear of being late, of losing everything. I know I'm doing the right thing, putting my daughter first.

Arriving back, I pull onto the drive alongside Olivia's car. Thank heavens she's not given up and gone. She bursts out of the house and greets me like an enthusiastic puppy, as if she lives here and I've been away for yonks. Then she's more serious. 'Mother, where were you?'

Her tone makes me barge past her and thud my handbag with car keys on the kitchen table. 'I've already told you. At a friend's.'

'What friend?' By the look on her face, anyone would think I don't have any friends. I wasn't expecting the third degree. So much for a pleasant day with my daughter.

'Just a friend.' I stomp past her, making a beeline for the kettle.

'You're blushing.' She hauls herself onto the counter. 'You've spent the night with some bloke.' She bursts into one of her raucous laughs.

'And so what if I have?'

'Mother, you're turning into a slut.'

The word *slut* cuts right through me. 'It's not like that. We've known each other for a few weeks and he's very nice.'

'That's what you say about them all. And you're telling me you haven't had sex?' She tilts her head back and lets out a hyena screech.

'It's none of your business if I have. Just be happy for me, for once.'

'All right, keep your hair on.'

Taking two cups out of the cupboard, I spoon coffee into them. After removing a carton of milk from the fridge, without thinking, I slam the door behind me, like a teenager in the middle of a strop. Jeez, she's really got my hackles up. I'm in need of the fortification of caffeine before I have the strength to deal with her. 'Why are you back anyway?' I don't mean to snap but I can't help it.

'That's nice, you're not being very welcoming.'

'If you'd told me you were coming, I could have planned around you,' I say more softly even though I'm close to tears. I've given up the opportunity of a lovely walk on the beach for an interrogation by my daughter. This wasn't how I imagined the day to be.

I take the mugs to the kitchen table, and she plonks herself on her favourite chair by the window. 'Pamela's left Dad.'

For a few seconds, I wonder if she's having me on. Her father has been married to Pamela for fifteen years. I thought they were rock solid. It's been cringe-worthy over the years hearing how happy they were. Vomit-inducing even. But Olivia appears to be deadly serious.

I feel my spirit lift at this juicy gossip, which is wrong of me because I should want him to be happy. At times his happiness has made me angry. I know I should want the best for him, and generally I do. I can't deny that it was hard when I found out he was getting married again. It led to some complicated emotions. And many questions. But I like to think that I've journeyed through the grieving and healing stages. Maybe that journey will never be over.

'Oh?' This is karma. Finally, he's got his comeuppance. It's been a long time coming. 'Any idea why?' I want to know all the gory details, but I doubt she's party to them.

'That's what I'm trying to work out. There's never a cross word between them. At least not in front of me. It's come out of the blue. Why do think they've split up, Mum?'

'I've no idea,' I lie with a shrug. I'm surprised Olivia's so blinkered. Surely, it's obvious. It's staring me straight in the face. It'll be his drinking and his bad moods. And if Nick and Pamela have been working from home during lockdown, that won't have helped. I can't think of anything worse than being cooped up with Nick for weeks on end. And how on earth has he coped with the pubs closed? He must be stir-crazy, and he's taken it out on her, poor cow.

As we finish our drinks, there's a change of plan––no surprises there. Olivia's been distracted by her phone and has arranged to meet up with an old school friend. So instead of us driving over to Piltdown for a picnic, we walk to Victoria Park which is just five minutes away.

The park is busy. Families are out in force––there's not much else for them to do. There's an air of happiness and under the blue sky the grass is dotted with colourful picnic blankets and cool-bags and there's plenty of laughter as we cut through the tall trees up the hill to the kiosk. Children on scooters are zipping up and down the pathway that loops around the park. Some are playing ball.

With Neros and Costa only serving takeaway drinks, people have flocked to the kiosk, Tory's. It's doing a roaring trade and we join the long socially-distanced queue, ordering their finest hot chocolate, the most delicious I've tasted. The wall around the patioed terrace and the benches are occupied, so we aim for the far side of the park overlooking the football pitch. I'm just commenting on all the rubbish flowing from every bin, when Olivia makes her big, bold, brash statement.

'You and Dad could get back together.'

I stop walking and stare at her, incredulous. My heart goes out to her, and I touch her arm. There was me thinking she was all grown-up, now in her twenties and living miles from home. Inside though she still has a child's emotions. And daydreams. And that's okay.

'Things can never go back to the way they were, sweetheart.'

She gazes off into the distance, a sad expression in her eyes. 'Divorce doesn't have to be a forever thing.'

'But we're not Elizabeth Taylor and Richard Burton.'

'You loved each other once. You must have done. You walked up the aisle together, you made promises, you had me.' Her voice trails off.

If we'd recently got divorced, I could understand her denial, her coming to terms with our separation, this being her way of coping. She wants to believe it's possible. But she was too young-- only a toddler when we split--and cannot remember us as a family or hanker after something she's not experienced. Except that sometimes in life we do grieve for all the things we've never had. A life plan, a wish or goal never realised. It's easy to brush those 'losses' off as small and insignificant compared to what others go through. But they do matter because the pain is real.

I want to tell Olivia what I went through, the abuse I suffered because of his alcohol problem, but of course I'm not going to. If she did witness anything, she was too young to remember. She must work this out for herself. I can't believe how clever he must have been to hide his drinking from her. I don't want to turn this into a blame game of who was responsible for the break-up and turn her against him. That wouldn't be fair on either of them. He's been a good dad, and that's what counts.

We sit on a bench, and I close my eyes to the sun wondering how on earth I'm going to reply. This is like walking on broken glass. Painful. I must choose my words with care, but I can't glaze over the marital cracks, fob her off.

'Sometimes things just don't work out. When a relationship breaks down for whatever reason, it's very hard to go back to the way it was.' I don't want to talk about the love I once had for her father. She'll clutch onto it, and it will just confuse her, give her false hope. 'Would *you* want to be around someone you didn't get on with?'

'But you must have got on well, you were together for how long?'

'Ten years.'

'That's such a long time.'

At her age, ten years must seem like an eternity, but really, it's no time at all.

'Have you ever talked to him about our marriage?' My eyes follow a cute black puppy. Its lead shakes as it skips along the path, head up, proud, then down when it catches a scent.

'Dad doesn't talk about feelings. But something he said got me thinking.'

'What?' I take a sip of my drink enjoying the warm sweet taste and glance at her.

'That he regrets leaving you.'

'He must have been drunk when he said that.' That was

stupid of me; I don't mean to imply that he has a drink problem. I'm so careful not to slag him off--I always have been. I try to diffuse my comment with a laugh and a light comment. 'We all say things when we're pissed.'

'You don't, Mother. You never drink. You hate drink. And you hate other people drinking.'

I'm not aware that's how I come across. But if I do, it's probably because I've seen what alcohol does to people. How my husband became nasty when he'd been drinking. No wonder I'm wary of it. But have I turned into a complete killjoy?

'Dad doesn't drink either.' She looks at me, frowning as if waiting for me to furnish her with the basic facts about her dad's habits. 'But when I arrived at his house a couple of nights ago, he was sitting at the bottom of the stairs drunk.'

Maybe he did stop drinking after we split. Bit late. Like waiting until the horse has bolted. I find that bizarre. He's managed to hide it well--clever really--but sometimes people do, often for years.

'He wasn't crying but he was close to tears. He wasn't making much sense, but he did say he still loves you.'

I'm worried now. What if he *has* started drinking again? If he did stop, he's done so well, this will take him back to a dark place. I wish there was something I could do. I must protect Olivia. She is my number one concern.

The conversation moves on as I'm still pondering how to address the issue of his drinking. All I can do is bide my time, see what happens, see if he really has fallen off the wagon.

She stretches towards the overflowing bin, ramming her empty cup into it and sending rubbish flying out. 'I feel cheated. I've never known a family. Sometimes it would just be nice to go home to you both. Like my friends do. I don't want to come home to strangers roaming round the house. If you were together you wouldn't need to scrape by, fill the house with lodgers. Dad has a good job. You'd be well off. And you wouldn't have to clean old ladies' bums either.'

My heart goes out to her but there's nothing I can do or say to make that sadness go away. This is part of growing up, accepting that family life is rarely like *The Waltons*. Cosy and idyllic. If only I could order an Argos-style family, ready packaged, delivered straight to the door.

I feel affronted. 'I like my job,' I say defensively.

'I don't want to watch as more men break your heart, Mum.'

I sniff. 'Darling, I'm too old for a broken heart.' That's not strictly true. I'd be gutted if Colton dumped me, but I have a good feeling about us. Maybe this time things might work out. 'My skin is tough like Teflon.'

'My friend Alice's parents have just got back together and that was after being apart for twelve years.'

Now I understand.

'I can't imagine getting back with your father.' And I really can't. If he'd agreed to go for couples counselling, we may have stood a chance, but he turned the idea down. Wouldn't even consider it. There wasn't an ounce of remorse for what he'd put me through.

I must stay out of her dad's problems. I don't want to stir. She's an adult now and that comes with harsh truths and realities. She must make her own mind up. If he has started drinking again there's going to be a rocky path for both of us because I'm sure she's going to be ringing me upset and in need of my advice. She'll be back in Leicester in a couple of days. His issues won't be her problem. Suddenly I'm grateful she's miles away. I don't want her embroiled in his mess. She's got her studies to think about.

CHAPTER 28 - A DIFFERENT NAME

onna

WHEN I ARRIVE at Colton's house the following weekend, he's leaning casually against the doorframe, grass trimmings on his tatty deck shoes with his arms folded, beaming at me. His front garden is immaculate, the lawn freshly mown. Reaching to kiss him, I breathe in his scent––freshly laundered clothes and Imperial Leather soap mingled with grass. He tells me I give the best hugs ever and that I'm so much warmer and more tactile than his ex-wife was. His breath is on my cheek. There it is again. That intense sexual attraction, the sort that is rare and coveted. But when he pulls away it isn't to lead me up the stairs to the bedroom; there's a worried look on his face and he's suggesting a coffee. Reaching for mugs in the cupboard, he turns to look at me.

'Donna, there's something I need to tell you.' He's downcast. He's going to end it. I thought this was too good to be true.

My heart is quietly sinking. 'What's up?' This is bound to be bad. Why does this keep happening to me, this disappointment, when will I meet someone that's not going to let me down and just love me for who I am?

'My name's not Colton. I should have told you before now.'

My brain is briefly paralysed. 'Who the hell are you then?' This, I wasn't expecting.

'Colton was just my screen name because I hate my real name. I thought it might put women off. Colin is such a wimpy name.'

'You should have said. Doesn't change how I feel about you.' I throw my arms around him and kiss him on the lips. 'I'll call you Col.'

'Most people do.'

I pull away and look at him. 'I thought you were going to say something awful, you had me panicked.'

Even though this isn't a big deal, there's a tiny part of me that feels deceived. As if there might be other things, he hasn't told me. It's slightly unnerving.

'Sorry.' When he smiles, I see the blueprint of future wrinkles in his face, the starburst of lines around his eyes. He's so handsome and although it's early days, I'd like to think he's mine. 'I don't know why I didn't tell you on our first date. And then when you kept calling me it, I didn't like to correct you.'

'I'll let you in on a secret.'

He raises his eyebrows, steps back.

I explain to him how I hadn't a clue what he was going to look like and because of his name, I imagined meeting a cowboy on horseback.

He pulls me towards the settee where we collapse in a heap of laughter.

'I hadn't thought about it being a cowboy name. I guess it is.'

'My dad was always watching Westerns. Mind you, back in the '70s there wasn't much else on the telly.'

'Mine too.' There's something about his posture as he swiftly gets up, changing the conversation. He looks uncomfortable. 'Come on, let's not bother with a coffee, let's get to the beach.'

WE TAKE the long route through Bognor and Pagham, weaving through housing estates until we arrive in the village of East Wittering. 'Locals call it God's pocket,' Col says as we park and get out of the car. I can see why. It's so pretty. There's a fudge shop, a couple of cafes and rose and honeysuckle-festooned cottages and a fisherman's hut selling local fish.

You could be forgiven for thinking it was the summer if you saw a photograph because it truly is a glorious day. The sun is bright, the sky and sea a deep shade of denim. On the horizon the sea and sky merge in a blurry haze. As I look out over this stunning stretch of exposed coastline the wind is raw and bitter. But even though the wind is biting and burning into my hands and cheeks, there's something beautifully refreshing about it. We zip our puffer jackets, and I pull my woolly hat over my ears.

The sea is peppered with sailing boats, windsurfers, and kayaks. We stand and gaze around us in awe, commenting on everything we can see.

'The water looks different every day.'

'There's something dreamlike about being at the sea. It's as if I've reached my destination, the edge of the earth and that vastness in front of me can take me anywhere I like.' He takes a deep breath, filling his lungs with the briny air.

'I think it was JF Kennedy who said we are tied to the ocean. And when we go back to the sea whether it is to sail or watch—— we are going back whence we came.'

'I assume he's referring to the womb when he talks about going back.'

'Probably. I'd like to live by the sea, Eastbourne perhaps. I love the idea of swimming every day in the summer and going for long coastal walks up the cliffs,' I say.

'Me too. I'd feel landlocked if I wasn't by the sea. I don't live close enough. I'd like a sea view.'

'You'd pay a premium.'

'Not necessarily. I've been looking on Rightmove.'

'I'm torn. I've got friends in Haywards Heath, it's nearer to London and I do like my trips to London. To the theatre, museums, shopping. And Gatwick's only ten minutes away.'

'You'd have a better life by the sea.'

'True. And I'm always on Rightmove too, planning my future.'

We start walking along a path which takes us past a row of large grand houses. Each house and garden is unique, but large windows seem to dominate their features, a stage set to show to the world how vast and splendid their living quarters are. Large tables to entertain their many friends. French doors onto a decked area for barbecues or resting in the sun. But this is Britain and most of the time they are sitting under the same grey clouds that the rest of us must endure.

'I'd like to think we have a future,' he says, taking me by surprise.

'I'd like that too.' It's early days, but to have someone to talk to, be close with, share troubles with––wouldn't that be wonderful? A team. Together. A couple. That would be my ultimate dream. My skin tingles at the thought and makes me think, this time, maybe, just maybe I've got it right.

Reaching West Wittering, we trudge over the sand dunes and find a spot on the beach to sit.

'We came here years ago for a family picnic,' he says, lying down and shuffling onto his side to look at me. 'That was the last time I saw my sister, Emma. There was an endless stream of digs and jibes. It was one of my kids' birthdays. She plunged her fist into the birthday cake.'

'What the hell for?'

'No idea. She's always had a grudge against me. My dad and her, they'd gang up against me. They're arrogant snobs. I didn't make it in life.'

'Nothing wrong with a manual job.'

'Not if you've gone through private education. There's a certain expectation that it will lead to a well-paid job.'

'But you've done well for yourself. Your dad should be proud of you. Not many people have three properties they rent out.'

'They're an extra income, but they're mortgaged.'

'You mustn't put yourself down.'

'Thanks.' He rubs my arm. 'It's so nice to be with someone who doesn't constantly criticise me.'

'Give me time,' I laugh. 'I'm no angel.' I run my fingers through his shaggy locks and kiss him on the cheek. As he stares at the sun, I take time to study his features. They are so symmetrical that his face looks as though it could have been cut from a piece of paper folded in half.

'This beach doesn't have the happiest of memories,' he says, eyes closed against the sun.

'You should have said. Next time we could go to Seaford.'

'I've never been there. It's near Brighton?'

'Yeah. It's a bit run down but I like it because the parking's free, the seafront is uncommercialised and you don't have to check the tide times. It doesn't go out very far.'

He tilts his head to the sun. 'I try to practise mindfulness.'

'Is that what you're doing now? I've heard of mindfulness, don't know much about it.'

'It's a sort of meditation. It's about focusing on the present, being intensely aware of what you're sensing and feeling in the moment.'

I run my fingers up and down his neck.

'I like what you're doing.'

'We waste too much time dwelling on the past and worrying about the future. I'm guilty of doing that.'

'The past can be a roadblock.'

His family situation is odd. It's not just the fact that his mother walked out, and his father was a brute. His kids don't visit either and he hasn't spoken to his sister in years. His family are a bunch of cranks. And he seems so lovely, so normal. Maybe his father has poisoned every relationship. They all seem to be under his spell. There's no desire in Col to repair these fractured relationships. Too much time has passed. Too many jarring events have left scars and wounds that run deep through the seams of their blood ties. He appears resigned to how things are.

We walk back along the sands to East Wittering, the cold penetrating our clothes and hurrying us along.

IN THE EVENING he cooks a delicious beef stew. He lets me chop mushrooms and onion, but mostly I stand in the doorway listening to the sizzle and clang. Soon there's a riot of dirty pans and chopping boards splayed across the granite worktop. His kitchen is cosy in the evening light. It looks like a relic from the 1980s with its farmhouse units and scenes of fat-cheeked pigs and sheep on the wall tiles.

'I love your kitchen.' I take a sip of wine as I watch him mash potato.

He turns and politely thanks me. There's a lot of politeness between us, even in bed. He thanks me for every compliment, every act of kindness. I wish he'd relax.

'I fitted it myself.'

'Wow, you are clever.'

'Thank you,' he says serving the dinner onto plates before turning to beam at me. It's as if compliments are a rare occurrence in his world. 'Can you grab some cutlery?' He nudges a drawer open before grabbing the plates and heading for the table. When we're seated and I've taken my first mouthful, lavishing him with more praise, he says, 'My sister and her arsey accountant husband came over one evening not long after the kitchen was finished. She stood in the middle of the kitchen and deliberately said nothing at all. As if she'd planned not to say anything. She gave one of her prim sniffs, a haughty look I've seen many times and said, "that's Laura Ashley wallpaper. Looks dated." '

'What wallpaper?'

'I took it down. Painted the wall instead because of her comment.'

'Bet it looked lovely.'

'The worst of it was, Anne, my wife, joining in, mocking my work, pointing out to my sister anything however small that wasn't perfect.'

'How horrible, looks great to me. Very professional.'

'Thank you.' There we go again. I wish he'd chill. He doesn't need to shower me with gratitude.

After dinner we cosy up on his mustard-yellow velvet settee and for a few moments we are in our own worlds checking our phones for social media updates and texts. Leaning towards me he says, 'Show me the houses you've seen on Rightmove.'

'Okay.' I've been dying to show him ever since our conversation on the beach.

He laughs when I show him my favourites. 'No way. They're the same houses I've seen.'

I scroll down clicking on a house that overlooks the sea. 'This one is gorgeous, but a bit over my budget.'

'We could buy it together.' He's grinning.

'That's daft.' Do I take him seriously? Seems like a throwaway comment. 'We've only known each other five minutes.'

'What does it matter? We clicked from the moment we met. The way we see the world, the way we think, we're so similar.

Being with you feels so natural, as if you're the one I was supposed to meet years ago.'

Such beautiful words. They leave me with a tingling wave of longing and I move closer to him, kissing him lightly on the lips. He takes my hands in his. 'I'm in love with you, Donna.' He beams at me. 'We're in love.'

'You're like a squatter.' I giggle nervously. 'You're in my head, now I can't get you out.' Every man has made my life worse. Every man's knocked my confidence. Every man has sapped my energy. And yet here I am again, willing to throw caution to the wind and give love another go. Because that's what we do––the human spirit is not broken where love is concerned. I just want to settle into a relationship. Stop that endless merry-go-round of swiping and dating and deleting. It's exhausting.

I throw my leg over his and we meld together. When we kiss–– a tongue in the mouth job–– it's delicious and soaked in the remnants of wine, the kind that almost stops you breathing and after a few minutes when I pull away and stare into his maple syrup eyes, I feel excited and dizzy like after a fairground ride.

I nibble his neck while his hand slides inside my jumper, his fingers reaching inside my bra and gently circling my breasts and making me shudder. Heat radiates across our bodies, our faces burning as we kiss. Desire thunderbolts through me as we tear each other's clothes off, collapsing onto the thick wool rug by the crackling woodstove.

He hasn't yet switched the lamps on, but the firelight illuminates the room and dances over our naked bodies, turning our skin gold and making his muscles appear supple. There's longing in his eyes as we lie down in the warmth. He leans over me, planting kisses like tiny darts along a trail from my neck to my belly button and beyond while I press my fingers into his back, clutch his buttocks tight. When he finds my special place, pleasure spreads through me, blood pulses, and my brain spins off to another planet. He knows how to use his tongue. A skill he's long mastered. Gentle flicks send fireworks shooting through me. I can't hold it in. My stomach tightens and I climax. It's so intense, so intoxicating, a sensation I can never experience again with someone else. For this is the best. Truly the best. It's the difference again–– between shopping at Asda and shopping at Waitrose.

I return the pleasure, taking him deep into my mouth, my hands kneading his inner thighs, touching, feeling, until he begins to moan, and I withdraw, straddling him and easing him into me as we begin to pump up and down before collapsing on top of him when we are climax together.

And in that moment, I smile to myself as I think of all the smug married couples who believe my life is over because I'm divorced. Marriage may have given them lasting love and deepened their affection for one another, but for many, the magic goes, leaving them as familiar as siblings and with a sex life that's bland and predictable.

CHAPTER 29 - LET'S GO AWAY

 onna

THE FOLLOWING MORNING, we wake wrapped in each other's arms.

'Morning, gorgeous.' Col plants kisses on my forehead. I know his love is genuine because his warm smile reaches his eyes. 'An idea came to me in the night.'

This is intriguing. 'Oh yeah?'

'We should go away for a long weekend.'

Lockdown is easing, hotels are opening soon. My heart soars. He likes me enough to go away with me. Inside, I'm jumping for joy even though common sense is telling me it's too soon. We should wait until the relationship has matured and when we know each other better and feel comfortable to be in each other's company for that long. But instead of voicing my doubts, I allow myself to be excited and watch him fire up his laptop and Google places to stay in Dorset. Within minutes he's booked a four-poster room in a pub on a cliff overlooking the sea.

Butterflies dance in my stomach as I begin to waver. This could be a deal-breaker or a dealmaker. We'll either discover endearing things about each other or some nasty habits. I hope every sound I make in the bathroom isn't overheard. Every sprinkle, tinkle and plop. Or will it be him making all the toilet noises?

It's a long journey down to Dorset. What will we talk about on the journey, will there be awkward silences, whose car are we going in? Will we play music or listen to the radio? Hell, I don't even know what his music taste is. Can't believe we've not shared our favourite tracks.

And is he paying for the room? Is it rude if I offer to pay?

All these thoughts are crowding in and dampening the thrill of the anticipation of a romantic weekend away. And what about my lodgers? I don't trust them not to leave all the lights on. One lodger left the front door open the last time I went away.

I need to slow down. Stop looking for problems. Relax. It will all work out. I want to spend quality time with him; it will give us the chance to get to know each other.

THAT EVENING I head home excited at the prospect of our weekend away. Until now, my love life has felt like Groundhog Day. Stuck—never going beyond date three or four. Always moving on to the next guy, then the next. Over and over. No progression. No moving on to the next stage. I felt doomed, but this time something feels different. Finally, I am happy with someone, and he seems happy with me. I've broken a cycle. Col and I are heading somewhere. It's too early to say where that will be, but I haven't felt this hopeful in ages.

We never call each other in the evenings because I hate phone calls and so does Col. It's as if I'm allergic to picking up the phone and dialling someone's number. It's another demand on my life. I feel uncomfortable on the phone and never know what to say. I'd rather meet up or text. At least with texting I can multi-task and consider carefully what I want to say, whereas on the phone I get all tongue-tied and self-conscious. It's a relief that Col feels the same. I found it exhausting when guys used to call every evening. It was so time-consuming and what is there to talk about?

It wasn't always this way. Years ago, long before the invention of the mobile, I used to sit on the bottom stair winding the curly cord of the telephone around my fingers doing the, 'you hang up first,' 'no you,' routine with boyfriends late into the night, or jabbering with friends because we had nowhere to go, no money and this was our social life. The landline was my lifeline back in the day.

Col and I aren't constantly texting either. If we were, it would be a red flag. It's not a good look to be overly available. He pings enough to make me realise I'm in his thoughts and to feel valued and appreciated. Our texts drive the relationship forward. He tells me sweet things like, 'I love looking in your eyes and kissing you is wonderful.' 'I love your company, I'm so fond of you.' 'I haven't felt like this in a long time.' 'I keep waking up thinking about you.' 'Let's hold onto each other, now we've found each other.' 'I get butterflies when I think of you.' 'So much to look forward to and plan.' 'Let's have a no-time-to-lose attitude to our plans, darling, I love you.' And I reciprocate with similar words.

In the evenings there are text exchanges about the TV programmes we are watching.

Him: 'You watching *Location, Location, Location?*'

Me: 'I do love a Kirsty and Phil!'

Him: 'An orange kitchen. Wow! Love It!'

Me: '£750,000 budget. Bloody hell! But imagine living in the Midlands?!'

Him: 'I couldn't stand that. I'd feel imprisoned!'

Me: 'I need the sea.'

Him: 'Me too, darling.'

Me: '"We should shimmy on in" Kirsty said.'

Him: 'Estate agent cheesey charm.'

WHY IS it that a watched clock never moves, a watched kettle never boils, and a watched smartphone never pings? I think it has something to do with the fact that I am mad about Col. I'm like a lovesick teenager. When we aren't together, I'm thinking about him all the time. And when he doesn't text, I'm panicked. But if he suddenly starting texting too much, it would make me think he's clingy, needy, and smothering. There's a fine balance. Part of me hates all this texting––the feeling that we must be in constant contact, airing our every thought, sharing the minutiae of our day-to-day life. It's too full-on and I find it off-putting. Dating was so much easier in the past when there were boundaries and distance and we phoned each other mid-week for a catch-up. It was more relaxing to step away from the other person. I don't like living in someone else's pocket.

I find myself constantly checking my phone for messages from Col and looking at when he was last online. That's the price of love, I guess. I know it's not healthy, but I can't help myself. And the more I do it, the more anxious I become. I don't want to have questions buzzing around my head, that uncertainty, that doubt. But the fact is, he's not mentioned any friends and yet he's constantly online. That's the problem with WhatsApp and Messenger––you can see when the other person was last online. I find myself wondering if he's still chatting to other women. But I'm not a controlling person and I wouldn't dream of asking him who he's texting. It would feel like an interrogation and make him defensive.

When we go from texting all the time to no texts at all one day, I wonder what's going on. I scroll back up the thread to check for indicators as to why he'd suddenly stop messaging. The last conversation was about Covid and now I'm wondering if he found my views upsetting. We were chatting during Channel 4 News, and this was the conversation:

Him: 'People dying in India. The other side of the coin where no action on Covid has been taken.'

Me: 'The media don't care when thousands die from poverty and poor sanitation. The media keep us locked in fear about Covid.'

Him: 'I really don't believe that Channel 4 News are reporting this to support a propaganda campaign to keep us locked in fear. 200,000 people have died of Covid in India -we could have seen those numbers here had the government not put restrictions in place. It's Covid that has stolen the past year, not the government. I have listened to your opinions & digested them but really cannot begin to agree with them.'

Me: 'I think what I'm trying to say is yes, it's awful people are suffering in India but India suffers every day from appalling poverty and disease yet we don't get to hear about that suffering. When I went to India, I saw it with my own eyes, and it was shocking and given we used to rule India until 1947 we don't seem to have done much to alleviate that poverty. I think we should at least be trying to now help with their Covid crisis. Re propaganda the trouble is people here now believe we will get a new wave and it will kick off here again, but it won't as we now have herd immunity thanks to the vaccine. I don't believe we can keep worrying forever about each variant that comes along otherwise we'd never lead a normal life. Lockdowns aren't sustainable. They have been shown to cause more deaths than they save. Missed cancer treatment, suicide, etc. And you can never completely lock down because essential services must continue so it will always spread, and thousands of lorries enter the country each day. It's an impossible situation. At the start of the pandemic a top scientist called Dr Mike Yeadon said 33% of us were already immune from previous Corona viruses and that the young and healthy should carry on working but we should just protect the elderly and vulnerable. To my mind that makes more sense. Here endeth my essay!!'

Him: 'I had forgotten my own agreement to the idea of sheltering the elderly & vulnerable instead of everybody going into lockdown. I think I was shocked by the situation in India. Hopefully we will start to send aid...'

Me: 'Yes, I am shocked too by the situation. It's a reminder of those early days when we saw people dying in Italy. We are very lucky and privileged here that we've been offered the vaccine and we take our wealth for granted while others suffer. Being a worldwide problem, really it must be dealt with like that rather than in isolation. Oh another thing, there have been studies in the USA of states that have and haven't gone into lockdowns and there's very little difference in death rates. E.g. North and South Dakota, Florida etc'

Me: 'Am I too feisty for you?!!'

Him: 'I agree, we are all in this together. People in the same country, county, town or street still haven't got that. How long will it take the global population? I think it would take burning all the money in the world.'

Me: 'Trouble is it's predicted that worse pandemics will come due to man's abuse of animals. David Attenborough's "Extinction" is well worth watching.'

Him: 'We've exposed ourselves to a virus that was locked away––the burning of the rainforests will release even more apparently. What are we doing cutting up bats?'

Me: 'Crazy.'

Him: 'Goodnight, Donna.'

It's Wednesday and the communication's stopped. I've not heard a bean from him all day. My political rants have put him off, I just know it. Jeez, if people are this fickle, can I really be bothered with a relationship? I have my views and I'm not backing down and pandering to him just to keep the peace. If he can't see that we won't always agree about everything, if he's this tetchy, he's not worth pursuing.

I'm niffed though. Feel deeply wounded. I really like him, and I do want to keep the peace. But I'm not going to be the first to break the silence. I don't want to be the needy one. Maybe he's just very busy; I'm pretty sure he's thinking about me. We've booked a romantic weekend away; he's really into me otherwise he wouldn't have done that.

Thursday dawns. No good morning text or even a simple how are you? No mid-morning update about work or lunchtime report on what he's eating. I can't bear it. I'm itching to break the silence, but I'll wait until mid-afternoon and if he hasn't messaged by then, I'll send a friendly line or two. I hope nothing's wrong. He could have been in a car accident or dropped his phone down the toilet.

I'm obsessed. This must stop.

At 6.10 the following morning, a message pings. I lie in bed staring at the ceiling, my heart soaring. I smile to myself and punch the air. Savouring the thrill of the anticipation I wait precisely five minutes before so much as glancing at my phone. I didn't expect to be behaving like this at my age. I'm like an excitable puppy.

I open WhatsApp and read his paragraph-long message.

And then my heart plummets.

CHAPTER 30 - JUST FRIENDS

onna

I READ HIS TEXT, baffled.

Him: 'I kept waking up in the night almost feeling panicky--I am going to work on the house today to make good where the electrician has chased into the walls & I want to spend all my spare time on finishing this house after waiting so long. I feel I need to step back from our 'fast track' relationship. The last thing I want to do is cause you any hurt. I want to put all my time, money & energy into this project which has already been delayed by over 10 years. I am, of course, your friend.'

Friends--after everything?

I'm too flummoxed to reply. I need time to think.

Me: 'It would have been much nicer to have had a phone call or conversation in person even if it meant dropping over to yours for half hour. I'm struggling to understand. I wouldn't have minded spending all our time doing up your house, or just spending time with you while you worked on it. I could have read in your garden, made you cups of tea, helped you out. It just didn't matter. But I think you knew that already. So can only conclude what I think was going through your head: you feel panicked. New woman. Everything too fast. You weren't prepared. You feared being controlled again, losing control over the things that mattered to you. You have had trauma in your life, and you need to recognise that it will affect how you react. Either that or you changed your mind about me. Something you didn't like.

I'm struggling to understand why someone would say all the things you said to me, booking a few days away in Dorset. It doesn't add up. I was just so looking forward to getting to know you, being with you whatever we did, it didn't matter. And if that meant putting you and your house first, that would have been fine with me. Give yourself headspace, time to think, figure things out. There is a way around most problems. No rush, no pressure, I'm here if you do think we can work it out x'

Him: 'Thank you, Donna, for your lovely message & I am so sorry.'

HIS REPLY SOUNDS FINAL. I can't understand why somebody would say all those lovely things and talk about a future together, then end it. I spend the day walking round in a daze, unable to focus. Arriving at my first client's house, I completely forget to administer the correct medication and it's only much later when my supervisor rings to ask me to fill out an incident report that I realise all the time I'm in this state, I'm a danger to others––my efficiency and profession-alism sacrificed on the altar of my emotions. I'm supposed to park my own problems at the door of the client, walk in with a cheerful smile and be caring, but how can I do that when I'm crumbling inside? On a normal day I sometimes feel despair. I cannot make them better, or reverse the effects of old age, serious illness or disability and the problems I see cannot be dealt with by me alone. But today I feel completely helpless and just want to curl up under my duvet and remain there.

I very nearly have an accident with one gentleman who has no legs, when I absentmindedly press the reverse button on his wheelchair rather than the up and down button when he is about to shuffle from his bed to the wheelchair. It's a scary moment and I rush forward and push him back onto the bed hoping I'm not going to cause bruising to his body.

'Stupid fool,' he shouts. 'What did you do that for?'

I know I'm a stupid fool. I was a fool to trust Col when he said he loved me. I can't get anything right. My life is a mess.

On the doorstep of my next client, an elderly man, I check my phone for the umpteenth time while I wait for the door to open. But I know I won't hear from Col, and I need to accept his decision. When at last the door opens, my client is standing there in a dressing gown and slippers. His face is ashen and unshaven. He ushers me into a hall that smells of disinfectant and grubby clothes. He tells me he's been in pain all night from loin to groin and it's painful passing urine. There's blood in his urine. I give him painkillers and a large glass of water before ringing his doctor. My job involves raising the alarm when things don't look right.

Everybody needs me, but something inside me is quietly dying, simmering, fizzing and petering out. I cannot be the strong person I am supposed to be. It's as if I am being extinguished like a lightbulb. I feel it in every cell of my body from head to toes: in the sluggish way I walk, each step a massive effort, the way my heart drags in my chest, the way I slump into a chair. I can't eat. It's as if my stomach has collapsed. Every morsel is an effort and the taste of the food I normally love is like soggy bread and makes me feel all queasy. Yet I'm holding on to the embers of our love, replaying the happy moments. I find myself itching on my eyelids and neck--my eczema has returned.

Col--why, why, why?

I wish I knew. What's wrong with me? Why can't I hold onto a good relationship? All I want is lasting love, the happy-ever-after. It shouldn't be this difficult, except that it is, and it has been for many years now. Are we all so damaged that we cannot trust another human being? We cannot put a lid on the past and move forward. It shouldn't be this way. Life is short--it's never felt as short as it does right now that I'm steamrolling to sixty and beyond into old age. I just want to grab life by the horns, and I thought Col did too.

A day later and I'm still feeling light-headed and dizzy. This is how I was after my mum and dad died. And yet my relationship with Col was so short. A matter of weeks. How can this pain feel so much like grief?

And then anger kicks in. It bubbles and fizzes up from somewhere deep inside me, catching me unawares and causing a stabbing pain behind my eyes. How dare he treat me like this, string me along?

Memories flit through my mind. I see the love in his eyes when he told me he'd fallen in love and fancied me more than anyone he'd ever met. Was he lying? What did he get out of it? It's deception of the cleverest kind. Maybe there are people out there who get a kick from falling in love, having sex for the first time. Maybe he's addicted to romance but then his interest wanes. I just wish I understood.

I want to meet him to hear the truth because all this nonsense about needing to do up the house to sell-- it's rubbish. He's made it up. His house looks lovely. It's virtually finished. He shouldn't use the house as an excuse--it's a feeble one.

A few days later, I can't help myself; I fire off a text.

Me: 'I wouldn't normally say this, but I would really like to meet up with you even just for half hour. I really need to understand. It just doesn't make any sense at all. I think you owe me that much. Half hour of your time.'

I wait for his reply and when it doesn't come even after I see the two blue ticks indicating he's read the message, I feel a right idiot and ping another.

Me: 'Ignore that last message. It feels like I'm putting you under pressure and I don't want to do that. Give yourself time but I think you've already made up your mind. For whatever reason, I'll never really know or understand. Take care.'

Why am I being so kind? I'm pandering to him.

He reads the second message but it's hours before he replies. He's treating me mean to keep me keen and even though I doubt that's part of his plan, that's how it feels. How could he not be missing me, missing us and what we had? I just don't get it.

Hearing the bell chime––his special text notification––my heart flits, and I brace myself and delay looking at the phone for ten whole minutes. I want to savour the delicious thought that he might just have changed his mind and realise what a twat he's been. I so want him to want me. But I know that's not going to happen.

Him: 'I'm sorry.'

That's it. He's got nothing more to say. How dare this end, it was so beautiful and promising. I must move on, but it's too soon. I feel wounded and flat and the thought of going back on the dating site leaves me feeling sick. I can't do it. I feel too unsure of myself. No man is a patch on Col. He was perfect in every way.

As I stare at the wall in the silence of my lounge, my phone rings out. It's Olivia. She is the last person I want to speak to right now. I can't be all jolly and cheerful and how a mother should be.

'Hi, Mum, how are you?' She's bright and upbeat. I can't believe she's ringing to find out how I am. Cynicism tells me she wants something, but I have nothing to give; I just want to be left alone to wallow in my own self-pity.

I can't rustle up enthusiasm. 'I'm okay, and you?'

'You sound down. What's up, Mum?'

'Nothing.' Tears spring to my eyes. It's the first time I've cried. I realise I've been bottling it, holding it all in.

'It's that new guy, isn't it?'

I know I should keep my personal life from Olivia. It's embarrassing, I'm the parent yet I'm always the emotional wreck. Weak. Inadequate. She has a way of wheedling information out of me, the true matriarch that she is. I so wanted to turn my life around, to show her that I'm capable of a stable relationship. Caving in, I spill every little detail: the past weeks with Col, the plan to go away to Dorset, his unexpected text message. I don't expect her to be kind and sympathetic. Olivia never is but when I've finished telling her, I somehow feel soothed and cleansed. Like washing away my inner clutter. I needed to tell someone.

'The first thing you need to do, Mother,' she says taking control as she prepares to bark orders. 'Stop putting him on a pedestal. He's an idiot, he doesn't deserve you.'

'Yeah, yeah.' What the heck does she know about love? She's less than half my age.

'Stop feeling sorry for yourself, you're a disgrace to the female race.'

I didn't expect this, even from her. 'That's harsh.'

'You're acting like your life is over because of some trivial break-up with some random man. Get a grip. You need to reclaim yourself, have some pride and respect.'

'But the things he told me. I'm sure he didn't make them up. He seemed so genuine. He's just confused. Emotionally damaged.'

'You're making him sound like a vulnerable five-year-old who needs to be taken into care.'

Sometimes her blunt words are helpful. Maybe she's right. I am pandering to him, but that's because I love him, and I want to help him even if it means unpicking his difficult past. Just to be able to talk to him, that's all I want.

'Say yes to every social invitation, reconnect with old friends, take up a new hobby, get yourself a new look.'

'That's not easy.' My tone is depressed.

'Covid rules let you can meet up to six people indoors. Throw a party.'

Six is a stupid number. The mark of the devil. One person is bound to be excluded and half my friends are paranoid about Covid. My lounge is tiny. We'd all be sitting on top of each other. 'Suppose I could have a small barbecue.' Government adverts are always telling us to *blow Covid away*. The smoke from the barbecue should do that.

'That's the spirit, Mother. You so don't need a waster in your life.'

CHAPTER 31 - CRINGE

onna

THE NEXT FEW weeks are tough, and I cope in the only way I know--throwing myself into my work, taking on extra shifts just to keep busy and to stop myself from dwelling on my thoughts. I meet up with friends in my spare time, and when the welcoming arms of summer reach out, I venture down to Seaford for my first swim of the year. The water's bracing and I gasp as it brushes my shins. I watch the waves building. I must time it right. I don't want to meet the biggest wave of the set. When it's calm, I hurry in, not wanting to change my mind or appear a wimp to onlookers. I feel the tug around my chest and shoulders, and splash hard to keep warm, my body pinking as I turn to enjoy the view across to the lighthouse at Newhaven and in the other direction the cliff rising majestically, a tower of white chalk, stark and dramatic against the dowdy buildings fronting the sea. I'm not in long, for this is my maiden dip, I'll need time to acclimatise and with more sun to come, the water will warm. I'll set myself some goals as the summer progresses and aim to get fitter.

There's that little annoying voice I've been fighting for the past weeks ever since it told me to start doing something. To get fit. To lose weight. To be more attractive.

Stop, Donna.

The next man I meet will surely love me for who I am. But I am overweight and it's good to set goals. Have something to focus on and help me to recover from Col. The thought slams into me––I'm not over him at all. I've been pretending to myself, keeping busy, hoping I'd heal. But my heart still aches for him.

I hurry up the beach dripping wet, the soles of my feet numb with cold. Grabbing my belongings, I towel myself as I climb the pebble banks to the concrete wall where there's a kiosk serving hot drinks and deckchairs arranged across the beach.

Damn it. I'll message him. What have I got to lose? What's the worst that can happen?

I order a cup of tea and slumping into a deckchair, pull out my phone to compose a text. Sometimes it's best to be impulsive; if I think for too long, I won't do it.

Me: 'Hi Col, I hope your decorating's going well. Your house will look super nice when it's finished. You're a clever man.'

Cringe, cringe, did I really type that?

Shit, he's read it. He's still out there. Hasn't blocked me. He's typing a reply. My heart is in my mouth and there's a buzzing noise in my head. I need to calm down. This is ridiculous.

Him: 'The wiring's going well. Lots of noise and mess but it's good progress. I'm filling the holes and painting afterwards. I've decided to open up the kitchen and have a breakfast bar.'

Me: 'That's a great idea. Will you do it yourself?'

Him: 'That would be fun, but it needs building regs first and a builder who knows what he's doing.'

Me: 'Weather's amazing. I'm on the beach. Had my first dip.'

I rub the towel through my hair, staring out to sea, waiting for his reply. But it doesn't come. I cannot send another, I'll look desperate. I've planted the idea in his head that I'm still out there and thinking of him, now it's up to him.

All I end up doing is causing myself more distress and now I must spend the evening beating myself up for contacting him.

After a restless night, I switch on my phone and the bell signifying a text from him arrives. I'm in seventh heaven.

Him: 'I absolutely panicked Donna - I didn't realise I had an issue! I've been treated cruelly by those closest to me––I'm not used to love, warmth & kindness––but I handled it badly – I'm so sorry for the hurt I caused you. Could you bear to meet me again?'

Me: 'Col, I have been out of my mind these past weeks, wondering what I said and did to put you off me!'

Him: 'You didn't do anything. It was me.'

Me: 'I knew the decorating was just an excuse.'

Him: 'Can I see you at the weekend?'

Me: 'I'd love to see you!'

He starts texting again regularly. Mid-week we have a long chat about the easing of Covid travel restrictions.

Him: 'They're announcing 'green light' countries for travel today.'

Me: 'Yippee! Gibraltar will be on the list. A rock with a monkey!'

Him: 'A list of countries nobody's heard of, or nobody wants to go to. Like the Falklands!'

Me: 'I just want to go to Spain.'

Him: 'Patience!'

Me: 'You can talk! You've got the patience of a gnat! Getting me into bed on the third date!'

Him: 'Sorry! Oh my God, sex with you is amazing. You turn me on so much.'

. . .

PART of me knows I shouldn't be meeting Col. If I hadn't pinged him, I doubt he would have contacted me and I wouldn't be sitting here now, in the car opposite the Martello Tower in Seaford waiting for him to arrive. It's a beautiful sunny day and my swimming stuff is sitting on the passenger seat beside me. With my stomach doing summersaults, I brace myself, glance out the window for his car, not knowing how we will be together. We've been texting every day, so it does seem as if we are back on track. Every relationship has minor blips--but he likes me, I know he does.

I spot his Panda rounding the corner. Beaming at me, he appears relaxed. Happy? I can't decide. Clutching my towel under my arm, I head over to his car as he pulls into a space. When he gets out, he gives me a sorrowful smile and then we collapse into each other's arms. The agony of the past weeks melts away in his warm embrace. I'm so glad I sent him that text. I don't regret it for one minute. We cling to each other for several moments, saying nothing and when he pulls away, there's a serious expression on his face, and three familiar lines across his chin which I notice are deeper.

'Can you forgive me?'

When I see myself reflected in his eyes, I know he's annihilated all strength inside me. 'I'll have to.' A feeling of intense happiness sweeps through me, ruling me.

He dips his head slightly as if by way of an apology. 'I love you, Donna, very much. I've been an idiot.'

'Let's get this swim over with, shall we?' I laugh. 'It's probably going to be chilly, it was last week.'

He's a much more competent swimmer than I am. Attending classes at his local pool to perfect his stroke and increase his speed, he also zips up and down the fast lane several times a week. No wonder his muscles and abs are firm and well-toned. I on the other hand am a fair-weather swimmer--sea only, I hate local pools. They are basically a huge blue toilet bowl. Let's be honest we've all peed in them at some point in our lives. It's disgusting. And then there's the thought of catching a veruca or athlete's foot. People who wouldn't entertain going in the sea complain about weaver fish, seaweed, and sewerage. I try not to think about what's in the sea. I'm hypnotised by its energy, the sound of the waves crashing on the shore, the smell of the briny air. I'm mesmerised by it––that great heaving body of water. The pool isn't the same. It has no life. It's a false setting and the bright lights and chlorine air make me think how artificial it is.

We cross the road to the beach, glancing up at Seaford Head. 'Incredible.' It's hard not to be impressed by the breathtaking white cliff, seams of flint woven through the iron-stained chalk.

'You haven't been here before?' I love introducing a new place to someone and seeing their reaction.

'No.'

Most people don't; they flock to Eastbourne and Brighton. 'I'd describe it as understated. Rundown, sleepy, grubby. Not your traditional seaside town but I like the fact that it's lowkey. You won't find anything vibrant about this place. But there's a beating heart here and a strong community. You have to discover that for yourself. Look hard and appreciate what it does offer. It's almost like the town is saying to visitors, we're out of service. But it's not an unwelcoming place.'

'And you can park right on the seafront for free.'

'Don't tell everyone. They'll all descend.'

It's turning into a fantastic day. There's a gentle breeze, but it's not chilly or unpleasant. The sky is baby blue and laced with fluffy clouds which for now aren't hiding the sun. We clamber across the pebbles, pulling our towels and swimming shoes from bags.

There's an excited flurry of words as we survey our surroundings. 'Wow,' 'beautiful,' 'stunning,' 'lovely,' 'amazing,' and in that moment something overwhelming slams into me. This is incredibly special. A shared enthusiasm. And I realise then that I've not had this with any other human being. As we comment about the sky, the fluffy clouds, the lighthouse in the distance, the twinkling sea and the crashing waves, we are like two excited children at Disney. We're so enraptured, it's as if we're gazing at the Grand Canyon or the Niagara Falls rather than the boring English coast. What a funny pair we are.

Further along the beach a gaggle of women in dry-robes have already been in and are now pouring tea from a Thermos flask and towelling their damp hair.

Hand in hand, we scramble down the steep bank of shingle and rush to take our clothes off. Laughing, we wait for a wave to crash before heading down.

Sometimes the water looks murky and brown and off-putting, but today it's an enticing shade of aquamarine. Tiny darts of light flicker across the water. There's a rush of adrenaline––that moment of being caught between apprehension and the thrill of immersion. It will be cold, it always is, but we've made it down here and we're now in up to our knees. It's not so hard. We can do it. It takes courage, but it's an achievement. A personal battle of the senses.

My pain threshold is low. I can't tolerate the cold, but I thrash my arms around frantically and kick my legs, in the hope that I'll warm up. It's still early in the season but as the weeks progress, I'll bear it for longer. Col on the other hand slices a trail through a patch of blue, aiming for a red buoy a short distance out. After a few minutes, shivering, I stumble onto the bank of shingle, a huge wave having spat me out. Wrapped in a towel I watch Col, his slender tanned arms dipping in and out of the water. His body is graceful, and the waves don't deter him.

Swimming to shore, he's chased out of the sea by crashing surf. Shivering and goose-pimpled, he scampers up the shingle and reaches for his towel.

I smile up at him. 'I enjoyed watching you, but I was sitting here wondering why we swim when evolution has shaped us to excel on land.'

His skin is turning a mottled blue and purple. We need coffee. 'I guess there's something that seduces us to water despite the dangers.' He pulls on a sweatshirt, then sits, his lower half covered by his towel as he yanks off his skimpy trunks. Without turning my head, I watch him from the corner of my eye hoping to catch a glimpse of his groin.

'Most of the planet is covered by water.' I stare out to sea. 'Just look at it. How awesome it is. Stretching out to infinity.'

'When I look out to sea, I think of adventure and the unknown.'

We're silent for a moment as we consider that thought. 'Most of the planet is covered by water and humans are mostly water.'

'And about half of us live within sixty miles of the sea. When you're in a plane circling Gatwick you can see where most of the urban development is. Brighton, Hove, Eastbourne, Worthing, Hastings. They're vast conurbations stretching right along the coast. And then it's mostly fields apart from inland towns like Crawley.'

'I'm looking forward to the summer. That whole wonderful feeling of gliding weightless, staring up at a blue sky, watching seagulls and paddle boarders. It's the most exhilarating experience.'

'Me too. I can't wait. Most of all I'm looking forward to doing it all with you, Donna. I'm sorry for pulling away. I don't know what came over me.'

We scramble up the beach, crossing the road and ambling towards the town centre.

'I like it,' he says with enthusiasm as we wander along a street of old fishermen's cottages, past an antique-junk shop, a chic florist, a greengrocer and a butcher with slabs of meat hanging in the window. 'It's a hidden gem. One day it'll get discovered and end up trendy and hip like Hastings and Brighton. What are the house prices like?'

'A fraction lower. Still expensive. It's the South Coast after all.'

There are several cafes in the main street. Evinas, is Turkish and the staff are friendly. As it's packed inside, steam blurs the windows so that it's impossible to make out the street outside. We head through the café to the back where there is a tiny garden with tables under a pergola.

I always say that if you want to see the true measure of a man, watch how he treats café and restaurant staff because his manners reflect his value system. It's a test of moral character. Col is not condescending and is as gentle and respectful with them as he is with me. These cues confirm he's a genuine and kind person. There's a part of me that feels sorry for the way he's been treated by previous women and his family. I can't understand why anyone would want to be nasty to him. There doesn't seem to be a bad bone in his body.

But there's still a part of me that's hesitating, asking the question; if he is a considerate person, why would he dump me by text?

He takes my hands in his as we wait for our full English breakfasts and tea.

'Sorry to bring it up again, but are you sure you're okay with us? What if you pull away again? I couldn't cope a second time.'

'No, darling, I couldn't do that to you. Part of me went into shock. I've not had someone nice come along in ages and we were so full on and fast.'

I won't talk about the future. One day at a time--mustn't scare him off.

CHAPTER 32 - CLIFFTOP SURPRISE

*O*ur next date is to Hastings Old Town––that little enclave of loveliness snuggled between two cliffs. After parking and hoping we don't return to a car smattered with seagull splats, we wind our way through twittens and narrow passageways that link streets and lanes, past weather-boarded cottages, and half-timbered houses along All Saints Street and up many steps to the top of the cliff. Puffed out, we look down over the view, pointing things out and commenting. Old Town is a hodgepodge of old houses, pubs, shops, and churches. They look tiny, like a model village.

Turning, we continue our walk over the short, springy grass, surveying the view over the vast expanse of flat glassy sea. Gulls wheel carelessly on the light breeze.

Col stretches his arms in the air. 'I feel so free up here.' He laughs, tilting his head to the sun.

'Freedom, it's a great feeling.'

'Freedom from fear. For months it's as if we were living in a prison of fear, terrified of mixing with other human beings because of a virus. Look at the seagulls, no net ensnares them, they can go anywhere, do what they like.'

'I was thinking about being free from an oppressive marriage. Living life the way I choose.'

Why did he let himself be controlled? 'How did she control you?'

'She decided we were getting married.'

He was a grown man; he didn't have to go through with it.

'Just like my dad decided to parcel me off to boarding school. Then turning his back on me when I let him down, hating me because I wasn't academic.'

'Parents don't realise how damaging they can be.'

We aim for a bench flanked by spiky gorse, covered in yellow blossom. 'My wife's jealousy ruined our relationship. I couldn't look at another woman without her having a go at me. She wanted to know where I was, what I was doing at all hours of the day. We never mixed with other people. It was as if she didn't want me encountering other women.'

Seems a bit extreme. 'Why was she so jealous?' What I'm really asking is, did you do anything to warrant her behaviour? Her lack of trust? Did you have an affair? But I can't ask him this. He'd deny it even if he had.

We only ever hear one side of a story. I wonder what her defence is. I'll never know.

'It was just part of her psyche. Jealousy is a disease. It's like a fungus that penetrates every area of a relationship, destroying what goodness there was. It's considered to be one of the five poisons in Buddhism.'

'I've been lucky, I've never had a jealous partner. What are the other four poisons?' He talks a lot about Buddhism and the power of meditation. I think it's given him meaning and comfort in recent years, helping him to make sense of his situation.

'Anger, desire, pride, ignorance.'

'Angry men. That's my territory.' I laugh, but it's a cynical laugh.

We won't get far if we sit here, so I rise to my feet and Col follows. We fall into step across the cliff. Part of the coastal path is blocked off, but we find another route which takes us through bushes. We dip our heads under low hanging trees, following the muddy tracks, stepping over rocks and tree roots until we find ourselves on a platform at the cliff edge surrounded by gorse. We're too close to the edge, but we step back and find a dry patch of grassy chalk to sit on. It's secluded here, not a soul in sight and below the rocks are rugged and dramatic. This could easily be Cornwall or Devon. So close to Hastings, yet so remote. In the far distance, the cliffs look like coffee swirls and merge with the hazy sky.

It's so isolated that we could have sex here, feet from the cliff edge.

I turn to him, my pulse quickening as our lips touch, mouths open. Mustn't stay here long––besides, it's dangerous. One wrong move and we could slip. It's a sheer drop below, we'd tumble to our deaths.

Inching up the bank, but enjoying the thrill of our vulnerability, I lift his jacket and finding the zip to his jeans, I yank it down. Reaching inside, my fingers trail over his pants, feeling his bulge. My fingers slip inside, uncoil him and moments later he's ejaculating into my mouth. Right here on the cliff edge. To the sound of breaking waves.

There's something naughty, risqué, and dodgy about alfresco sex. Something to tick off the bucket list.

After adjusting our clothes and exchanging cheeky looks and comments, we are back on the main path continuing our walk, skirting an inaccessible cove and climbing about a hundred steps to the top of the next cliff before deciding to turn back.

'The walk goes all the way to Fairlight,' I tell him.

'We should do this again and park two cars––one in Hastings and one in Fairlight.'

· · ·

WITH ACHING LEGS, we make our way back down to the Old Town, stopping to admire a converted chapel. 'That would be my absolute dream,' he says taking a picture of the building. 'To refurbish an old church. And look at the lighting.' He's pointing to the industrial-style light fittings hanging from the ceiling with large globe-shaped smoky glass bulbs with orange filaments twirling through them. 'Love the quirky bulbs.'

We are like two children in awe of a decorated Christmas tree.

'And exposed brickwork. Love it. Imagine living there.'

'I'd never thought about living in Hastings.'

'It's a great place,' I say with excitement. 'The best thing is the music scene. They have festivals with singers and bands in every pub.'

It's hard to tell, as we gaze at the church, locked in our own thoughts, whether he's visualising an 'us', renovating a house together. I certainly am. This is what I've wanted for so long–– to meet a hands-on practical and creative man, interested in home design and renovation. I'm excited. I want a project with him so much, but I'm aware of jumping ahead and misreading the vibes sparking between us.

In the window, I see more than us in our reflection. I see a dream. We could be so much. Do so much. But does he see what I see, or am I being deluded, hoping for more than he can give? He's pulled away once, he could do it again. I couldn't have pulled away from him. I want to spend every moment with him and yet he was okay closing the door, forgetting all about me. I realise now, I'm not over what he did and to my shame I realise also that what I did up on the cliff was partly to keep the excitement going. I want to keep him keen.

Am I just a passing fancy, not someone to plan a future with? His relationship history is chequered. He's been treated badly–– so he says. Controlled, shouted at, talked down to. Why would he want to sail full pelt into the next relationship? It would have to be pretty amazing for him to want that. He has trust issues, I'm sure of it. He'd never commit again. He's hinted that much.

If only he could open his eyes to us––there's so much potential. My heart aches for more. We could be so happy together. We get on well. There are no disagreements, no awkward moments. We appreciate the same things. We could pool our resources, join our equity, buy a place together, open a small hotel. Or we could rent somewhere here and move abroad to the sun. Or travel the world. The possibilities are endless.

Steady on, Donna, you're racing ahead. Still early days.

Wandering down to George Street to find a café, we pass an eclectic mix of shops selling retro and vintage goods, art, bohemian clutter, antique and bric-a-brac. Near the seafront, opposite the black towering wooden sheds with pitched roofs, there are stalls selling freshly caught winkles, cockles, and shrimp. We find a tiny café nestled between an old-fashioned sweet shop and a tobacconist and grab an outside table.

After choosing, I put down the menu and glance across the road. 'See that pub?' I point to the quaint old timber-framed pub called Ye Olde Pumphouse. 'How old would you say it is?'

'Tudor.'

'Wrong.' I beam at him. 'It's actually less than seventy years old.'

'Wow. How deceptive. Maybe it was built from the timber of a shipwreck.'

'Shiver me timbers.'

It's wonderful to be sitting here, sharing thoughts and ideas, observing the quirky world of Hastings from our little table as we sip tea and munch on sandwiches.

This is the perfect place for good old-fashioned people-watching. Our eyes follow a woman wearing what looks like the tail of a raccoon pinned to her bottom and an enormous red hat with a colourful feather poking out in all directions.

'I love it,' Col says, still watching the woman. 'People like her, they push the human race forward.'

'I wish I was a free spirit like her. I care too much about what others think, that's my problem. She's happy in her skin. Like him over there.' I nod towards a guy dressed in a canary yellow jumper, black bow tie and tight white leather trousers. He has a pointed beard and huge black glasses that cover a third of his face.

'It's hard not to care. Most of us want to conform, to fit in, not stand out or attract attention.'

Looking around me, I find that most people are wearing jeans. They're conformists. Sheep. Happy not to be noticed. To blend in.

Col takes a sip of tea. 'We're free to be who we want to be. In theory. Except that from the day we're born other people clip our wings and make us conform so that we fit into their neat little box. Freedom is the only condition for happiness.'

'Very profound.' I laugh.

We spot a couple browsing in a shop window. They're holding hands but there's something that doesn't seem to fit together. We take a moment to brainstorm scenarios and before long we are creating an elaborate scenario of how they met. We speculate they met on Tinder and decided to give it a go, but they haven't hit it off and neither of them has the guts to say no to another date.

As we banter contentedly, there's a moment when I'm sure of one thing. There's only one true happiness ––sharing. There's no joy or delight in new adventures, making new memories if they're experienced alone. The more we share, the richer our lives become. I want to be connected to another human being, someone who thinks in a similar way and appreciates the same things. Otherwise, what is life about?

CHAPTER 33 - COP-OUT

livia

GOD, what is wrong with Mum? She's pathetic. Quite literally.

I've just arrived at the house to find her slumped on the bottom step of the stairs, right outside the lodger's room. It's wretched. My fifty-six-year-old mum is sobbing. Nobody's died. A bomb hasn't dropped on the house. She hasn't lost her job or found out she has cancer. Such a drama queen.

These tears are for a man. Another waster, another arsehole. His name is Colin. I don't know much about him; I don't want to know to be honest. He's just some random guy. The idea of my mother dating makes me cringe. I've lost count of the number of men who've broken her heart or messed her around. Maybe I should apply for her to go on *Married At First Sight*.

Hugging her knees to her chest, Mum is surrounded by balls of used tissues. I spot a bottle of Jack Daniels by her feet. I know I should feel sympathy, but I don't. It's a pitiful sight and not how I want to think about her when I close my eyes at night. I just feel despair. It's not that I'm a cold and callous daughter. Sometimes she seriously worries me. And that is ridiculous because parents are supposed to worry about their kids, not the other way around. At least not until they're old and decrepit and in danger of having a fall and breaking their hips.

I love my mum and just want to see her happy. What would it take for her to be happy? I wish I knew. Having a daughter hasn't made her happy. I've never been a substitute for a man.

'Mother, come on, get up, he's not worth it,' I gently coax. I only have scant details of what's happened. I can't believe she'd fall for Colin's tricks a second time around. He clearly does not want a relationship with her. For whatever reason.

Shrugging off my coat, I sling it over the newel post, step over her snotty tissues and perching on a higher stair, I tell her how it is. I bet her friends are all, 'oh poor you.' There will be no platitudes from me. I'm not sugar-coating the truth.

'Mother, why are you crying over a guy?' I realise my voice is harsh, but jeez she is so feeble. 'Have you blocked him yet?'

'No, I can't bring myself to. I gave him a week to reflect.'

'Reflect? That is pathetic.' I spit out my words and watch her flinch. 'He either loves you or he doesn't. It's not complicated.'

'It is complicated. He's complicated. He's had a difficult childhood and a controlling marriage. I just want to understand him better. I know it sounds silly, but I want to be the first woman in his life to show kindness because that's something he's not experienced a lot of. There's no point in getting angry with him and blocking him. If I'm patient, he'll be back, I know he will. And I've got nothing to lose.'

He's another victim. She likes victims. A challenge. Alcoholics, gamblers, diabetics--if they have a problem, my mother is there. I think she's under some illusion that she can fix them. All her men play the victim role. I hate the thought of grown men behaving in such a weak and useless way. Blaming others. Nothing is ever their fault. Refusing to take responsibility for their own actions. She can't see it. She panders to them, lets them off the hook. Allows them to treat her badly.

I cut her down with short, snappy words, like gunshots. I don't want to hear any more absurd explanations. 'No. Stop. Mother. Stop. I'm seeing more red flags here than in Les Mis.'

'Listen to me'. She sounds squawky. Flustered. 'You never listen.'

And before I can open my mouth, she's rattling on about the supposedly lovely dates she's had with waster Colin, but if she took her rose-tinted glasses off, she'd see those dates for what they really were. 'We went to Hastings and Bexhill and East-bourne. Had a great time. He gave me no reason to believe he was about to dump me.'

'Sounds like an old people's coach tour of coastal towns. Did you take your flasks and a packed lunch?' She gives me a withering look. 'You said something on the phone last night about a walk in Shoreham.'

'That was the last time I saw him, two weeks ago,' she says flatly.

'He's not going to contact you now. Forget him. Time to move on.'

'We had such a great day in Shoreham. We walked past the quirky houseboats along the estuary. We didn't stop talking and laughing. He's relaxing. Easy-going. I've not felt like that before with anyone.'

'He clearly doesn't feel the same way, otherwise he'd be here right now.' I can't help it, I laugh. It's a sarcastic laugh.

Men are like dogs—give an inch, they take a mile. Put them on a long lead, they gnaw their way through.

'There was nothing to suggest he was going to pull away. We walked a few miles on the tow path, bought a coffee, sat on the bridge. As we looked out at the view, he apologised for being quiet. Which he wasn't. Then he told me he was having the relationship jitters again. Said he likes being on his own. Might even live in a caravan and buy a dog.'

A flash of irritation shimmies through me. 'What the hell.' I can't believe she's falling for this crap. She's a basket case. I study her. Her stomach is straining in a pair of pink jeggings. She probably thinks they're fashionable, but they emphasise all the tummy ripples. She used to dress better than this, back in the days when she took fashion advice from *Trinny and Susannah*. She could do with shedding a few pounds. I've tried to get her to download a diet and nutrition app, but she's not interested. Loves her cakes and puddings too much. Especially clotted cream rice pudding. And those shoes. They are horrible. Enough to give any man the ick.

I'm not sure what's going on with her hair. So dull and life-less. If she trained it, got into a routine, teased it with curl cream and watched a few TikTok videos, it could be lovely and curly. I wish she'd treat herself to a good cut and style. 'All that wasted energy, Mother. So much stress. It's not worth it. None of these men make you happy.' I realise I'm shrieking but if this is what it takes to make her see what an idiot she's being.

She sighs, her body slumping. It's a weighty, clouded sigh as though all hope is leaving her. With tiny dimples of tension appearing on her chin and a hollow look in her eyes, I see it–– just how much he means to her. Creepy Colin is her world, her everything.

Why am I even surprised? This has become my life. My heart has hardened to it because throughout my childhood a string of men came and went.

Don't get me wrong––I'm not spoilt, or under some illusion that everything in Mum's life should revolve around me, her daughter, like the planets orbit the sun. I don't demand to be centre stage, but it would just be nice to feel my life gave meaning and purpose to hers. I wish I had a key to lock away the memories that stain our fractured past. I stow bitterness and contempt in my heart because our relationship is defined by these things. Not coming to my GCSE award ceremony because she had a fancy dinner date. Dumping me with random blokes while she attended work courses and meetings. One of them even smacked me. Brutal git.

At fourteen, I struggled with maths. I begged Mum not to go out, but she'd arranged to see a tribute band with some geezer. I really needed her help; I had an important test the following morning. Tunnelling through my mind there are so many of these incidents. Birthdays were always huge let-downs. A twatty boyfriend of Mum's who stank of sweat was roped in to perform a set of magic tricks at my tenth birthday. Mum spent most of the afternoon in the kitchen guzzling wine and giggling with magician man, content to stand by while Auntie Sasha took charge. I envied my cousins; their mum was amazing. More loving than Mum, she showered them with a plethora of praise and affirmative words and would happily have sacrificed her soul for her kids.

Scraping her chair back, Mum stands like a weary pensioner and flicks her phone across the table. 'Here, read the latest messages. See what you make of it.' She enters the passcode even though I know what it is. Her mother's birthday. The same number she's used for years, for every bank card and every phone. She heads to the hallway loo and as soon as the cloakroom door is closed, I hastily add Colin's number to the contact list on my own phone and look at his profile picture, before reading their messages.

Mum: 'The conversation on the bridge in Shoreham has left me panicked. It's like playing a game of chess. I don't know what will happen next.'

Cut to the chase, Mum.

I read on.

Mum: 'It might be that you've sort of decided you prefer being on your own, that actually you've enjoyed the peace of the last year. Maybe your gut is trying to tell you that? Maybe you can't admit it even to yourself? I'm worried that at some point you're going to turn round and say, sorry I've decided I want to be on my own, I'm planning to live in a caravan with a dog. It now feels like I'm taking a big emotional risk being with you, getting deeper into it, that I'll invest time in you and ultimately get hurt. When I got your original text, it was a big knock, and I did wonder if I could trust you going forward and now after yesterday's conversation, I'm finding myself back in that uncertain place. It would be just nice to relax and enjoy each other's company, feel loved. We both deserve that, but I'm not sure you can. There seems to be something in you stopping you and it's very upsetting because I feel we are so good for each other and it's frustrating because I've never loved someone as much as you.

'Maybe we need this coming week to yourselves to take stock? It's okay to do that. Maybe you need to reflect? Decide if you do want a relationship? Or just have time to yourself. Maybe you need more balance and don't feel you have it. I don't want to give you pressure and hope I'm not. Let me know what you think. No pressure xx'

Yawn, yawn.

God she rambles. Wish she'd get to the point––just tell him to sling his hook.

There's a fine balance between loving and smothering. She's a smotherer.

Colin: 'Thank you for your message. I really don't want to play any games. A week of reflection will be good.'

Huh. Colin the Cop-Out. Letting Mum down slowly.

The loo flushes and Mum returns to the kitchen, her head dipped, hands in pockets, hovering meekly beside me as if waiting for my blessing, my endorsement.

'Well?' God, why ask me?

What the heck do I know about relationships? I've had a few

disastrous dates and there's a nerd on my course with a crush on me. And sex, in my humble opinion, is grossly overrated and just gross full-stop but I guess if I fell in love with someone and there was an emotional connection between us, I'd feel differently. I've only done it once and that was more a drunken fumble, which doesn't count. I think Mum lives for sex. Just the thought of that makes me icky. I found a Rampant Rabbit in her knicker drawer once and I've heard her at it. The walls are thin in this house. Stud walls everywhere. Even she admits she hears the lodger farting in the bath above her head.

'You pander to these men. Yes sir, no sir, three bags full, sir. Read your messages again, you'll see what I mean.'

No matter how hard Mum tries, she'll never teach a gorilla to put down the toilet seat or write her notes of sweet nothings.

'I don't.' She's on the defensive. Why ask my opinion, then ignore it? 'I'm just trying to be understanding. Poor guy's had some tough experiences. Hasn't been treated nicely. He needs patience, love.'

Jabbing my finger on the table, I hammer home my point. 'And so have you, Mum,' I shriek. I can't bear it. She's so frustrating. I'm banging my head against a brick wall; she doesn't get it. 'Pull yourself together.' Hark at me dishing out advice. I've been watching too many TikToks. 'Are you just going to mope around waiting for his emotional recovery? He's messing with you. You have needs too. This isn't all about him. You want a committed relationship—set a high bar. He doesn't love you otherwise he wouldn't keep pulling away. He's playing with you. He doesn't care about what this is doing to you.'

'Suppose not.'

Weak-willed, Mum has no backbone. She treats each break-up as a crushing defeat, a devastating blow. You'd think by her age she'd have grown a thick skin. God, I hope I'm not like her in middle age: miserable and lonely with a battered self-esteem. These dating apps can't be a good thing; I'm sure they bring on mental health issues. She never learns from her mistakes either. It's time I took matters into my own hands now that I have Colin's phone number. I haven't worked out what I'll do, but I'm not sitting back and watching the toll this is taking on Mum. Once she's completely free of this creep and all the emotional energy she's wasting on losers, I'll encourage her to focus on herself. Some big changes are needed, starting with her hair and clothes.

'He's not good-looking.' The cruel comment flies from my mouth. Sometimes I can't help myself. I just want to show her that he's not Mr Amazing. He's just some old guy. Nothing special.

'Give me back my phone,' she says. Ha hah, she's aware of all the things I could do with it.

Laughing, I hold it up and out of her reach, only because I love teasing Mum; she always takes the bait.

'Thankyou.' There's relief in her voice. What did she imagine I was going to do? Little does she know what I'm planning to do though.

CHAPTER 34 - MISSED YOU

onna

Collapsing on my sofa, I ease my swollen feet out of my shoes, rubbing at an inflamed patch of skin on the back of my heel. It's been a tiring day, twelve hours with only one snatched break between clients. I'm grateful in part for these long shifts because I'm too busy to dwell on Colin, but as soon as I'm back inside my four walls the pain returns. That crushing loneliness. The sense that I will never be good enough, for him, for anyone. It cuts across my chest and there's a ringing in my ears. Is this the pain, the agony of heartache? These past days it's crept up and over me like an incoming tide. He still hasn't been in touch, not even to apologise or to finish the relationship properly.

If I can't have him, I don't want anyone. I'm aware I sound like a silly impetuous teenager and really, how could I possibly get back with him now? Too much time has passed. I couldn't trust him not to pull away again. I don't want to question his integrity and I wouldn't know where I stood with him and that would make me act uncomfortably around him. There's something closed off about him, a side to him that I think he keeps hidden. He's a mystery and I'm better off forgetting him, blocking him like Olivia suggested.

But it's not easy. I cannot forget and move on. Even after two weeks. I can't believe I'm still hoping he'll text me after this long. If he loved me, he wouldn't have needed to reflect. It was absurd of me to be so accommodating, so naive. And at my age too. I must have been hoping for a miracle. What an idiot I am.

Picking up the remote, I flick the telly on. *Eastenders* is about to begin. I've been watching a lot of soaps lately. Escaping into the lives of fictitious families is a good tonic.

Just as it's ending, I check my phone for the umpteenth time, my heart sinking as I stare at the black screen and on a whim without any thought, I send him a text.

Me: 'Gorgeous weather.'

Shit, that was stupid of me. I could click to unsend the message, but he'd only wonder what I'd written. I should not be the one breaking the silence. Doing the chasing. Acting all desperate. If he likes me, he will contact me.

Except that he won't. Not unless I do the running. This is how it works unless two people are equally mad about each other.

I stare at the phone, almost willing him to text and just as I'm getting up to pour a second glass of wine, my screen lights up. When I see his name, my heart skips a beat.

Him: 'Amazing isn't it? I had a dip in the sea yesterday & today. Sorry I haven't been in touch which is very rude of me.'

Two minutes later, as I'm pondering how to reply, the screen lights up again.

Him: 'I've been doing a lot of soul searching--I have developed commitment issues! Not surprising perhaps after a long marriage where I was treated like an absolute idiot. I've enjoyed very much the time we've spent together. You may not want a part-time lover, but that is all I seem to be able to manage x.'

A huge howling sob tears through me. A part-time lover? After all the special and wonderful times we've had together. The long days out. The love I've shown him, the interesting conversations, the soul-searching. Talk about a future together. That's all I'm good for–– a shag buddy. What an insult.

It's as if I'm a piece of dog dirt he's scraped from his shoe. I know exactly what I should do. My head is screaming to tell him to fuck right off, then I'll block him. Bastard. How could he treat me like this? All my friends, and especially Olivia, would tell me I deserve so much better.

But I can't. I'm railing against it. Something's stopping me. I sense that deep down this isn't him, not really. He's built a steel girder around his heart and is protecting himself. He doesn't want to get hurt again, he can't cope when someone shows love and support.

It's like an itch I must scratch. I reply.

Me: You need to decide what's important in your life, what it is you want and where you imagine yourself going forward. If you think long term you want to be with someone then maybe you need counselling, particularly learning how to trust again, because it might manifest itself in a relationship as a form of mental abuse. (E.g. giving love then withdrawing it, giving mixed messages) or you might be better on your own and happy enough or you might want just sex and lots of men do go along that path just to satisfy that one area of their life. I don't want a fuck buddy. I want a proper relationship.'

Him: 'I'm sorry.'

This is going nowhere. I have standards. I will never be somebody's shag buddy, a door mat, especially someone I'm in love with. This is so grossly unfair. I feel cheated, hard done by, as if I've been offered the chocolate icing of a cake but not the cake itself. I will not settle for this. I turn my phone off, go to bed.

I long for my brain to find sleep quickly and my mind to switch off but I'm still reeling from the shock of Colin's appalling text and the sheer disappointment of it all. It's another early start tomorrow; I need to be rested. In the morning I'll be with my most demanding of clients, the dreaded Violet Evans. She micromanages me and is preoccupied with order and exactness, watching me like a hawk while I line up crockery and pots and pans in her kitchen cupboards, complaining and criticising until they are 'just right.' She has her fun side too though and sometimes asks me to watch a Christmas movie with her. She's obsessed with Christmas and eats Christmas pudding all year round. She even wears dangly Brussels sprout earrings. The Brussels sprouts have Santa hats. She wears these even in the summer months. She sings on the toilet, she gives her poos different names as they plop into the pan.

Sunlight slanting through a gap in the curtain drags me from a restless sleep. I'm thinking about Colin again. He's sapping my energy. I'm a weak lightbulb. I wish I could purge him from my soul, but I'm stuck. If we'd argued, it would be easier. Something lies unresolved between us. I want to understand his mind. I cannot be at peace until I know. I want to meet him, make sense of it all.

My phone lights up with a text from him as soon as I switch it on.

Him: 'I was trying to find a compromise but in retrospect that's just selfish.'

Extremely selfish, but I won't tell him that. I want him to see the nice person that I am. Being nice is hard to sustain. Inside I'm hurting.

Me: 'As we've enjoyed each other's company maybe we could meet up for a swim sometime.'

Shit, why did I send that? Does he think I'm happy to be a

part-time lover? I have standards, I am worth more. He's a parasite and I'm the host.

Him: 'I'd love a swim.'

As I wash and dress, several more texts fly in.

Him: 'I've missed you so much xx.'

'Seeing your lovely smile & being with your happy personality will be so good.'

'So much to tell you.'

'It'll be fun xx'

'I love you, Donna.'

What's the matter with him, why's he giving me these crazy mixed messages? I'm not settling for a toxic kind of half-love. And yet I still believe we are good together. That he's worth hanging in there for.

Driving to work, I'm annoyed with myself. I settle for crumbs when I deserve the whole cake. He's playing a game–– throwing tokens and gestures, giving me the illusion that I deserve a place in his life without him having to commit to more. I shouldn't allow him to drop back into my life after this period of ghosting. I should value myself more. I'm making it too easy for him.

Why?

Because I love him like crazy and my heart is soaring as I read his texts. This is what I've longed to hear these past weeks. And I want him to love me. I want to turn this around, make it the best relationship he's had.

Throughout the next few days until our swim, we banter back and forth via text and it's as if there's never been a gap in our relationship. Driving down to meet him at our usual parking spot opposite the Martello Tower in Seaford, I realise something. Despite the anguish he's caused me, he's been a good influence in my life. Every relationship, even the bad ones have had positivity, but it's all too easy to let the good times be swallowed by the bad. Over the years, in various relationships,

I've discovered new skills and interests, as well as places to visit. Thanks to Colin encouraging me to overcome my dislike of public swimming pools, I'm now a regular at the local leisure centre and I feel so much fitter for it. I've also started a diet. The last time I sat on the beach next to Colin I was aware of how fat my legs were compared to his. After my recent birthday celebrations, I felt like a complete pig and vowed to quit the gannet lifestyle. Olivia's constant digs about my weight, and photos she's delighted in showing me to prove my plumpness, made me start a diet. It's early days and I'm doubting Colin will notice because I've only lost a few pounds to date. I'm not losing weight for him I remind myself; I'm doing it for me.

When I spot him standing casually by his car, his swimming bag slung over his shoulder, my heart flips and my throat goes all dry. With a mixture of nerves and excitement jangling inside me, I park up and stroll towards him. His head is dipped slightly in that pose I know so well but he's beaming at me. His skin looks darker as if he's been sunbathing in the garden, or it could be the black t-shirt he's wearing that's enhancing his tan. He knows I love him in black, so sexy, and those torn faded tight jeans–– my favourites. Is this as deliberate as me rushing out yesterday to buy a more flattering swimsuit? I chose red because he loves red underwear.

'What gorgeous weather.' He looks up at the blue sky.

'Amazing, isn't it? But it should be, it is August after all.'

'Yes, if it can't be nice in August when can it be?'

'Sunshine is the best medicine.'

I'm grateful for this age-old conversation starter; it always helps to dispel awkward tension.

He glances behind him. 'It's so nice here. We should walk up the cliff.' I love that enthusiasm he has for simple pleasures, simple places. He's like a city child arriving at the beach. Seaford really is nothing special. It's rundown, low-key and today it's busy. We were lucky to park. His enthusiasm is infectious, and I find myself agreeing to climb the steep cliff.

When we've trudged up the steepest ascent, panting and out of breath and with achy legs, we gaze at the view, counting the boats dotted across the twinkling expanse of blue. The sea sparkles and glows like a land enchanted in a fairy tale.

I'm squinting against the sun. 'I wonder if they're passenger ferries heading for Newhaven or cargo ships. There are so many. It's a busy highway.'

It's a simple act but when he rests his hand on my shoulder, I feel my insides tingle. I've missed his touch. I just want him to hug me. 'I'm really sorry for everything.'

'I'd like to understand, Colin, what was going through your head.'

'I think I've got commitment issues; I've been so cruelly treated in the past.'

I sigh. This is well-worn territory. 'Yeah, I know that.'

'I never stopped thinking about you. I really missed you.'

I pull my gaze from the sea and stare at him. How can I believe him? Believe anything he says anymore? 'Do you mean that? If you like someone you wouldn't want to risk losing them. You wouldn't pull away. You couldn't bear the thought of being without them. Something keeps nagging at the back of my head. I'm not good enough for you. Just admit it.'

His face is pained, skin slightly leathery. 'You are. You're lovely, intelligent. There's nothing wrong with you. It's me.'

'My self-esteem is pretty low, I'm always questioning myself.'

He pulls me into a bone-jarring hug that seems to go on for so long, I gasp for breath. He draws back, looks at me, love taking a shape in the air around us, mixed with longing and regret.

'I have missed you. I love your company.'

'It doesn't make sense then.' I don't know what more I can say. We're going round in circles. He either doesn't understand his emotions or he's being deliberately guarded. 'And I don't want to be a part-time lover. Or it put it crudely, a fuck buddy.'

'No, Donna.' He grabs my arm forcing me to look at him. 'I don't know why I said that. That's not what I want at all.'

'What do you want then?'

'I just love your company.'

Not enough to keep in touch with me, but I don't say this. We'll only spin in a vortex again. 'I enjoy all the things we do together. It's always fun,' I say flatly, trying to take the enthusiasm from my voice in case he's hesitant about us. I'm careful not to say *being together* or using the word *relationship*. It might scare him off again. 'Don't pretend to feel something if you don't.'

'I never want to do that, I'll never lie to you or pull the pull over your eyes.'

I'm not sure right now how I feel or how I should respond. I'm being stupid. I shouldn't be here. I'm the fly going straight into the ointment. I can't stop myself. I love him. I want him. Just being with him again is making me breathless.

'Come on then, let's go for that swim,' I say when he goes quiet. I'm annoyed with myself for not getting the truth out of him, for not digging deeper. I know I should confront him––, really confront him, it's the healthy thing to do, but it feels like pressure, and I'm scared. He's here, that's a start, maybe he'll talk in time. I'd rather play it cool. I don't want him running off again. But the problem is, I never confront, not until I'm so pissed off with the other person that I explode. Psychologists would call this passive-aggressive. I struggle to be assertive. I don't think I can be reprogrammed at this late stage in my life. This is how I'm wired. I didn't confront Nick's drinking until I'd reached rock bottom. Come to think of it, I've never confronted the big issues that crop up in relationships. I think I've always secretly hoped that the problems would go away, be resolved with time.

Maybe I'm being hard on myself. It felt impossible to talk openly to Nick; he always ended up shouting and blaming me for his behaviour. Col wouldn't do that, he's gentle and calm. It won't take much to lose him again. I've got to be careful, patient. It feels as if we're skating on ice.

By the Martello Tower, a string of campervans, all shapes and sizes, are parked up. Strolling past, I steal a glance inside the open doors. People are making tea, sleeping under duvets, their belongings are spilling out-- all the essentials of life and four wheels to take them anywhere. There's a waft of weed, laughter, tanned faces and a man sitting on a bench playing a banjo.

'I wonder why there are so many of them. I guess the parking is unrestricted and right on the beach.' Col stops to read the signage. 'But it says no overnight parking. Maybe they don't check at night.'

We trudge over the pebbles and down the shingle bank to find a spot on the beach, before pulling threadbare towels and swimming shoes from our bags. 'I think they're waiting to board the ferry at Newhaven. It's only ten minutes from the port and with the free parking, it makes sense.'

'Yes of course.' As he looks at me, I can see envy and longing tucked behind his pained expression. 'God, imagine travelling round Europe. I'd love to do that, get away from rainy England. You could live cheaply, cook on a stove, watch the stars, enjoy the sun, explore. Go where you like. Beaches, mountains, cities. I wonder how much you could pick one of those vans up for.'

'Sounds wonderful, but maybe they're parked up because they've had their ferry cancelled. I've lost track of Boris's stupid traffic light system. Can we even go to France right now? The rules are constantly changing. There's so much confusion and all this ridiculous testing and different Covid rules from one country to the next. I don't even know which countries you can and cannot go to. It's a complete muddle. And worst of all, you could go to a green country only to find it turns red because a new variant has been detected and be ordered to quarantine. Makes me so cross. People have had to cancel holidays at the last minute, they've lost thousands.'

'Hard to remember a time when we could travel freely. Jet off at a moment's notice.'

'Travel's never simple. Remember that ash cloud. And what about when we were kids and our parents worried about the PLO blowing up planes.'

'I just need a holiday, I'd go anywhere,' he says glumly.

'I've heard it's the law to wear a mask on the beach in Spain.'

'I was going to suggest we go to Spain. That's on the green list, but no way am I wearing a mask outside.'

'Me neither.' He's gone from wanting to be a part-time lover to planning a holiday. It's bizarre, but I don't care, I'm throwing caution to the wind, I'd love to go away with him, if he's serious about the idea.

'A work colleague was raving about Anglesey, in North Wales. You ever been there?' he asks, pulling his jeans off to reveal slender legs, then slipping his t-shirt off.

'I don't know North Wales at all.'

'He said I'd love it there. There are beautiful beaches and forestry and lighthouses perched on rocks.'

'It's definitely better to holiday here, for the time being, until things are back to normal.'

'Will we ever be back to normal? Covid will eventually disappear, but it could take years and by then the climate lobby won't want us jetting round the world.'

'They won't stop campervans though.'

'We should get one.'

'Steady on.' I pull my top off and tug my jeans down. I've shaved and creamed my legs. 'We're only just back in touch, Col, let's see what happens. Let's not rush.'

'Wow, that's stunning.' He reaches out, and with longing in

his eyes as they rake over my body, his finger trails down the side of my swimsuit.

My pulse quickens as he moves towards me, his lips parted as his gaze falls to my boobs then my mouth and just like that, I drop my guard. Every sensible thought inside me floats out with the sea breeze. He's handsome and intelligent and perfect for me. His fingers stroke my hair, tilting my head up to meet his lips and we kiss. He takes my hand and squeezes it. It's a simple gesture but one that says, "we're back on and I'm not going to let you down again."

He pulls me onto my feet and we pick our way across the uncomfortable pebbles, taking short, soft steps despite the added protection of the special swimming shoes we're both wearing.

At the foaming water's edge, he drops my hand and staggers in, legs wide apart, his arms flapping comically to avoid waves coming at him. When the water is up to his waist he dives in and under, emerging a few metres out, shaking the drips from his hair and turning to beckon me in.

I laugh and he turns away from me, his muscly limbs slicing rhythmically through the water, an athlete's front crawl. I stand for a while watching him, transfixed. There's something about today. I feel such hope. I can't quite put my finger on it, but it's as if this is a new chapter in our relationship.

The water suddenly feels so inviting. It tickles my ankles, my knees. It's exhilarating. Anticipating the next wave, I'm wary, fearful of the water crashing over my head, but when it's calm, I plunge violently in, gasping, the saltwater teasing my lips. My arms and legs cut automatically through the water until I'm out of my depth. When I've acclimatised to the temperature, I stop and lie for a few moments on my back, my hair splaying around me, my arms gently flapping to keep me afloat as I squint towards the sun, watching the circling gulls.

CHAPTER 35 - MUM'S CREEP

livia

I DON'T BELIEVE IT. My stupid mother has only gone and booked to go on holiday with Colin the Creep. To be fair, after I caught her sobbing her heart out, and judging by her appalling past record with men, nothing would surprise me. But I am disappointed she went back to him. Just to have had the guts to block him; it doesn't take much. That's the beauty of all this technology. I just hope he doesn't keep messing her around because to see her like that again, so upset, I don't think I could cope.

The odds aren't great. It can't last. He's shown his colours. He's a commitment-phobe. The moment she gets too close for comfort, he runs the other way. I wish Mum could see what's happening. I've tried explaining all this, but she won't listen. Colin the Creep is Mr Big in *Sex in The City* or Chandler Bing in the first few seasons of *Friends*. He gives Mum all the signals that he's head-over-heels in love with her but pulls away when things start to get serious. He leads her on and the moment she falls for him, he backs out. He's an altar-jilter and I don't reckon he'll show up the day they leave for Wales. She probably knows it too but would never admit it. One blessing––at least this holiday is in Britain, there won't be flights to cancel.

A week in Anglesey staying in a pub. That's all I know about the trip. I'm not interested enough to ask a ton of questions. It always rains in Wales, but I doubt they're bothered. They'll pass the time shagging because let's face it, that's all he's after. Ew, I don't want to imagine my mum in the sack.

It's time to take matters into my own hands. To protect Mum. To stop her from making a complete fool of herself. I've been mulling it over for some time now and I know what to do.

Propping the pillows behind me and plugging my phone in to charge overnight, I get comfy. Dad's up late, downstairs playing *Death Loop* and *Psychonauts.* Ever since Pamela left him, he's become addicted to those rubbish computer games. The walls are thin in this house and the repetitive loud audio is jarring and so annoying. Slipping out of bed, I huff. Damn it, I want to be up early for a jog round the estate. It's a great energy boost to kick start the day and stop me feeling sluggish.

From the top of the stairs, I shout down. 'Dad, you've got work tomorrow and you're keeping me awake.'

Opening the lounge door, he storms into the hallway and with one hand on the newel post barks up at me, 'Go and stay with your mother if you don't like it.' He hasn't shaved in days; he looks a mess.

'You know I can't stay at hers. It's full of bloody lodgers.'

He ruffles his hair. 'I won't be long.'

'You need your sleep.'

'You sound like your mother when you nag.'

It's pointless arguing with him. Turning, I head back to bed, slamming my door behind me. Knowing I won't be able to drop off to sleep now, I switch my phone back on. This is a good time to put my plan into action.

It's time to fire off my first text to Colin the Creep.

Me: 'Hi Colin, it's Julie from the dating site. *Lucky in Love.* It's been ages since we chatted. How are you? Just wondered if you'd found anyone?'

My heart is thumping with fear. I shouldn't be meddling. It's wrong and scary, but as I stare at the screen, I chuckle to myself because this is quite exciting. I'll be so disappointed if he ignores me, which he probably will because he'll be thinking who the F is Julie?

I don't have to wait long for his reply. And to think of Mum, bless her, checking her phone every minute of every hour for the text that never arrived. What a slime ball. He doesn't deserve her.

Him: 'Hi Julie, nice to hear from you. I'm good thanks. No, I've not met anyone yet. What about you?'

Doesn't question who I am. Unbelievable. He must have chatted to that many women, he's lost track of who they all are. As the Americans would say, he's a complete douchebag. I want to call Mum immediately, but how can I? Taking his number from her phone was a terrible thing to do, a violation of privacy. She'll be more shocked at that than Colin's response to my text. Until I can work out how to break the news to Mum, I'll carry on texting him, see what I can find out.

Me: 'I didn't want to butt in if you had someone! I'm well thanks! Had a few dates, no one special yet!'

Him: 'You're not interrupting anything. I'm still single! I'm up early, chat tomorrow?'

Me: 'Sure.'

A surge of horror swamps me. Liar. Cheat. He might be good-looking, for an old guy, and charming and witty and all the other traits Mum was sucked in by--but I'm repulsed. I just want to punch him in the face, send him packing. Anger wants to explode out of my body right now but in order to sleep, I dial it down, reassuring myself that I will fix this for Mum. Revenge is sweet, so they say, but best served cold. Retribution is coming.

THE FOLLOWING EVENING, I text him early, after dinner, allowing plenty of time to chat before he can make the excuse of needing his precious beauty sleep. All that rubbish he gave Mum about recovering from a traumatic marriage and the stuff about his mum walking out on them when he was little--it's all bullshit. I reckon he's an attention seeker. And even if it isn't, he's using it to excuse his behaviour. He probably stays up late chatting to all sorts of women online, getting a kick from how many likes he can notch up. A capsule full of women who would, in his mind, sleep with him. I'm surprised he doesn't get fed up with the games and the flakiness and the waste of time that dating apps can be.

I can't think of what to say so I go for a bland message. I'm sure he's used to dull chit-chat.

Me: 'Hey Colin, how was your day?'

Him: 'Good thanks and yours?'

He doesn't seem keen to chat unless this is what he's like. I need to cut to the jugular and suggest a drink.

Me: 'Fancy a drink sometime? Shoreham next week? *The Bridge* is nice.'

I've no idea whether The Bridge is any good. Never been there. Only been to Shoreham once. Can't remember it at all. There's a big M&S on a roundabout near there which Mum is obsessed by. The satnav on my iPhone will find it but I'll go early to orientate myself. Shit, now I need to make up a career for myself. It's too easy to lie.

Him: 'Hi Julie, sounds great. Thursday, 7.30? Shall we eat?'

Hell, eating will complicate the evening on many levels. Me: 'Just a drink this time?'

Him: 'Fine with me. See you there. Look forward to it.'

This is ridiculous. He's no idea what I look like. What's he going to do, walk in, scan the place like a dork hoping I jump up and wave my arms frantically at him? I suppose that's exactly what I'll have to do unless he has the good sense to ask me for a photo. What kind of a plonker would go on a date without knowing what the person looks like? He's either desperate or doesn't care.

CHAPTER 36 - HOLIDAY BOOKED

onna

As I sweep into the car park at Tide Mills near Newhaven early one Sunday morning, a series of images pop into my head of us in Anglesey. We're sitting on a rock overlooking a lighthouse. It's a cold day–– it's Wales after all. But I don't care about the wind making my hair fly and my ears burn with the cold because I'm with the man I'm madly in love with.

Colin. Colton.

I don't care what his name is.

He's the one for me. The one who makes me forget everyone else in my past. He's the best, the cream. If I hadn't messaged, reminding him I was waiting and still out there, I'd be back on the dating site, chatting to dross. Our break was just a blip. A detour. It's firmly back on track and here we are, doing what we enjoy together, swimming in the sea.

It's early and we're the first ones in the car park, but it won't be long before it's full of dog-walkers, swimmers, and cyclists.

The sheer joy I'm feeling radiates from every pore. I turn and smile at Col. These days, I can't stop smiling, ever since he suggested the week away. Like my smile will never fade.

It's not long now. We've booked a room in a cosy-looking wisteria-clad pub in the centre of the island, in a town called Llangefni. There are so many place names that start with a double L. LL is a real peach of a sound––hard to get my tongue around, but it's fun practising.

Out of the car, we follow the concrete path towards the beach. Either side of us the hedgerow is a tangle of brambles and nettles with fields beyond. We stop to watch a blackbird in a tree singing a beautiful melody, his voice travelling far.

To the right are a smattering of industrial buildings around the port of Newhaven. A docked P&O ferry dwarfs the houses tucked on the hillside. To the left are the outskirts of Seaford.

The path crosses the rail tracks of the route from Seaford to Brighton and a few metres along there used to be a station, Tide Mills. Lichen, and thickets of dandelions have worn the stone of the disused platform. A bored Network Rail security guard in a high-vis jacket is leaning against the gate monitoring pedestrians as they cross. Apparently, there are plenty of near fatalities, teenagers especially, dashing across seconds before the train approaches.

We're now on the site of the derelict village, once a thriving community of several hundred people. Ruins are all that remain––low walls of workmen's cottages near where the mill once loomed over the landscape. If I listen hard enough I can almost hear the ghostly whisper of voices of the past, see shadows flit across the tall tangled weeds where furniture stood.

Over a bridge crossing a muddy lake and on until we reach the shingle; it's suddenly chilly.

'Oh my God, fog.' Stopping, we look ahead in disbelief. It's as if we've stepped into a fridge, it's that cold. Behind us the sky is an intense blue, but ahead a thick sea mist envelops the coastline, tendrils clawing like fingers across the shingle, turning the sun to milk, obscuring the view and shrouding the cliff beyond the sea wall in a haze. The veil of mist creeps like a cat stalking its prey, swirling around the lighthouse, inching on towards Seaford.

'Sea mists disappear as fast as they appear.'

'Let's hope.'

The pebbles drop in terraces to dramatic waves crashing the shore, too large and overwhelming to swim in; they'd knock us over. But further along, the beach sweeps around in a crescent ending at the sea wall where the shingle falls away to an expanse of wet sand. The sea, gently rippling to the shore, is tantalisingly smooth as bath water on this stretch of beach. Today, it's eerie in the reduced light. To swim at most beaches, you need a tide table and a military sense of punctuality, but not here. The tide never goes out too far.

After we've undressed, we head towards the water. I feel like a tree in the wind with branches that creak. I breathe in deeply, clasping my hands behind my back to stretch out my arms and shoulders, shivering in the chilled air as I take those first tentative steps. I feel the tug around my chest, shoulders, letting the coolness surround me. Then I'm in and splashing around. Surrounded by mist and glancing out towards the horizon in the murky light, I imagine the Loch Ness Monster emerging from the depths.

The sun suddenly explodes through the misty veil bringing everything back into focus and warming the air. Light scatters tiny diamonds across the water as I cut through the salty brine, turning my head, closing my eyes towards the sun, basking in the warmth.

Colin gets out first, clambering over the killer pebbles on his bare feet, scrambling to wrap an old greying towel around his shoulders before sitting down and shivering. His face is mottled with purple patches. Scissoring through the water, I glimpse at him every so often. He's now glued to his phone. Is busy texting and his face is intense. Who's he chatting to? I'm curious. He never mentions any friends. Just a few work colleagues he occasionally has a pint with. There's an uncle in Yorkshire. His daughters who sporadically communicate. His fingers are still typing as I reach the sea wall and turn. He's in his own world, looks troubled by something. I cannot ask who he's texting, that would be too nosey.

Out of the water, I'm renewed and restored. I stagger to my towel, wrap it around my goose-pimpled body and collapse onto the stones. It's as if he hasn't noticed me get out of the water, a shadow blocking his light. Still glued to his phone, fingers flying across the screen; he doesn't glance up and speak.

'Everything okay?' I ask.

I see tension across his upper body and with a heavy sigh he slips his phone into the pocket of his jeans and turns to smile at me. It's a forced smile, courteous, as if he's wrestling with his emotions. Something is going on.

'Yep, all good.' His voice is stiff; is this how it's going to be? Parts of his life kept hidden? Whoever he was texting, it seemed important, intense, as if he was arguing with someone. Or is it me, just being paranoid? I don't want to come across as controlling. He's had a lifetime of being controlled. If there's something to share, he'll tell me in his own good time.

'What do you love most about swimming?' I ask as I towel my hair.

He stares out to sea, looking sad. It's obvious he's still dwelling. Someone has annoyed him. It's a few minutes before he answers. 'That intense satisfaction, losing myself.'

'It's one of those confusing sports. Sometimes we do it for fun, at other times it's for survival. And sometimes the water is so cold, you'd die before you swam. I'm thinking of the Titanic.'

He appears more relaxed. 'I've always loved anything that involves water. Canoeing, surfing, snorkelling, diving. Makes me feel alive. I miss just splashing around with the kids. Messing around in rubber rings, playing catch in a pool. When I look at holiday photos, I get all teary-eyed and long for them to be little again, doing all those fun things with them. But now that they're older, doing their own thing; doesn't stop me having fun.'

'My mind goes into free-float mode when I'm out there. Makes me feel fresh and rejuvenated.'

'Lazy summer days on the beach. I wish it was hot all year round. I hate the winter. Thank God that mist evaporated. It was chilly.'

'I could sit here all day, every day, if I'm covered up. Hate getting burnt.'

We're dressed now, lying down looking up at the cloudless sky. He turns to face me. 'Don't you love the glow of a tan?'

'Couldn't care less. It's Factor 50 for me. I'm not out to impress others. Just don't want to get skin cancer.'

'I'm not out to impress either, but I still love a tan. Makes me feel healthy and handsome.'

I nudge him. 'Hey, don't be so vain.'

'I'm anything but vain, I hate an audience.'

That's hard to believe. Everything he does is about improving his physique, his stamina, toning his skin, his muscles. What's he doing it for? To stay young, keep fit? I stare out to sea, mulling over that thought. Or was he secretly hoping to attract someone younger, more attractive, to bolster his ego? They say that men are simple creatures. He's different to all the men in my past. None of them cared about their body like Colin does. They unashamedly cultivated big bellies and sagging chins and the only exercise they did was to walk to the car or the fridge. One guy used to say, 'it's better to have loafed and lost, than never to have loafed at all.'

What does he want in a woman, what does he see in me?

My thoughts are broken when Colin asks, 'Where to next?'

'Brekkie in Eastbourne?'

'Or Seaford?' He prefers Seaford, but we're always going there. Be good to go somewhere different.

'If we go to Eastbourne, we could have a walk up on the cliffs. Selfie time before we go.' I hold my phone up to take a photo of us, but he ducks out the way. 'What's up? I wanted to post it on Facebook, show everyone we've been for an early morning swim.'

'Facebook?' He stares at me in horror.

'You're on Facebook?' I'm sure he's mentioned promoting his business on social media. Maybe he uses Instagram instead.

'I am. Don't use it much.'

It's odd that he doesn't want me to take a picture of us. I've taken pictures of us before. Something claws at me--a sense of unease, as if there is something not right between us. Can I trust him? Will he ghost me again? Damn it, it will never feel right because I don't properly understand why he pulled away--not just once, but twice and we still haven't properly talked about it. It's become the elephant in the room. I can't believe we've booked a holiday together; I must be mad.

He's here and that's all that matters. He's chosen to spend today with me, come on holiday with me. This is about him and whatever demons he's carrying. I mustn't question myself or let my lack of self-esteem ruin this relationship.

'Are you being vain again?' I tease.

'Me, vain? Most definitely not. I'm a private person that's all. Don't want my picture all over social media.'

'Are you on the wanted list? What dreadful crime have you committed?' Gathering my bags, I laugh, keeping our banter light-hearted. I don't want to scare him off, but sometimes it's like treading on eggshells. I shouldn't have to worry what I say.

As soon as he nips to the loo, I do a quick search for him on Facebook to settle my mind. But I can't find him despite typing every variation of his name; nothing comes up. Strange. I go to

Instagram and Twitter--same thing. He's not on social media. Do I dare to think the unthinkable, that he's blocked me?

The day is tainted by that thought, crouching at the back of my mind. I should ask him if he wants to friend me on Facebook and clock his reaction. But I can't do it.

After driving across the Cuckmere Haven, I steel a glance over the valley to the magnificent meandering river that cuts through the South Downs while trying to keep my eye on the road ahead. The famous oxbow river weaves towards the sea, a glittering ribbon under the sun, and the iconic coastguard cottages on the cliff edge. We pass through the village of East Dean and up a hill. A cluster of houses on our left. The landscape is breath-taking up here. Gentle undulating fields, rolling away in every direction, like a quilt of green and dotted with sheep. There are views over the sea in each direction. A whole panorama. Every time I drive across this stretch of Sussex, with Beachy Head to my right, I'm in awe. It's truly magnificent and as we come to the crest of the hill with Eastbourne below and to our left, we both gasp. From above, the town looks enormous. I pull over, cut the engine. I just want to get out, admire the view, forget my niggling worries.

There is it. The place that really matters to be. The town where I long to be, one day. It holds a special place in my heart.

Eastbourne.

Memories of happy times, days of bliss too brief. Of fun and laughter. Carefree days with Olivia when she was tiny, playing on the beach, drinking ice cream soda in Macari's, pantomimes at the Devonshire Park Theatre at Christmastime. Tea with my parents on the lawn of the Hydro Hotel. Old people crammed along the promenade benches as far as the eye could see, dozing in the sun. The men, their bald patches covered by knotted hankies, the women in Crimplene floral dresses.

'Wow, it looks huge from up here.'

'Too big,' he says.

'Bigger than I thought. It's almost a city. Sad. Soon it will be another Brighton.'

'You don't want to live here. Move to Seaford instead,' he says.

As I study the dense tapestry of houses, churches, tall blocks of flats, the sprawl of warehouses trickling into the distance, I wonder if maybe he's right. From up here looking down over the town, there's sense of perspective that only distance can provide. I'd go to Seaford, if it meant being with him, carving out a life together, exploring, joining activities, making new friends. But Seaford is not where my dream is and never has been. A niggling voice inside me questions whether he sees a future for us anyway. When he mentions living in Seaford, he's not thinking of us together.

We're living in the present, enjoying each weekend as it comes along, but I don't know where this is heading. Maybe we will go the way every one of my past relationships has––there'll be an explosive ending or we'll peter out but stay loosely in touch. Happy-ever-after doesn't exist. I let that reality sink in a long time ago. I just want to reach a point in my life when the messiness and the anxiety stabilises. But heck, I'm not naïve. My next big birthday is sixty after all. That sense of security I so deeply long for isn't waiting for me at some point in the future. I can't live my life with the conviction that someday I'll reach my so-called destination––a stable place where I will no longer suffer, crave, or worry. And yet despite knowing that, a part of me yearns for that dream.

CHAPTER 37 - POOR MUM

livia

THURSDAY ARRIVES, and waking early, I remember the task ahead. A thick wedge of fear and panic lodges in my throat. My nerves are a signpost, screaming at me not to do this, to leave Mum's love life well alone. Nothing good can come of it. She'll discover soon enough what a shit this man is, and when he bails out of the holiday, she'll be devastated but try to rope me into going to Anglesey with her instead. Typical of Mum. I'm tired of playing second fiddle to her men.

I can't meet him. I'm scared. I've no idea what I'll talk about or what I'm hoping to achieve. I did wonder about making a dramatic scene––pouring a pint of beer over his head–– but that would be a waste of good beer and I would be made to look silly. I don't know if I'd have the guts to do it anyway. It's not my style. He might even report me for assault. Either way, would it make him feel guilty about how he treats women? I think I already know the answer to that one.

I hate the idea of internet dating. It's forced and artificial. Does it even work? If Mum's record is anything to go by, she's only ever met a bunch of wasters, lost damaged souls, excuses for men. I'd rather meet someone in a bar or a nightclub.

All I really wanted to do was talk to him, find out more about the creep and try to understand why Mum keeps falling for the wrong sort. It's maddening to watch her go through this heartache.

I make a snap decision. I'm going to cancel him. Instantly I feel better. From Dad's in London, Shoreham is a long drive and expensive on petrol. I could do without the aggro, and yet, a part of me is curious to meet him.

When I switch on my phone, there's a message from him.

Him: 'Oh Julie, I'm so sorry but I need to cancel this evening. I'm no longer in a position to see you for a drink. My apologies, take care.'

Relief sweeps through me.

I take my time, mulling over a suitable answer. This needs to be good, got to cut him down to size. No longer in a position to see me—why? Because of Mum? Maybe this is positive, he's loyal after all, not the bad guy I'd imagined.

Me: 'Oh dear, Colin. My loss then. I will save the new dress for perhaps another drink evening. Please feel free to text when you can. Thankyou for telling me.'

Him: 'I mean I can't see anyone as I've met someone, sorry not to be clear. I feel bad about it. And the dress.'

Such a crafty, sneaky bastard. He was tempted to two-time poor Mum. Wonder what happened, why he really decided not to meet me. Maybe he had a change of heart, his conscience was pricked. I guess even he realised how low he'd stooped.

I'm glad I'm not driving to Shoreham. I didn't fancy getting dressed up, shoes cutting into my feet. Finding the pub. Walking in alone. How scary that would have been. I'm not sure I would have had the guts to go through with it. Being jostled by people struggling to carry a round of three pints with two hands or being ogled at by the locals. Texting him was one thing--meeting him, a perfect stranger was something else entirely.

Feeling sorry for Mum after interfering in her life, I decide to head down to Sussex to see her. She's not working today. Washed and dressed, I peer out of the window, changing my mind when I see how grey it is out. I sense rain is going to start at any minute and not stop for the day. Can I really be bothered to tackle the M25 and M23? I'll ask Mum if she wants to come up here instead, take me out for a meal at Pizza Express or somewhere. And if she's not keen, then at least I will have made the effort to see her. There won't be many more chances to meet up before I'm back in Leicester for the autumn term.

As soon as I hear Mum's voice on the phone, I know something is wrong. That flat, dull voice, the pain tucked behind every strained word. I don't ask, I just know it's to do with Colin. It's always to do with men. No man will reduce me to the sorry mess I see in my mother. You can't force happiness, it's not a key in a stubborn lock. Happiness is fleeting, elusive like a butterfly, the more she chases it, the more it will frustrate her. I grab my bag, leave the house, start the car. She can't see the wasted years piling up. I wish I could change her mindset. She's watched me grow up under a cloud of failed relationships. I've no doubt she does love me in her own way even though she never says those special three words and even though I always come second to the latest man in her life.

Arriving at Mum's, I find her outside in the garden sitting on the patio staring at the hedge. She's clutching her phone as if it's a lifeline. Still wearing her pyjamas--not a good sign. Her hair is un-brushed and matted. This is an image of her I know too well. The impact of yet another heartache. I see it in her eyes as she jolts when I open the patio door, turning to smile at me--a forced smile that makes me feel like an extra burden in her life she can do without right now. I see it in the slump of her shoulders and in the way she slams her phone down on the metal patio table, balling her fists in frustration. She feels a failure. In her head these men are never to blame; she takes it all to heart, chastising herself, moaning to me that she should have acted differently. I'm her daughter, I don't want to hear the nitty-gritty details of her love life.

I can tell she's been crying.

Now is not the time to break my news.

My big news.

When she's like this, like a lovesick teenager, she's of no help, no support. She's obsessed with her own issues.

As usual the latest wreckage that is her love life will take priority. Everything is always about Mum and her harem of men. It's no wonder I've always longed for my parents to get back together, just to stop this madness. I crave stability. Continuity. It was a fantasy. How naive. Whatever had led to their break-up––and I doubt I'll ever find out why––they will never reconcile. Too much time has passed.

I step out onto the patio, put a hand on Mum's shoulder, feel her quiver beneath me. I see the pain she carries. What comes of pain like this? It's so pointless, self-absorbed, deliberate, sabotaging. Does it slowly dissipate, or will it congeal and turn toxic, pervading every cell of the body, turning Mum into a bitter old woman?

Years of internet dating have changed her, pulled at her face. Her hair is grey. There are bags under her eyes, eyes that lack sparkle. She must stop this madness. It has become like an addiction, all-consuming, she's a woman on a mission, must have her fix.

I plonk myself down opposite her. 'Things not good?'

'He's ghosting me again.'

'He's one of those guys who keeps letting women down.'

She stares into her tea and sighs.

'Come on, Mum. How could you trust him again? You'd buy a house and he'd pull out at the last minute.'

'Men need their caves. What if he's one of those guys that need space, to get away, then they bounce back and they're okay again? Men are more menopausal than women.' She laughs, but it's tinged with cynicism.

'Is that what you really believe? I think he's playing hide and seek with your emotions.'

She raises her eyebrows and looks up at the clouds. 'I don't know what I believe any more, but we had a holiday booked.'

'So what? Go on your own.' She can do it. 'Or find a friend to go with you.'

'At this late notice? It's in two weeks' time, Olivia. Most people need to book time off work well in advance. Anyway, I don't want to go with a friend. I wanted to go with him.' She looks irritated at my suggestion.

I note that it doesn't even occur to ask me. I'm not doing much else, just waiting for the new term to start. But I'm damned if I'm going to offer, only to see that glum face, knowing she'd rather be with him than her own daughter.

He's a player, he preys on women and Mum can't see it. He's like a serial killer. If I had the chance, I'd wipe the floor with him, but he turned me away.

'You should report him to the dating site.'

'And say what?' There's torment in her features. Lines around her eyes and mouth.

'Dunno. He shouldn't be allowed to get away with what he's doing. He's a wolf in sheep's clothing.'

The perfume from the flowers in the bed beside us is intense. I feel my eyes itch.

'Men get away with all sorts of things,' she says in a voice drained of strength.

I shake my head. 'If you let them.'

'He's blanking you because he's met someone else. I'd lay a bet on it.' I let my words settle on her like dust.

'He might come round.'

I raise my voice. 'Mum, you're just kidding yourself.'

'You don't know that.'

'Men like him just want to use women. It's a feeding frenzy. Let's hope you don't meet another like him.'

CHAPTER 38 - A WEEK BEFORE

onna

HERE WE GO AGAIN. I know he's blanking me. I sent my usual "good morning how are you?" text when I woke on Monday after what I thought had been an amazing weekend together, and now two days later and he still hasn't replied.

I'm not going to chase him. That would look desperate. Maybe he just needs space. Again. This is becoming pattern-forming. I must step back, be patient, let him make the first move, allow him time to miss me. That's where I go wrong. I act too keen. But two days. It's a bit much. Anyone would agree with me there, even Olivia. Doesn't take a lot to be polite and just reply. It's rude. Hurtful. I don't deserve it.

I hate being suspicious, wary. But it's a gut feeling, and I trust my gut. The facts speak for themselves, I have little reason to doubt Colin. We have a holiday booked. We had a wonderful weekend together.

And yet, something doesn't feel right.

I replay the events of the weekend, searching for answers, little red flags. On Saturday we climbed the cliffs and walked across the Downs to Belle Tout lighthouse and down to Birling Gap where we sat on deckchairs and chatted for ages before walking back to Beachy Head and driving onto Eastbourne. It was such a relaxing weekend. I can't remember what we talked about. Nature, climate change, travel, Buddhism. In Eastbourne we parked along the front and having talked about Greece we'd decided to try one of the Greek restaurants along Terminus Road. I wanted him to take a picture of me outside an old haunt of mine, sadly now closed after many, many years. Notarianni. It was a proper old-school café, run by the same Italian family for decades. Unchanged, steeped in the past, it was rundown in a charming sort of way. A bit oppressive with drab '50s décor–– dark wooden panelling, brown vinyl seats and the menu unchanged: Bovril to drink, one of my childhood favourites. And banana boats and Knickerbrocker Glories for dessert. Liver and gravy. Mashed potato. Yuk. It was one of the only links I had to my childhood and now it's closed. Probably didn't survive the pandemic. In her teens, I tried to get Olivia in there, but she always refused. Glimpsing the customers from the window put her off––old men with gravy dribbling down their chins. Col kept saying he thought I was so cute the way I stood outside, sad, wanting my photo taken, animated as I reminisced. Every restaurant and café along Terminus Road tells a story of my past, and I wanted to share it all with Colin. He was inter-ested. Or was he? Maybe his mind was a 1,000 miles away. I often sense he doesn't listen to me. He has a rubbish memory. Doesn't recall things I've told him. Is it because he's uninter-ested, thinking about something else or even someone else or does he genuinely have a poor memory?

It's midweek when he finally replies to Monday's text. I rush to my bag, grabbing my phone.

Him: 'Sorry, Donna. Yes, I'm okay.'

He doesn't ask how I am, so I don't bother to reply.

The following day my heart gallops when my phone pings with another message. Excited, I open it.

Then I go cold.

Numb.

Him: 'Sorry, Donna. I've been a tired, miserable git. And the truth is I feel very much in one of my withdrawal stages again. X'

I wish I had the guts to tell him how hurtful he's being. How I've listened for hours to his woes about how women have treated him. Don't I deserve an explanation? And we'd booked a holiday.

I manage to go for two whole days without replying, but this is tearing me apart. It's all I can think of. My anger, the disappointment, the sadness, the loss of his company, his friendship, us. I loved everything about him––apart from this. Dwelling on my sadness and the thought of never seeing him again makes me feel completely flat and lifeless. The loss of him feels like an actual pain, a dull ache around the heart that drags and tugs as I walk in a haze wondering what to do with myself, where to go from here.

On Sunday I head down to Tide Mills to swim, but really, I'm just hoping I'll bump into him. I imagine his car parked up and us falling into each other's arms, his apologies, my forgiveness, kissing.

After my swim, on a whim I text him. It's like an itch that needs scratching or a cream cake that needs eating. I am weak, I am pathetic. This is as low as I can possibly go.

I tell him how cruel he's being and then I press send. Only one grey tick has appeared. He's blocked me. Disappointment curdles inside me. I resist the urge to go bombing round to his house to find out exactly what's going on. I don't want to make a fool of myself and what would it achieve?

Sniffing back tears, I force myself to be positive. Even

though my heart and head aren't ready to consider the holiday, I go into the Airbnb website and peruse a variety of organised activities. Within minutes I've booked a canoe trip, a cycle ride around Beaumaris, a meditation hike in the hills, a walk with a lady in Welsh costume around Conwy and a bus tour of the castles in North Wales. For the first time in days, I feel energised. Despite my sadness, I think I might just enjoy this break. Because of the lockdowns it's been a while since I went away. I wish I wasn't staying in a pub though. It's not ideal, but I don't have to eat there, I'll buy food from a supermarket and eat it in my room. It will be a tad grim, but better than feeling conspicuous all on my tod. Billie No-Mates is not a good look. Already I'm starting to feel cheerful and finding the humour in my sorrow. I will make the best of this week away.

CHAPTER 39 - CON ARTIST

*O*livia
Mum seems to be enjoying her week away. I'm glad I encouraged her to go on her own; it will do her good, maybe even help her to reflect on where her life is going. Quitting these dating sites might be too much to hope for, but she could surprise me. Good on her for booking a canoe trip and a cycle ride. I'm almost envious, but in my condition, I can't do active sports.

My condition.

I can't believe this has happened to me––of all people. My old school friends, maybe––the careless ones who don't think about what they are doing, then they get caught out. I'm the sensible one. Always have been. Until now. It happened during one drinking evening with my flatmates. Two minutes is all it took to change everything. The whole course of my life. One drunken shag. I did think about having an abortion, but I couldn't go through with it. It didn't feel right.

I am certain of one thing.

I will not let this child be a burden.

I will not repeat Mum's mistakes. I will nurture, treasure and protect the bean growing inside me. The love between a mother and child is as fragile and delicate as a spider's web. It cannot be taken for granted or pushed aside. My child will not be a millstone around my neck. My child will come first. I will make sure of it. Like any love it will grow and blossom with time and support––two ingredients that were in short supply during my childhood.

I wonder if Mum harbours regrets––all that time she's spent dating. Palming me off on Dad when she went on dates.

I want him or her to have a full-time grandma who picks them up from school on occasions, who looks forward to fun days building sandcastles on the beach, days out at cute farms looking at baby goats. Playing hide and seek in the garden. LEGOLAND. The zoo. Fulfilling the role assigned to her. She made her mistakes with me. She will not do it again with her grandchild. I will make sure of it.

On Mum's third day in Anglesey, to my horror and complete surprise, Colin messages me.

Him: 'Hi Julie, have you met someone or would you still like that drink? The woman I was with turned out to be a complete lunatic. She's dumped me. She has so many issues and I'm not sure it's going anywhere.'

Oh my actual God. My heart races. Didn't think I'd hear from him again.

What's he playing at? Is he referring to Mum, or some other woman or making himself look like a victim?

This time around, there are no doubts in my mind. I'm ready to confront him.

I WASTE NO TIME, don't want to change my mind; I arrange to see him that very evening. I'm open-minded, don't have a plan. I might reveal who I really am, or I might just treat it like a fact-finding mission to glean as much about him as I can. I'll play it by ear, see how the evening pans out.

Here I am. Standing outside a pub in a village near Brighton peering up at the trailing Virginia creeper threatening to suffocate the brickwork of this quaint old pub. I head inside. It's a warm and characterful place with a wood-panelled bar and an impressive array of beer pumps. A rich red carpet. A huge wagon wheel attached to the wall. I don't know why I notice all these details; I'm as nervous as hell. I manage to resist the urge to run back out or head straight to the loo to empty my guts.

He's already here, propping up the bar with his elbow, and looking as nervous as I feel. His eyes dart up at me, but he looks away, takes a sip of the pint he's nursing, clearly not expecting a twenty-something to be his date for the evening. Let's get this over with. Taking a deep breath, my legs all wobbly, I tamp down my nerves and march right up to him before I can back out of this.

'Colin.'

He doesn't believe it's me. He does this peculiar meerkat routine, twisting his head from side to side and scanning the pub as if he's on the lookout for prowlers.

'I'm Julie.' I smile at him but feel bloody awkward. I must be about the same age as his daughter.

Out of the corner of my eye, I clock the barman chuckling to himself as he vigorously dries a glass with a tea towel. Clearly amused by our mix-up, I wonder if he's worked out that we're on a date. He's probably witnessed all sorts of weird liaisons from behind this wooden counter.

Colin has read my thoughts. 'Christ, you're about my daughter's age.' He moves away from the bar, lowers his voice. 'I set the age range from forty to sixty.'

'You can't have done.'

He's all red and flustered. So much for the confident man that Mum painted. 'I don't remember matching with you, and I'd definitely remember. I mean you're stunning.' His eyes check me out from head to feet but not in a lustful way.

'I can leave if you want me to.' I adjust my bag on my shoulder and glance towards the door.

He looks panicked, touches my arm. 'No, no, no, don't do that.' Unbelievable. He thinks he's in with a chance. I'm half his age and more. God, some men do flatter themselves. Already I can tell he's vain and believes he can have any woman he wants. I bet he sees these dating sites as one giant candy jar. I'm going to have some fun with him. Suddenly I know the purpose of my evening. I'm looking forward to winding him up then dropping him like a lead balloon. 'What are you having?'

'Glass of white wine, please.' Alcohol. Dutch courage. But just the one--I'm driving.

'You find a table; I'll bring them over.'

I choose a table opposite the bar and study his behind as I wait. Nice arse. Long legs. Slim. No beer belly. Full head of hair--that counts for a lot at their age. He's good-looking--for an old git not far off drawing his pension. He's the best Mum's been out with. She scored lucky with him, and I think she knows that which is why she clung on for so long. Like a barnacle. Looks are superficial though. Where people are concerned you can't judge a book by its cover. Despite her age and experience, Mum was suckered in by this prize fucker.

Bringing our drinks over, he perches on a stool, his legs wide apart. 'Still can't believe I was chatting to someone so young. How old are you? I'm not a cradle snatcher or a paedophile.' He gives an awkward laugh. He takes a sip of his beer, leaving froth on his upper lip. Looks nervous as hell. 'Wouldn't you rather meet a guy your own age?'

I haven't prepared an answer to that question, so I trot out a string of cliches about age. 'Age is just a number Older guys are more mature; they know how to treat women like ladies.' I rattle on, warming to my theme. He laps it up.

This is weird, like going on a date with my dad. I try to push that uncomfortable thought from my mind. It will be over before I know it. There's a clock above the bar. I won't need to keep checking my phone. Thinking about it, even if there's half a gentleman lurking inside him, he won't want me to drive home late. He'll probably suggest we leave at a decent time. Men of his era are supposed to be more chivalrous.

'What do you do?' he asks. 'You're not still at college, are you?' I want to thump him. How patronising.

I reinvent myself as the lies trot with ease off my tongue. 'I'm cabin crew. I work for EasyJet. I've been on furlough for months but went on my first assignment last week. To Brussels.' Shit, I hope there's an airport in Brussels. It's lucky I have a friend who works for EasyJet. I can't imagine a worse career. A glorified waitress, clearing up puke, dealing with irate customers.

We chat about travel. Mum's already told me about their shared passion to jet round the world.

After a while, I cut to the chase, otherwise I'll be here all night talking about irrelevant crap. 'Tell me about the woman you were dating. The lunatic.' What a word. Does anyone use it anymore? Doesn't sound very PC. Bit insulting.

'She was Spanish.'

I'm about to take a sip of my wine. My hand freezes in mid-air and it's as if the world has gone on pause. The realisation hits that he has probably been cheating the whole time he's known Mum, hits. He's Colin-the-con-artist. 'How long were you together?'

'A year.'

'A whole year?'

'Don't sound so surprised. Us oldies aren't all flaky.' He laughs. This is anything but funny. It takes effort not to glare at him. What I'd really like to do is stab him.

'What attracted you to her?'

'What is this, 101 questions?'

I don't answer. Thoughtful, he's either choosing his words carefully or God forbid, he's not sure. I stare at the swirly carpet. All I can think about is poor Mum driving all the way to Anglesey on her own and eating Tesco sarnies in her hotel room.

'There was something exotic about her. Dark glossy skin, like burnt caramel.' I look at him. His eyes are twinkling. 'Her parents were from India. Her accent was sexy.'

'How shallow.'

'It was more than looks.' His face is turning red. Embarrassment. 'I was dazzled by her. She was vivacious. Captivating. Charismatic. I don't think I'll ever meet someone like her again. She was so totally unique. But intelligent with it, creative and I loved her accent. She was younger than me. Only forty-two. I disappointed her.'

'You don't want to meet an English rose then?' I'm being sarcastic. 'Someone with classical beauty and wind-flushed cheeks and just-bitten lips. A Princess Di or a Kate Winslett?'

He shrugs. 'Not really my type.'

Bastard.

'You're describing my ex-wife. I'm done with the English rose types.'

What did he see in Mum? I don't understand.

'She's the only one you've dated in the past year, this lunatic exotic woman?' I can't keep the sarcasm from my voice.

'Of course. I'm not a two-timer. I know a lot of men are but I'm not like that. I could never cheat on a woman.'

No, of course you wouldn't. He doesn't flinch, no tics give him away, no visible indicators like rubbing his nose or crossing and uncrossing his legs. He's brazen. Bold. A prize cheat.

'Has she lived in this country long?'

'Twenty odd years but she wants to move back to Spain.'

'Would you have gone with her?'

'Yes of course.' I despise him. He'd follow true love to the ends of the earth. I want to slap him round his conceited chops. I bet he wouldn't have followed Mum even to the next town, but he'd do anything for this floozy.

'I started learning Spanish.'

Jesus. I doubt Mum even knows he was learning a language. 'I've always wanted to move to Europe. For the weather mainly. That's my ultimate dream but Brexit kind of got in the way. I'm not sure it's going to be possible anymore, but that's my plan.'

I'm flummoxed. Don't know what to say. This is dreadful. He's two people, leading two lives.

As he chatters away, everything blurs around me, I'm barely listening anymore, I'm so incensed. I zone out, maybe it's the shock. His voice is white noise mingled with the pub noises.

I need to get out of here. I feel sick. I will puke if I sit here a moment longer. And my condition isn't helping. 'I need the loo.' As I get up, I'm light-headed and something whooshes through my ears. It's not far to the door. To the car.

He's not getting away with this. I peer down at him. 'Does the name Donna mean anything to you? Donna Radcliffe?'

The colour drains from his face. I step away as he stares up at me in horror, his brain ticking over, then the realisation.

'Her daughter?' he whispers.

I rush towards the door and he's behind me grabbing my arm.

'Get off me,' I scream. 'You fucking paedophile.'

'Hey,' the barman calls. 'I don't want no trouble.'

Ignoring the fat inarticulate barman, I swing my bag in a vicious arch. He turns slightly, doesn't see it coming. I clobber him across the side of his head, catching his face with the buckle. A graze. Blood. His glass shattering across the floor. Beer frothing and puddling.

He's dazed as I grab the copper handle, yank the door open.

Moments later, with trembling hands and a thumping heart, my Corsa screeches out of the car park sending gravel scattering in every direction.

THE FOLLOWING MORNING, I set off on my journey up to Anglesey to surprise Mum.

CHAPTER 40 - SOLITUDE IS BLISS

 onna

IT'S a warm mid-September day and not a cloud in sight. I'm sitting on the dunes appreciating the peace and tranquillity of this stunning view. The dense pine forest of Newborough Nature Reserve is behind me and in front, the sea gently ripples to shore. Further along, waves crash around the outcrops of jagged grey basalt pillow lava rocks that jut out giving the coast-line its distinctive character. A small sailing boat tethered to a rock gently bobs on the water.

I never knew such beauty.

Anglesey.

It's been a magnificent week. I want to come back; I love it so much.

It's early, just after eight and the water is mottled grey in the subdued light. If I was strolling across Beachy Head, it would be teeming with walkers. A busy thoroughfare, the chalk cliffs are being eroded and nature trashed. But here, it's deserted. Not a soul in either direction. Miles of golden sand. Silence apart from a pair of seagulls squabbling over what looks like a cuttlefish. In the distance, the sea is framed by the majestic rolling mountains of Snowdonia and the Llyn Peninsula.

Alone here, I'm at peace in a way I never imagined and for possibly the first time in my adult life. There are no demands on my time, no lodgers asking me questions or taking up my living space, no crazy clients leaving me feeling exhausted at the end of the day.

And no man.

I smile to myself. I've pleased myself these past few days. It's been liberating, freeing. I've gone where I wanted, done what I wanted. I've not had to compromise. I'm not sure I want to live a life of compromise, at my age. This is my time, to be who I want to be. I stretch my arms, running my fingers through the soft sand. Is this contentment?

For the first time in days, I realise something powerful. It overwhelms me with its intensity. Although I have thought about him––too much––I don't need Colin. Heck, I don't need anyone. To be in a relationship––what a drag it had become. Time-consuming. Stressful. Demanding. The ups and downs, having to talk to that person when I want silence or having to listen to their prattle. The arrogance of some men. Their selfish ways. The snoring, farting, their narrow interests, their disregard for my needs. I can survive on my own. I will invest time in building interests and passions.

This week has stirred something inside me. In the same way that eight hours in a prison cell did. I feel stronger and smarter.

Some stories are unfinished. Incomplete. For all the years and all the effort invested in dating, there is no happy ending. It's impossible to know what is really going on in someone else's life and in their mind. There's little transparency with some of these men. They lie, they bluff, they play a game. My love life will always be a work-in-progress, a painting waiting to be completed. I try hard not to feel sorry for myself. Why can't love go my way? Just once, and be for keeps.

I curl my toes into the cold sand like brown sugar, then rising to my feet, I continue my walk across the sand towards the lighthouse on the tiny tidal island of Ynys Llanddwyn. On a rugged mound there's a cross and the ramshackle ruins of a church. I get a sense of what this stunning place means. Pilgrims once crossed the sea from far and wide to come here. It's spiritual, sacred, poetic, magical, wreathed with tales and legends of long ago and as I look around me, my heart is filled with a sense of majesty. I am truly blessed. Incredibly, I could be in any decade, in any century. It's timeless. And best of all, I've not had to step on a plane or take a darn Covid test.

I thought that nothing could disturb the silence apart from the cry of birds and the distant thrum of a boat, but on reaching the lighthouse along a sandy track, I hear voices through the crackle of the wind and waves. Brushing against the white wall of the lighthouse, I see a man and a woman peering over the rocks towards a cove, taking it in turns to peer through binoculars.

Turning, they look as if they are expecting company. They smile, put a finger to their lips, beckon me over and raise the binoculars to my eyes.

I gasp when I spot them.

The sight of fins. Three dolphins ducking in and out of the water. The joy of this shared experience bonds us in an instant and it's as if we are the only three remaining people left walking the earth. After the dolphins swim away, disappearing into the depths of the dark waters; we chat. They tell me about the wildlife they've spotted: red squirrels in the forest, cormorants on the rocks, osprey hunting for fish, a colony of seals in the bay at low tide.

As we chat, a subtle change comes over the woman. She

looks away, there's the odd tut and raised eyebrows, and suddenly I'm aware that they are not the blissfully happy couple I'd imagined. She glares at him with a sullen expression. Appears bored. With him? While she loves this adventure; he's the one who is passionate about birdwatching and wildlife. She goes along with what he wants. That's what I've always done, it's been my greatest downfall in most of my relationships.

The men I've lived with or dated, fit into three categories.

The victims.

The arrogant.

The oppressors.

Why can't I just meet someone normal?

As I walk back along the pathway, I glance up at the stone cross that commands the bay and make a pact with myself.

I will never be a doormat again.

Not to a man.

And not to Olivia either.

Olivia. I've thought a lot about her these past few days. She's heading up here on Friday to join me for the weekend. I'm not sure how I feel about that. But I'm touched that she wants to spend time with her old mum. That hasn't happened in many years. She has her own life. I'm wallpaper. She tears around, seeing different people, never has time for family. I should feel happy about seeing her, but instead there's a stone of anxiety at the pit of my stomach. She unpredictable, she flares up so easily. I don't know what harsh home truths or aspersions she'll throw at me. She pokes fun at my feelings or challenges them. She invalidates my emotions. But whatever I feel, these are my feelings. I own them and they are not up for debate.

She has something to tell me. She could wait until I'm back or call instead. I'm thinking the worst. She's been chucked off her course.

The following day, spent in Llandudno on the North Wales

coast, is marred slightly by the thought of Olivia's arrival. It's a shame that I'm anxious because I'd be enjoying LLandudno much more otherwise. It's a treat to visit a new seaside town, to explore every inch, be surprised by what I find. Very soon I dub it the Eastbourne of the north. But here, there's no rundown feel about the town. No boarded-up shops or homeless on the pavements. Or hardened alcoholics singing from park benches. It appears to be prospering, despite the setback of lockdowns. And then I see why. Coachloads of old folk spilling onto every pavement, bringing their pensions to spend in the shops, chattering in Liverpudlian and Mancunian accents. It's a mecca for the population of those northern towns. Flocking here to soak up the Victorian charm, quintessential cafes and knitting shops, strolls across the vast sands. A Mr Wimpy for an afternoon treat. Bingo and a meat-and-three-veg dinner.

The air sizzles with candy and fried onions as I pant from the climb up to Happy Valley Botanical Gardens. Reaching a bench, I collapse onto the wooden slats taking in the view over the pier, the beach and the long row of guest houses painted in shades of sugared almonds. Behind me is an emerald manicured lawn with a fresh just-cut smell. Established trees flank the park and beyond there's a quaint rockery garden.

The sultry heat is unusual for a British summer and even more unusual for Wales. I haven't felt this oppression of a long hot summer since I was a child, but it's beautiful and I'm not complaining. It can't last. As I gaze out to sea, a thought pops into my head.

I scratch a fingernail over the grainy wood of the bench. I could live here.

I smile to myself because it's so totally absurd.

Maybe it's being somewhere different. There are no memories here. No attachments. It's pure, untarnished, a clean slate. Waiting to be discovered. New people, new adventures.

Gulls wheel overhead, screeching. One dives down a short distance from me, pecking at a discarded packet before flying over and perching on a bench. He fixes his beady black eyes on me and it's as if he is reading my thoughts and warning me not to move here.

CHAPTER 41 - FAMILY IS EVERYTHING

onna

'THIS PLACE IS HORRIBLE. You could have booked somewhere better.'

'Shush.' Typical Olivia, no filter, complaining already and doesn't care who's listening or who she will offend. She has her father to thank for that trait. Doesn't get it from me. 'The nice man on the reception will hear you,' I whisper.

Bounding up the stairs towards my room on the second floor, I glance down at the ugly frayed worn-out swirly carpet and the scrapes on the walls. It's seen better days and needs updating. When Colin and I booked to stay here, we were taken in by the cosy exterior and the pictures showing luxurious four-poster bedrooms. Colin would have hated it. The room is drab and dark, the bathroom is poky, and the shower is a dribble. It's hard to get to sleep because outside it's so noisy. Motorbikes screeching, revellers shouting and laughing well into the small hours. One night I yanked the sash window up and screamed at them to shut the F up.

'Oh my God, Mother. This is ghastly.' She's looking around the room, her face a picture of horror. Spoilt madam, she has no idea what holiday makers had to put up with back in the '50s. Things have barely changed in some parts of the country. She's had it too good. 'I can't wait till we can go abroad again, bloody Covid restrictions. We shouldn't have to put up with this shit.' She turns towards the mahogany dressing table and eying the hospitality tray, grabs the complimentary Bourbon biscuits and laughs before dropping them into the bin. As if they don't matter. As if I don't matter. 'Thought those went out with the ark.'

Her rudeness makes me flinch. They are just biscuits, but logic can't quell the tears that spring to my eyes and the rush of different emotions welling inside me. Her mocking of me, my lifestyle, my choices. How different we are. She is my daughter, but I do not understand her. This is personal. I suddenly feel protective of my surroundings––this place, Wales. Everything.

'Don't do that.' I retrieve them from the bin, sniffing back the tears. If she sees me upset, she'll mock all the more. 'Let's find somewhere nice to eat.' No sooner have I said the words, than I realise there is nowhere much to eat in Llangefni. It's lacking in eateries––there are a few greasy takeaways and this pub which serves Harvester-type food.

As she strokes my shoulder, her tone is patronising. 'It's okay, Mother, I noticed an Asda over the road. We could buy sandwiches and eat them on a bench. I know that's what you'd rather do than spend money on me. Like when I was a kid, and we ate bread and Camembert every day on that awful holiday in France.

I can't take anymore. Losing my rag, I screech at her. 'That's what people do in France. Eat French bread and cheese. I was hardly going to feed you frogs' legs and mussels now was I?'

'Okay, keep your hair on. What do they eat in Wales then?'

'I've stumbled across some pretty pubs and boutique restaurants by harbours and coves but it's difficult eating in those places alone. I'd have felt conspicuous. I did get over my fear last night though. I went in a restaurant in Llandudno.'

She's not interested in my week and now seems to be blocking me out as I start to tell her about a café lunch next to Penmon lighthouse after my group cycle ride from Beaumaris. Dumping her case on the bed, she gives a heavy sigh. 'I'm not hungry anyway.'

I don't believe it; what was all that fuss about if she doesn't want to eat? I hate all this antagonism. It's unnecessary.

How I wish she hadn't come.

THE FOLLOWING MORNING, we drive over to Conwy. We do a guided tour with a Welsh lady in costume and visit the tiniest house in Britain, nestled at the end of a row of terrace houses down by the quayside. Afterwards we stroll along the path by the waterside away from the castle chatting about what it would have been like to live in such a tiny house. It's just 72 inches wide by 122 inches high. There's just enough room for a single bed, coal bunker and a fireplace.

'I can't believe a whole family lived in such a tiny house,' Olivia says, glancing back at the cottage in wonder.

'People coped. God knows how. I suppose they were out at work for long hours, even the kiddies and they weren't so bothered about the cold. When they weren't working, they probably sat on the quayside watching the boats being unloaded. Sounds romantic, bet it wasn't.'

She stops abruptly and stares at me. 'How does anyone cope? With kids?'

I frown at her. What's brought this on?

Gazing up at the dull overcast sky, I sense yet another tough conversation ahead and already I feel sick with the thought of it. 'Don't ask me. Sometimes it feels as if I'm the worst mother on the planet.'

She links my arm. 'You're not that bad, as mothers go. If you didn't always put men first.'

I glance over at the boats moored along the river, my eyes starting to water. There's truth in her words, truth in pain and pain in truth. My head is a tangled mess of regret, and my heart is weighted down with the sadness that I cannot change the past.

I reach out and touch her hair. Despite the way we are these days: awkward, ill at ease, and despite her rudeness; she's still my baby and always will be. 'I wish I could wheel back in time, just enjoy *you*. It's not the pain of childbirth that we remember or the struggles of raising a child; it's simply the regrets.'

A gull wheels above, crying into the breeze, taking me to another time and place. Trips to Eastbourne when she was little. Queuing for ice cream and Olivia always choosing a twenty-pence strawberry Mini-Milk. My voice wobbles but I carry on. 'And that regret hangs over me like a dark cloud. Wishing things had been different. But life's hard, and that's how it's been since your dad and I divorced. Single motherhood. All of it.'

'Do you regret splitting up from Dad?' We've reached the end of the towpath, turn and head back the way we've come towards the castle.

Reaching a bench, I stop and drop onto the slats. She joins me. I stare at the mountains in the distance wondering whether it's time to be honest or do I continue to protect her?

'I wish things had been different, that's all.' How can I possibly tell her that her father abused me, that he hit me on several occasions, that his drinking was the downfall of our marriage? Would she even believe me? It seems he's a changed man. Maybe he's had therapy. Support. They say that leopards don't change their spots, but maybe there are exceptions. 'Your dad and I...' Unsure how to finish my sentence, I let my words hang in the air. 'We were just unsuited. Just different.'

'Mum?' She's looking at me in a strange way.

What's coming––more probing? I want to move on from this conversation. Protect her from the details. She doesn't need to know.

'What is it?' I glance at her, trying to gauge what's on her mind, then fix my gaze on a boat.

'I'm pregnant.'

Nothing could have prepared me for this. I hear her, but my brain stutters, struggles to play catch-up, the words failing to sink in.

'I knew you'd be all awkward,' she says gruffly.

'I'm not awkward. I'm finding the right words.' I feel odd, as if I'm floating. 'You've taken me by surprise.' I stare at her. She's wobbly, fragile. I see something in her eyes. She needs me. Yet she's fierce too. I take her hand, squeeze it. So many questions to ask, but my head is a whirlpool. This is so monumental; I can't process it.

She looks down at her lap and I see the rawness of her vulnerability. Poor kid. Poor, poor kid. A rush of love sweeps through me.

'Obviously, it wasn't planned. I'm eight weeks.' Her voice is barely a whisper. She's slumped as if in shame.

How am I supposed to feel? Disappointment. Sadness. In this day and age––so unavoidable. But it's happened and I must support her.

She turns, melts into my arms. It's not the stiff ironing board hugs we are familiar with. This is the hug of strong arms, of love, that tells everything we are to each other. Something that was lost seems to reignite. As if we've come home. She presses into me, quietly crying and I breathe in her scent––Yves Saint

Laurent, Mon Paris, and the fragrance of her shampoo--almond. My hand is on her shoulder, her back--everything bony, slight. She's still so young. Soon she will have the body of a mother. And I'm going to be a grandma.

Grandma.

This is happening about ten years before I am ready and in difficult circumstances. But it's a blessing.

Do I dare feel joy in the midst of this crisis?

When we pull away, I dig in my bag for a clean tissue and wipe her smudged mascara.

Words find me. 'This is your decision, Liv, your body, your life. I'm here for you. I know this is coming at an incredibly stressful time for you. You can do this if you want, just tell me how I can help.'

'How will I cope? I've literally no idea.'

I squeeze her hand. 'We'll work it out. Together. It's going to be okay. I promise. You're not the first woman to face this challenge and you won't be the last.'

My phone pings with a text and I pull it out of my pocket and peer at the screen.

'Who is it this time? A new creep?' There's weariness in her voice.

I read the message and laugh. 'I don't believe it.'

'When it comes to you, Mother, I'd believe anything.'

'A random message from a guy I met a couple of times yonks ago. He says he's seen my new WhatsApp profile picture and is just imagining me walking all over him in high heels.'

'Don't reply.'

'I don't intend to.' Sighing, I switch my phone off and slip it back into my pocket.

As we sit here in companionable silence each in our own private thoughts, my mind floats to another time and place. The future. I see it with such clarity. There will be no regrets going forward, no misplaced responsibilities, no distractions, no barriers to helping her. And no more dating. I'm not going to mess this up. There's a lot to work out, but we'll get there. I will be there for her; I will be the best grandmother there ever was. Because family is everything, and family comes first. It's taken this to make me realise.

THANK YOU, DEAR READER

Thank you for reading *Slippers On A First Date?* If you enjoyed the story, I would really appreciate a short review on Amazon. Reviews are the lifeblood of authors.

If you would like a FREE digital copy of a similar book to this one, *A Time To Reflect* please email me at joannawarrington@ hotmail.com

Follow Joanna Warrington on Amazon: https://www.ama-zon.co.uk/Joanna-Warrington/e/B00RH4XPI6/

My best-selling series is *Every Parent's Fear,* inspired by the thalidomide crisis of the 1960s. You will find book 1: *Every Mother's Fear* and book 2: *Every Father's Fear and Book 3 Every Son's Fear* on Amazon. Just follow this link: https://www.ama-zon.co.uk/gp/kindle/series/B084KZ8NCB?

OTHER BOOKS BY JOANNA WARRINGTON:

Don't Blame Me

My Book

When tragedy struck twenty-five years ago, Dee's world fell apart. With painful reminders all around her she flew to Australia to start a new life. Now, with her dad dying, she's needed back in England. But these are unprecedented times. It's the spring of 2020 and as Dee returns to the beautiful medieval house in rural Kent where she grew up among apple orchards and hop fields, England goes into lockdown, trapping her in the village. The person she least wanted to see has also returned, forcing her to confront the painful past and resolve matters between them.

Weaving between past and present, this emotional and absorbing family saga is about hope, resilience, and the healing power of forgiveness.

Holiday

My Book

Determined to change her sad trajectory Lyn books a surprise road trip for herself and her three children through the American Southwest and Yellowstone. Before they even get on the plane, the trip hits a major snag. An uninvited guest joins them at the airport turning their dream trip into a nightmare.

Amid the mountain vistas, secrets will be revealed and a hurtful betrayal confronted.

This book is more than an amusing family saga. It will also appeal to those interested in American scenery, history and culture. This is part of a loosely related family drama collection. Book 2 is *A Time To Reflect*

A Time To Reflect

My Book

When an aunt and her niece take an epic road trip through
Massachusetts, their relationship is changed forever.

It's a trip with an eclectic mix of history, culture and scenery. Seafood
shacks. Postcard-perfect lighthouses. Weatherboarded buildings.
Stacks of pancakes dripping in syrup. Quaint boutiques. A living
history museum showing how America's early settlers lived. Walks
along the cobblestone streets of Boston, America's oldest city––the city
of revolution.

Everything is going well, until a shocking family secret is revealed. In a
dramatic turn of events, Ellie's father joins them and is forced to
explain why he has been such an inadequate parent.

An entertaining but heartfelt journey through Massachusetts from
Cape Cod to Plymouth, Salem, Marblehead, Boston and Rhode Island.

Every Family Has One

My Book

IMAGINE THE TRAUMA OF BEING RAPED AT AGE
FOURTEEN BY THE TRUSTED PARISH PRIEST IN A
STRONG 1970S CATHOLIC COMMUNITY.

Then imagine the shame when you can't even tell the truth to those
you love, and they banish you to Ireland to have your baby in secret.

How will poor Kathleen ever recover from her ordeal?

This is a dramatic and heart-breaking story about the joys and tests of
motherhood and the power of love, friendship and family ties spanning

several decades.

The Catholic Woman's Dying Wish

My Book

A DYING WISH. A SHOCKING SECRET. A DARK, DESTRUCTIVE, AND ABUSIVE RELATIONSHIP.

Forget hearts and flowers and happy ever afters in this quirky unconventional love story! Readers say: "A little bit Ben Elton" "a monstrous car crash of a saga."

Middle-aged Darius can't seem to hold on to the good relationships in his life. Now, he discovers a devastating truth about his family that blows away his future and forces him to revisit his painful past. Distracting himself from family problems he goes online and meets Faye, a single mum. Faye and her children are about to find out the horrors and demons lurking behind the man Faye thinks she loves.

Printed in Great Britain
by Amazon

84451646R00171